AMBUSH!

The building appeared deserted, the downlink apparatus quiescent, powerless. In one corner, thin partitions created a cubbyhole office . . . also deserted.

"Nobody home," Gomez said with barely suppressed excitement.

"This is too damn good to be true, LT!" Anderson exclaimed softly. "We done got ourselves another Russkie downlink!"

"*FREEZE, ALL OF YOU!*" The voice was amplified thunder, booming from a hidden speaker. "*DO NOT MOVE!*"

What happened next passed in a blur of sound and motion. The upper half of the back wall of the warehouse seemed to fold out and down . . . a hinged, steel wall masked by bricks. A trio of spotlights snapped on, riveting the Ranger team in a pool of blinding incandescence, while from several directions came the harsh snicks of drawn bolts on automatic rifles, of running, booted feet, of harsh commands and shouts in Russian. Hunter raised his pistol, seeking to fire into one of the blinding disks of raw light. . . .

Something clubbed him down, a stunning blow at the base of his neck that sent him sprawling to the floor. Someone kicked his hand, and his pistol was sent skittering off into darkness.

"*RESISTANCE IS USELESS, LIEUTENANT HUNTER,*" the amplified voice thundered. "*YOU AND YOUR PEOPLE ARE OUR PRISONERS!*"

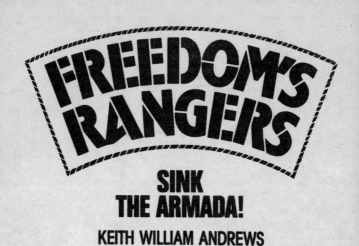

FREEDOM'S RANGERS

SINK
THE ARMADA!

KEITH WILLIAM ANDREWS

BERKLEY BOOKS, NEW YORK

FREEDOM'S RANGERS: SINK THE ARMADA!

A Berkley Book/published by arrangement with
the author

PRINTING HISTORY
Berkley edition/ October 1990

ISBN: 0-425-12300-6

A BERKLEY BOOK ® TM 757,375
Berkley Books are published by The Berkley Publishing Group,
200 Madison Avenue, New York, New York 10016.
The name "BERKLEY" and the "B" logo
are trademarks belonging to Berkley Publishing Corporation.

PRINTED IN THE UNITED STATES OF AMERICA

10 9 8 7 6 5 4 3 2 1

One

Paris was dark and filthy, a city made grim by the distant rumble of a rioting mob. Lieutenant Travis Hunter checked left and right, his eyes flicking from window to window of the brooding apartments that looked down on his Ranger team.

It was February twenty-second, and the air was raw and wet. The year was 1848—the so-called "Year of Revolutions"— a year of social unrest that swept the entire continent of Europe. It was a year of destiny, Hunter knew. Karl Marx's Communist Manifesto would be coming off the printing presses in London any day now; Marx would be here, in Paris, on the Rue Neuve-Ménilmontant, in another couple of weeks, challenging the tottering facades of the European monarchies. Seventy years hence, Marx's philosophical legacy would shake the world.

Hunter was more concerned with Marx's political offspring than with the man himself, however. This street, narrow, wet, appeared deserted . . . but they could be anywhere, watching the Rangers' movements by the dim light of the streetlamps.

"Looks clear," a voice with a soft, West Texas drawl said at his side. Sergeant Roy Anderson looked uncomfortable in the stiff collar and tailed coat favored by well-dressed citizens of this time and place. He held an old but lovingly cared for Colt .45 automatic in one hand.

"Yeah," Hunter said. His own collar was scratching at his throat, and he wished for the thousandth time that their mission

1

profile had allowed the U.S. Ranger team their usual fatigues and weapons. This time, however, the Rangers' incursion into the past was to be strictly covert.

Home for Travis Hunter was America of the year 2008, where most of the world was dominated by Communism and half of the United States was occupied by UN "peacekeepers" under Soviet control. Only Free America, protected by the ruggedness of the Rocky Mountains and by the remnants of the U.S. military, continued the struggle—a fight that could only end in eventual, inevitable defeat.

Unless they could win in time.

In time . . .

Free America's top-secret Chronos Project—a spin-off of the long-defunct Star Wars program which had carried American technology to new heights before the nation's failure of nerve led to disaster in Europe and the virtual triumph of Communism across the world—was the product of twenty years of research. Called "Time Square" by the hundreds of soldiers, scientists, and technicians who worked within the gleaming miles of corridors beneath the mountains of western Wyoming, the Chronos base had pioneered the use of time travel as a weapon of war.

The idea was simple, if its execution was not. If, for example, Vladimir Ilych Ulyanov—known to the world as Lenin—had died before the Bolshevik revolution of 1917 Russia, there might be no Communism to engulf the free world eighty years later. That particular mission had failed. But someday, Hunter knew, the Rangers would try again. There were so many variables to history. Change one and other factors might change as well, ending in a new history starkly different from what was anticipated by the mission's planners. If, for example, there were no Soviet Union in World War II, would the Allies still defeat the Axis, or would the new history be one of triumphant fascism and a worldwide police state? Hunter himself had visited such an alternate future briefly once, and the possibility was not an appealing one.

Rachel Stein came up beside Hunter with a rustle of petticoats and silk, her dark eyes intent on the glowing readout of the electronic device she held in her hand. The black-haired girl, the daughter of one of the senior scientists at Time Square, had accompanied the team on several previous missions to the past.

"Anything?" Hunter asked her. Rachel was attractive, even in her clumsy-looking period costume with its long dress, full bustle, and flowered bonnet. Hunter was in love with her . . . though that relationship had led to problems on previous missions.

She shook her head, not taking her eyes from the MSD scanner. "Not since we picked up that initial signal, Travis. But they're close."

"They," in this case, were the VBU, the *Vremya Bezopasnosti Upravlenie* or "Time Security Directorate" of the Soviet Union. The organization, composed of elements of both the KGB and the GRU, was the Russians' version of Chronos and the spearhead of their own attempts to fight and win this strange, twilight war across the pages of history. The VBU had already made two attempts to rewrite the outcome of the American Revolution, and their *Ochrana Brigadi*, or Guards Units, had foiled previous Chronos attempts to kill Lenin and intervene in the Russian Civil War. Any American intervention in the past had to assume that VBU forces were there, either watching for American activity or engaged in some project of their own. In many respects, the Soviet time program seemed to be far in advance of that of the Americans.

The device Rachel held was a magnetic surge detector, the one sure way the Rangers had of detecting and locating the Soviet equivalent of American time portals. Russian time-gate equipment was bulkier than the book-sized recall beacons that the Rangers used, but it was capable of operating independently. Usually, Soviet temporal downlinks were located in large, innocent-appearing buildings, though on their previous mission the Rangers had encountered a mobile downlink hidden inside a boxcar in an armored train during the Russian Civil War.

"Wait!" Rachel's eyes widened as LED readouts flickered on the MSD's screen. "There! Bearing zero-three-zero . . . and close! Real close!"

Hunter looked in the indicated direction, up the brick street. There were only more buildings, dark and brooding. This section of Paris seemed given over to warehouses and grimy-faced apartments. There was still no sign that anyone—locals or VBU—knew that the Rangers were here.

"Whatcha think, Chief?" Sergeant Eduardo Gomez was the team's demolitions expert, a small, wiry Hispanic from San Diego with an oft-declared love of loud noises and impressive pyrotechnic displays. "Time to call in the strike team?"

"Not yet, Eddie," Hunter replied softly. "Let's get a fix on it, first."

"Let me go across the street," Rachel said. "The signal's close enough I think I can get a triangulation on it from there!"

Behind her, Master Sergeant Greg King scowled. *He still doesn't trust her,* Hunter thought. *That could be bad.*

For all the times she'd accompanied the Rangers into the past, Rachel was still a civilian, and she had trouble at times subordinating her own ideas and impulses to the needs of the team as a whole. King, especially, had been angered by what he perceived as her lack of support during their previous mission in 1918 Siberia and had protested her presence on this mission in less than complimentary language.

"The bitch is going to be nothing but trouble," he'd warned Hunter before their final mission briefing back at Time Square. "Mark my words! She's on some bloody crusade of her own, and it's only a matter of time before she goes her own merry way and leaves us in the lurch!"

Hunter knew something of Rachel's personal crusade but resisted the idea that she might one day work against the team rather than with it.

Besides, I love her . . . "Go ahead, Raye," he said. "Eddie . . . go with her."

The two Americans darted across the street, their shoes ringing on the uneven pavement with an exaggerated clacking that sounded loud enough to wake all of Paris.

At least, that part of Paris not already awakened by the rioting at the barricades a mile or two to the north. The murmur of angry crowds sounded louder now, closer and more insistent.

The first clue that 1848 Paris might be of interest to the VBU had surfaced during interrogations of Russians captured during the Siberia op some three months earlier. Remote MSDs placed in 1848 France by Chronos scout teams had registered the magnetic surges associated with Soviet time downlinks in this general area of Paris. The four Rangers, with Rachel along to operate the scanner and take readings of the area to facilitate future time ops here, had come to confirm the automated MSDs. If they could locate a Russian time base, they were not to attack but to send for help. A specially trained strike force was being mustered at Time Square, waiting for the Rangers' call. The team's recall beacon would give Chronos the temporal lock they needed.

Hunter hauled back the slide of his .45 with a sharp *snick-snick*, chambering a round. There was still no sign of activity on the street. That in itself was sinister in this nineteenth-century city of labyrinthine streets and alleys.

A small eternity passed as Rachel and Gomez crouched at the corner of a building across the street. King and Anderson stirred at Hunter's side, watching in all directions at once. "C'mon . . . c'mon . . ." Anderson's low-voiced words were a litany of urgency, barely heard. The normally relaxed Texan fingered the thread of a scar barely visible by the dim light on the close-cropped side of his head, a legacy of that last sharp fight in a railway tunnel in Siberia. Anderson was nervous.

Hunter glanced at King, who had been uncharacteristically silent even in his good-natured grumbling since their arrival in 1848. *We're all on edge,* Hunter thought. *It's this going out time after time, always knowing that one tiny mistake could kill you . . . and everything and everyone you ever knew back uptime. How much longer can the team take this?*

He looked up as the *tap-tap-tap* of Rachel's shoes on the brick pavement sounded again. As she and Gomez returned, Hunter could see their excitement.

"Rachel's nailed 'em," Gomez said. There was a fierce light in his eyes, an eagerness to come to grips with their elusive enemy.

"I think it's that warehouse up the street," Rachel said, pointing. "Just crossing the street gave a definite shift in the bearing."

Which meant the source was damned close. They must be right on top of the Russian base. Where were their guards? "Is it still there?" he asked.

She shook her head. "No. Winked off right after I took the

second reading. There's no way to tell whether it was people going out . . . or people coming in.''

"Right," he said, uncertain as he sifted through the options available. They were damned few. Wait and watch, all the while avoiding discovery by VBU guards or stray locals; high-tail back to Time Square with an incomplete report; or . . .

"Right," he said again, with more decision this time. "Roy . . . on point. Greg . . . bring up the rear. Be ready with the recall beacon if we need it. Raye, stick with him.''

"This setup stinks, Lieutenant," King said grimly. "It's too damned quiet.''

Hunter nodded. "Maybe we can flush them, eh, Greg?''

King looked away. "Should we maybe trigger the beacon now? The damn thing takes twenty minutes to open up . . .''

"Not when our Russian friends might be watching with their own MSDs," Hunter replied. He looked from face to face. "Everyone set? Let's go.''

The team moved up the street, attempting to appear casual, but steel-spring-taut and ready for anything, their pistols concealed in pockets but tight-held in hands sweaty with anticipation.

And fear. In all his years in the U.S. Rangers, Hunter had known a number of men who genuinely enjoyed the prospect of combat. He was not one of them. Combat was a great place to get killed.

There was a chance—a good chance—that the silent ware-house was a trap. The Ranger team had foiled enough VBU plots in the past to make the Soviets wary. Hunter could only hope that if it was a trap, King and Rachel would have time to trigger the beacon and escape with the information.

The warehouse pinpointed by Rachel's scanner was a high-walled, rambling affair, seedy-looking with ragged scraps of posters still clinging to its coal-blackened facade. A nearby street lamp cast a cold light across windows high along the front. The place was silent and appeared deserted.

"Not even a sentry outside," Gomez observed. "I think they've pulled out.''

"Maybe they heard us coming," Anderson suggested. "If this is another one of their *Ochrana* units, maybe they didn't have more'n a couple of guys here in the first place and they split.''

"You think they'd just abandon a downlink?'' King asked. "Not bloody likely.''

The Rangers had captured a Russian downlink once before . . . in Russia, from just such a time guard unit as Anderson was suggesting. Perhaps the Soviet equipment had been abandoned. . . .

But there were other alternatives too. The VBU agents might be monitoring the barricade riots elsewhere in Paris or preparing for the scheduled arrival of Karl Marx two weeks hence.

Or they could be watching the Rangers at that moment on long-range IR scanners, waiting for the moment to spring their trap.

There was only one way to find out. "Greg . . . Rachel . . . you two stay here.'' He touched the tiny microphone of his combat radio clipped to the lapel of his coat. The receiver was a flesh-colored plug inserted unobtrusively in one ear. "Don't come unless you get the code on this.''

King patted the recall beacon in its leather pouch slung at his hip. "We'll be ready. You be careful, Lieutenant.''

"Always.'' Hunter managed a grin. "Everybody set? Let's move.''

The fifty yards to the warehouse door felt like fifty miles. Hunter studied the faded sign across the front: *Duplessis et Fils.* He scanned the line of tall, dirty windows, all far above the street level. How many eyes might be watching their approach?

But there was no challenge . . . no gunfire. With Anderson and Gomez covering his back, he raised the wooden latch of the barn-sized door. It swung inward easily. . . .

Hunter exchanged nods with the others. If the Russians were waiting for them, this would be the moment. He gripped his .45 in both hands, the muzzle raised. With a deep breath he rolled across the threshold and plunged inside.

The warehouse interior was dark, the air musty with dust and pungent, unidentifiable odors. A complex tangle of equipment loomed across the room, illuminated only faintly from the high windows above his head. As his eyes adjusted to the low light, Hunter made out the snake forms of thick cables winding across the wood plank floor, of busbars and power coils focused on a raised, empty stage.

Jackpot . . . !

Silently, Hunter signaled to his two comrades. They slipped through the shadows, probing, searching. The brick walls were stark and empty, with no way in or out save the broad door through which they'd entered. The building appeared deserted, the downlink apparatus quiescent, powerless. In one corner, thin partitions created a cubbyhole office . . . also deserted.

"Nobody home," Gomez said with barely suppressed excitement.

"This is too damn good to be true, LT!" Anderson exclaimed softly. "We done got ourselves another Russkie downlink!"

"Maybe the thing's busted," Gomez suggested.

A long, shivering sigh escaped Hunter's lips. He'd not realized how tense he was. "We'd better find out."

They made another circuit of the room without finding any sign of the warehouse's former occupants, save the silent electronic gadgetry. At last satisfied, Hunter touched his lapel mike. "Yankee Leader to Yankee One," he said. "It's clear . . . and it looks like Rachel has another toy to play with. Code Falcon."

"Falcon acknowledged," King's voice replied in Hunter's ear. "We're coming in."

Hunter scanned the empty walls of the warehouse again. They must have caught the Russians totally by surprise to walk in on their unoccupied downlink site. The magnetic surges they'd detected earlier would have been the last of the Russians leaving for their home base in 2008. There might well be other VBU agents monitoring the Parisian riots or Karl Marx, but they'd left their time machine unguarded and now the Rangers had it. In another twenty minutes, American troops would be here in force. He eyed the Soviet equipment squatting in the gloom. They'd learned a lot from the boxcar-mounted downlink during the Siberia mission. This time, they'd take the machine apart and ship it piece by piece back to Time Square, where they might be able to learn how to jam Soviet time-travel attempts . . . or track their operations.

He looked up as King and Rachel hurried in through the door, then began peeling off his uncomfortable tailed coat.

"Okay, Raye," he said. "See if you can unplug that thing so we don't have Russian time travelers dropping in on us. Greg . . . trigger the beacon. Let's see what Thompson's boys and girls make of *this*. . . ."

"FREEZE, ALL OF YOU!" The voice was amplified thunder, booming from a hidden speaker. *"DO NOT MOVE!"*

What happened next passed in a blur of sound and motion. The upper half of the back wall of the warehouse seemed to fold out and down . . . a hinged, steel wall masked by bricks . . . or perhaps by imitation bricks, molded from plastics unknown in the nineteenth century. A trio of spotlights snapped on, riveting the Ranger team in a pool of blinding incandescence, while from several directions came the harsh snicks of drawn bolts on automatic rifles, of running, booted feet, of harsh commands and shouts in Russian. Hunter held up one hand, trying vainly to penetrate the dazzling glare of light. He raised his pistol, seeking to fire into one of the blinding disks of raw light. . . .

Something clubbed him down, a stunning blow at the base of his neck that sent him sprawling to the floor. Someone kicked his hand, and his pistol was sent skittering off into darkness. He heard a nearby grunt as one of his men was knocked down, and the sounds of a scuffle mingled with a bitter curse from King.

He heard Rachel scream and came up fighting, throwing a wild swing at a shape half-glimpsed through the dancing afterimages imprinted on his retinas by the spotlights. The punch missed, but a heavy weight slammed into him from behind, bearing him back to the floor, pinning his arms and legs.

"RESISTANCE IS USELESS, LIEUTENANT HUNTER," the amplified voice thundered. *"YOU AND YOUR PEOPLE ARE OUR PRISONERS!"*

From flat on his belly, Hunter became aware of moving shapes all around him, of booted feet closing in from several directions. Hunter shook his head, trying to clear it. *How the hell did they know my name . . . ?*

A boot struck him in the ribs, sending burning pain through his side. "Don't move!" a harsh voice snapped in thickly accented English.

"Skaryehyeh!" someone ordered in Russian. "Quickly! Strip and search them!"

Rough hands yanked him to his feet, pinned his arms, tugged and tore at the clothing he wore, poked and probed in a harsh search for hidden weapons. His radio receiver was discovered and yanked from his ear. He felt the cold bite of handcuffs closing on his wrists behind his back.

The spotlights were replaced by a more even lighting, and, blinking the spots from his eyes, Hunter could make out dozens of uniformed Russian troops, elite spetsnaz by the look of them, closing in around them. A Soviet officer crossed his arms and grinned at him from a few feet away. "You took your time getting here, Lieutenant. We had about given up on you!"

Behind him, Hunter could see the details of the trap . . . a false, camouflaged back to the warehouse room where a company of spetsnaz could wait and watch. Only now did Hunter realize that the entire warehouse was a carefully crafted deception, a trap set specifically for the Rangers themselves. He had more than halfway expected an ambush as he'd approached the building earlier . . . but nothing as elaborate as this . . . !

Blue light shimmered above the empty stage of the Russian downlink. The warehouse might be a deception, but the time machine itself was real. Hunter watched the gateway open through time, leading . . . where?

Hunter's vision went black as blindfolds were dropped over the captives' eyes and tied tightly behind their heads. The cold muzzle of a gun barrel prodded Hunter's naked spine. "This way, American!"

He was aware of being herded into line with the others, of being shoved along up a sloping ramp toward the stage. Blind, he could hear the crude observations and laughter of their captors, could feel slick, cold metal under his bare feet. There was a sharp tang of ozone in the air as he approached the Soviet time gate. . . .

Someone shoved him from behind, and he stumbled through.

Two

Blindfolded, Hunter could see nothing of where they had been taken, but his other senses provided clues. He could hear the lap of water, and the laughs and voices and boot-scuffings of their Russian captors held a hollow, echoing quality that suggested a very large, empty chamber, possibly a cave or a concrete-walled room of some sort. The floor under his bare feet felt like concrete . . . and it was wet.

The most startling change was in the air. Paris in February had been cold and wet; here it was hot and humid. There was a salt tang in Hunter's nostrils that he immediately associated with the sea.

The sea? FREAM Intelligence believed the Soviet time-travel project was based at a place called Uralskiy in western Siberia. Wherever he was now . . . *whenever* he was, it was not Siberia!

With guards on either side holding his elbows, he quickly lost track of the twists and turns—left and right, up steps and down—as he was steered through mazelike passages. Once a harsh voice snapped "those two, to Interrogation" in Russian, and he sensed that he was being led away from the others, down a carpeted corridor. He heard the crisp rustle of men in uniform saluting as the party marched past.

The handcuffs were removed then, but only so his arms could be stretched above his head and his wrists and ankles fastened to an upright metal rack. The blindfold was whipped off, and he found himself facing Rachel across a white-walled room with tile floors and wooden cabinets. They were both chained, spread-eagled, and helpless. Some of the team's gear—the MSD and Hunter's radio—lay spread out on a table nearby. The leader of the Paris spetsnaz team held the American recall beacon in his hands.

"It is a pleasure to meet you at last, Miss Stein," he said, smiling at Rachel. His English was perfect. "We have an extensive file on you from . . . ah . . . past encounters, and I have been looking forward to making your acquaintance. I am Major Fedor Fedeevich Shvernik . . . at your service. We have many questions we want to ask. . . ."

Rachel twisted and struggled against her restraints. A husky guard looked on, leering unpleasantly.

Shvernik smiled again, examining the beacon curiously. "How this device works, for example. I think you can tell us, my dear. Oh, don't worry. You won't be hurt. Not yet, at any rate. As a senior American Chronos technician, you are most valuable to us in one piece." The cold blue eyes turned away from her then, meeting Hunter's. "Your friend here, on the other hand . . ."

Greg King paced the narrow confines of the cell restlessly. Their handcuffs had been removed, and he, Anderson, and Gomez had been thrust into the concrete-walled room, together with three sets of gray cotton pajamas and three pairs of cheap plastic sandals. Hours had passed since they'd been brought through the Soviet time gate.

"Where the hell are we?" Anderson asked. His back was to King as he searched the opposite wall. There was no furniture in the cell, nothing at all save a naked light bulb dangling out of reach overhead and a drain in the center of the floor. The steel door was featureless save for a sliding-panel eye slot for the guards outside.

"Not in Siberia," King replied. "Not yet, anyway."

Anderson turned then, questioning with his eyes. King touched his forefinger to his ear. There could be no doubt at all that the cell was bugged; there could be no other reason for the three of them to have been imprisoned together.

The Texan nodded, then tapped his wrist, again questioning with his eyes. King could only shrug. At least as important as *where* they were being held was *when*. If their VBU captors had not taken them to Uralskiy, it was a fairly safe bet that they weren't in 2008 at all. But what year was it? There was no way to find out unless they got out.

If they *could* get out . . .

King completed his fruitless search and slumped to the floor, his back against the rough, cold wall. There was nothing to be learned from bare concrete . . . and no way in or out save through the steel door.

They would be questioning Travis and Rachel now, King decided. That was the only explanation for their absence. The Russian had called both of them by name at the warehouse and mentioned some sort of file.

Bloody hell, he thought savagely. *We're notorious already.* It gave him a kind of grim satisfaction to know that the team had caused the VBU enough trouble to be known by name. Not that it would do them any good. Quite the opposite, in fact . . .

He thought about Rachel. How long would it take the Russians to break her?

"To Interrogation," one of the Russians had said. That suggested a strangely un-Soviet haste in the procedure. Usual Soviet questioning techniques called for a period of time—weeks or even months—of softening up, keeping the prisoners awake, ruining their time sense by irregular meals and questioning sessions, feeding them drugs.

They're in a hurry, he decided. *Why?*

He was fairly sure that any of the Rangers could stand up under almost any physical abuse the Russians could hit them with, at least over the short term. Anyone could be broken, given enough time, but time seemed to be what their captors did not have. That meant the interrogators would be concentrating on Rachel as the one to break . . . and that brought King's thoughts full circle.

How long would it take them to break her?

A rattle of keys came from the door . . . followed by the clatter of steel as it opened. Two Soviet guards propelled Hunter—naked, bruised, and bleeding—into the cell, while another covered them all with an AKM from the passageway outside.

"Chief!" Gomez exclaimed, going to Hunter's crumpled form.

A Russian officer tossed another set of prison garments into the room, then pointed at King. "That one next."

They clubbed him down with their rifles before he could even begin to resist. Half-conscious, he was dragged from the cell before the steel door was swung shut and locked with a hollow clang.

Hunter opened his eyes, and gradually the blurred shapes hovering above him resolved themselves into the anxious faces of Anderson and Gomez. His head was throbbing, and the mass of bruises over his body had merged into one vast, dull ache.

"What'd they do to you, LT?" Anderson's face was dark, flushed with anger. "Where's Rachel? Where'd they take Greg?"

Hunter reached up and touched the side of his face. His finger came away slick with blood. That goon with the broom handle . . .

Shvernik had limited the interrogation to a simple but extremely thorough and methodical beating, but Hunter knew with a gut-wrenching certainty that worse was to come. His beating had been for Rachel's benefit, an attempt to make her cooperate to save her friends further pain.

The Ranger lieutenant groaned. Greg must be getting a similar treatment now. "Just down the hall," he said at last, answering Anderson's last question. He sat up slowly. Anderson touched a finger to his lips, then his ear, then pointed to a wall.

Hunter looked around the room, taking in the absence of furniture or appliances. He touched his eye, questioning, and Anderson shrugged. If it was a foregone conclusion that microphones were hidden behind the walls of this place, the presence of TV cameras was less certain. It was possible, of course, that they were under visual observation, but the tiny cell had the look of a converted storeroom, and it seemed unlikely that they would be kept here for long.

"Here, Chief," Gomez said, making conversation for the

sake of eavesdroppers. He handed Hunter a gray bundle. "They left you something to wear, at least."

Anderson, meanwhile, used his hands to make quick, fleeting signs in the air. *Break out, all of us . . .*

Hunter nodded agreement. Their chances from this point on could only get worse as they became weaker under the questionings and beatings. If they acted quickly, they might take the guards by surprise.

It wouldn't be easy, Hunter reflected. Not knowing where they were, or what year they were in, their chances of getting home would be vanishingly slim.

Unless . . .

He used his hands to sketch the outline of the recall beacon. Gomez soundlessly mouthed the word "where?" Hunter replied with more signs. *The room where I was . . .*

It was a long shot but preferable to wandering an unknown countryside while spetsnaz teams hunted them down.

The best time to attempt an escape was now.

Hunter used his own blood, still wet across the side of his face, to rough out a floor plan of the part of the Russian base he knew . . . the interrogation room, just off the hallway beyond the cell door, down a side passageway and up a short flight of stairs. As he drew the diagram, Anderson used teeth and nails to tear off a strip of his own pajama top to bandage Hunter's head.

The action gave Hunter an idea. He gestured for Anderson to tear off a second strip, eighteen inches long and less than an inch wide. Piano wire would have worked better, but the cloth strip would make an acceptable garrote.

"Hey! You out there! We'll talk! We'll talk!"

The three of them crouched in the cell, Hunter in the middle, Gomez and Anderson on either side of the door. Would the ploy work?

Keys rattled outside, and the door swung open. . . .

The plan assumed that there would be two guards, one covering his friend from the passageway with an assault rifle. As the first guard stepped into the room, an AKM prodding menacingly at Hunter's chest, Anderson stepped behind the man and whipped the cloth garrote around his throat. Hunter sidestepped the assault rifle and knocked the muzzle aside, snapping the heel of his hand up and forward into the guard's nose. He felt cartilage splinter as the Russian's head jerked back. Gomez was through the door like a cannonball, colliding with the soldier outside, sending him sprawling as his AK skittered across the floor.

Then nothing went as planned. Automatic gunfire barked and ricocheted in the hallway as Hunter snatched the AKM from the first guard's unresisting fingers. There was a sound of running, booted feet outside, a shouted warning in Russian.

Eddie Gomez was pinned by the guard he had tackled, a big, heavy man. Hunter stepped through the door, bringing the butt of the AK down on the back of the VBU trooper's head. Gunfire crashed again from up the passageway, where another soldier shouted into an intercom mounted on the wall while trying at the same time to shoot Hunter with a one-handed grip on his assault rifle.

Hunter triggered his own AKM, a short burst from chest-high that spun the enemy soldier away from the intercom and pitched him facedown in the corridor. Somewhere far off, a deep-throated, whooping alarm sounded. Another trooper appeared from a branching corridor down the hall. Hunter fired again and the man screamed and dropped.

"That's done it, LT," Anderson said. He picked up the second AKM and helped Gomez to his feet. "Every Russkie in the joint'll be here now. . . ."

Their silently constructed plan had called for the three of them to head for the interrogation room. With surprise, they might have been able to free King and Rachel, barricade themselves in with the recall beacon, and hold off the enemy long enough to get through to Time Square.

That chance seemed vanishingly small now. With the alarm out, Shvernik would certainly assume that the Rangers would attempt just that. . . .

"Change of plan," Hunter said. He gestured with his AK. "Eddie . . . you and I'll give them a run for their money. How about it?"

Gomez showed his teeth. "Sounds good, Chief. A diversion, huh?"

"Exactly. Roy, you find the interrogation room. Eddie and I'll make enough racket that you have a chance to get in there."

"Maybe you should go, LT," Anderson said. "You've been there...."

"No!" Hunter was still hurting after the beating, and that could slow him up. Besides, the thought of running for help while Roy and Eddie held off spetsnaz commandos was repugnant. "No. We'll try to keep them off your back."

"You want me to get Greg and Rachel out . . . ?"

Hunter shook his head. "Not unless it's handed to you. Find the recall beacon. It'll be in there somewhere. They want Rachel to tell them how to use it. If you can get it away . . . find a quiet spot to hide . . ."

Anderson nodded sharply. "And get help. You can count on me, LT!"

Shots erupted from down the corridor. Hunter returned fire. "Go!" he yelled. "Go! C'mon, Eddie!"

Hunter and Gomez charged off down the passageway in one direction, pausing only long enough to retrieve a second weapon from the body of one of the men Hunter had killed. Anderson hesitated only a second, then hurried off in the opposite direction.

The alarm continued to shrill. . . .

Rachel closed her eyes and tried to look away, but Major Shvernik grasped her jaw with one hand and forced her head around. "No, my dear. You must watch. Grigor . . . again, please." The guard slammed the end of a broom handle into King's belly.

"I don't understand, Miss Stein," Shvernik mused, his fingers roughly caressing her cheek. "Surely you must care *something* for these men. Perhaps if we carve him with a knife . . ."

Across from her, King looked up blearily through eyes blackened and nearly swollen shut. "Don't tell 'em . . . a bloody damned thing. . . ."

"You can save your friends a great deal of pain, my dear, if you'll just . . ."

She twisted against his touch, her mouth closing on Shvernik's hand. He yelped and pulled away. *"Shooka!"* He slapped her, a stinging, open-handed blow that set stars dancing in front of her eyes. "Bitch! Perhaps we'll play with you for a while. . . ."

He looked up sharply as the whooping shriek of a siren echoed in the room.

A telephone rang. Grigor answered it, then handed the phone to Shvernik. *"Da, Tovarisch Polkovnik,"* Shvernik said after listening a moment. *"Kaneshna . . . neemedleena!"* He replaced the receiver, then spoke rapidly to Grigor in Russian. Rachel watched the major leave, struggling not to surrender to the panic throbbing in her chest. She knew that if she once gave in to that cold terror, it would rise up and overwhelm her, holding her more helpless than the chains.

Rachel sagged against the manacles. She feared pain. Worse, though, was the fear of what else the VBU troopers might do to her. She had been raped once, by Soviet soldiers in Boston months before her escape to Free America. Her recovery from that ordeal had been a long time coming. Travis, with his understanding and with his gentleness as a lover, had done much to heal that wound, but Rachel knew that her old dread of being utterly helpless lay just beneath the surface.

They'd done nothing to her yet beyond fondling her and making crude, leering threats, but she knew what would come next. The real horror lay in her own uncertainty in how she would react, in her fear that she would break and tell them what they wanted to know. The shame of holding firm while others—while Travis—were beaten and tortured in front of her, and then giving in when they turned on her, would be too much to bear.

Rachel yanked with a new desperation at the cuffs holding her wrists. So much, she thought, had depended on the American time-travel project. For her, personally, a successful rewriting of history meant that her mother, victim of an auto accident during the building of the Chronos complex, might not die, because there would never be need for the project in the first place. It meant that the United States would never have been divided and occupied by foreign armies . . . and that four drunken Russian soldiers would not have broken into her room one night two years before. . . .

But if the price of those changes was her own soul, the cost was far too high.

Across the room, Grigor's face cracked in an unpleasant smile and he set his AK assault rifle aside. "You maybe are uncomfortable, *devoshka*?'' He advanced on her. ''I could help, maybe. Is long time before Major come, *da*?''

''Leave her the hell alone!'' King bellowed.

Grigor turned on King and drove an elbow into the helpless man's stomach, where bruises already showed from the earlier beating. ''Silence, *Amerikahnets! Devoshka* and I no want be disturbed. . . .''

Rachel screamed as Grigor reached for her. . . .

Three

The Russian soldier spun as Anderson burst through the interrogation room door. With Rachel in the line of fire he didn't dare shoot, so he swung the butt of the AKM around as he stepped in close. The Russian crashed sideways into the wooden cabinets that lined one wall, then slumped to the tile floor, blood streaming from one ear.

"Nice one, Roy!" King managed through bruised lips. "You ever thought about taking up baseball?"

Anderson eyed the chains holding King spread-eagled against the metal rack. "Where are the keys?" he snapped.

Rachel watched wide-eyed from an identical vantage position across the room. "Shvernik has them," she said. Her voice was shaking, her breath coming in shallow, panting gulps. "The beacon . . ."

"God, yes!" King said. There was a sound of running foot-steps in the corridor outside. "Get the damned beacon, Roy! On the table behind you!"

For a second that felt like an eternity, Anderson wrestled with an impossible choice. If he stayed here, their captors would return; certainly they'd be back long before the twenty minutes it would take to open the portal back to Time Square. But he couldn't leave his friends like this.

"Don't worry about us, lad," King said. "Get out! Get help!"

And there was help waiting, Anderson knew. The strike force mobilizing at Time Square for the Paris op could be readied in minutes. If he left the beacon here when he stepped through the portal, he could return with a small army. . . .

"I'll be back!" he said, scooping up the beacon. It was book-sized, a black plastic box set with lights and a blank digital readout screen. "I don't want to leave you. . . ." The urgency he felt to reassure them was overpowering. "I'll be back!" he repeated.

"Roy!" Rachel's eyes were wild, filled with some undefinable horror. They flicked to the body of the VBU soldier, then locked with Anderson's own. "I . . . I think you'd better . . . kill me."

Anderson recoiled. "Kill you! Why?"

The horror in her eyes darkened "I . . . don't think I can hold out. . . ."

"Nonsense! I'll be back with half of Time Square in no time at all!"

"Roy . . . ! Please . . . !"

He turned and fled the room. What had those bastards done to her?

A pair of Russians met him in the corridor, more startled by Anderson's sudden appearance than he was by theirs. The AK bucked in his hand, spraying lead, driving them back in splattering blood and fragments of concrete chipped by ricochets.

He paused, suddenly uncertain, as smoke coiled from the AK's muzzle. Where could he find a place he would be undisturbed for the twenty minutes he would need to trigger the beacon and wait for the portal to open? The Texan looked up, inspiration dragging from him a grim smile. The siren continued its eerie wail, as gunfire slammed and nattered in the distance.

With Eddie and the LT kicking up a fuss elsewhere, there was one place that might suit his needs. . . .

A grenade clattered across the concrete floor, bounced from one wall, and came to a halt spinning at Hunter's feet. Without pausing to think, he lashed out with one foot, sending it skittering back down the corridor. "Down!"

Hunter and Gomez flattened themselves on the floor as the grenade exploded. Bits of metal pinged off the walls above them and the concussion hit them like a sledgehammer blow, but they struggled to their feet in the smoky hallway a moment later, battered and momentarily deafened, but unhurt.

The gunfire that had spat at them from down the passage had ceased.

"Let's go!" Hunter yelled. His ears were ringing so loudly from the blast that he could scarcely hear his own words, but Gomez nodded and plunged forward. Neither of them was sure where they were. Their escape had carried them a long distance through twisting corridors, up one level and far from the block of prison cells where they'd started the diversion. Hunter wished he had his watch. He could only guess that it had been at least ten, maybe fifteen minutes since their escape. Anderson should have reached the interrogation room by now . . . should have found the recall beacon.

If it's still there. If the Russians weren't there waiting for him. If . . . If . . .

Behind the endless ifs and doubts was a burning guilt. *Rachel! What have they done to you?* He suppressed mad, half-formed images of going to her, of rescuing her. . . .

No! Her best hope—the best hope for all of them—was Roy. "Let's go, Eddie!"

"Right with you, Chief!"

They pounded up the corridor, pausing only to discard nearly empty magazines for their AKs and replace them with fresh mags drawn from a pair of khaki-clad spetsnaz sprawled where the grenade had cut them down. Hunter looked both ways along the cross passageway. The farther they could get from the area where they'd been held the better, but the enemy must be tracing them, closing in on them from several directions by now. The underground complex was large, but not as deep or as intricate as the Chronos base underneath Wyoming's Mount Bannon. How long could two men hope to hold out against this base's entire complement?

The explosion slammed him against a wall. He dropped the AK and slumped to the floor. He rolled over, ears ringing, groping for the AK. It was out of reach. Gomez lay against the opposite corridor wall, nose and mouth bloodied, eyes glazed. Smoke choked the narrow passageway.

Concussion grenade . . . Hunter's thoughts were confused, a mumbling of half-formed images and words. *They want us alive....*

Booted feet appeared before his eyes, blurred as his eyes tried to focus on them.

"Quickly ... *quickly*!" Anderson was beside himself with urgency. "If they find where I left the beacon, they'll slam the damn door shut in our faces!"

"We're ready," a tall, dark-skinned man assured him. Sergeant Dark Walker was a Dakota Indian, refugee from an alternate reality where the British had beaten the American colonials in the 1770s. Before that universe had been edited out of existence by the Rangers, Walker had been a member of the British SAS, fighting the Communist monster enslaving his world. Now, here, he continued the fight. The monster, it seemed, was the same, whatever the shape of the history that spawned it.

The men behind Walker were new to the Chronos Ranger force, a motley collection scraped together from elite units scattered or broken by the Soviet occupation of America. They included Army Special Forces, Rangers, even a few Navy SEALs. Their commander was Lieutenant Jason Case, blond, blue-eyed, and hard, once a member of Delta Force before that half-legendary elite unit had been disbanded.

The Free American Central Command had been building a large and hard-hitting strike force. They numbered thirty now, and they'd been training for time ops with the original Ranger team for the past three months. While Anderson and the others had been tracking down the VBU in 1848 Paris, Walker and the others had been here at Chronos, waiting for a target.

Now they had one—not the time or place they'd expected, but a target nonetheless.

"Power levels are steady," a technician reported. "They can go through any time, sir."

Major General Alexander Thompson nodded, his face grave. "Sergeant Anderson ... Roy. You did well getting back to us. You don't have to return...."

"What, and leave them back there?"

Thompson's face creased with the trace of a smile. "I thought you'd say that." He turned and looked at Lieutenant

Case. "It's your show, Lieutenant. Move out."

"Sir!" Case snapped. "Sergeant Walker! Move 'em through!"

On the stage behind them, blue light gathered at the nexus of power coils and busbars, and ozone stung the air. Anderson hefted his M-60 machine gun, checking to see that the belt of 5.56 ammo was unkinked and properly seated in the receiver. Fresh fatigues and an MG in his hands made him feel ready to tackle anything. A pack on his shoulders held clothing for Hunter and the rest, as well as weapons.

Just pray God they're still around to take 'em when you get there, Roy old son. . . .

Thirty heavily armed men clattered up the ramp and vanished two by two into the blue light. Hiking his 60-gun on his shoulder, Anderson followed them through. . . .

Major Fedor Fedeevich Shvernik gestured at the winking lights on the console. "They've made contact with their base."

"Obviously," Colonel Primakov replied. "Kurayev reports dozens of intruders. You should not have left the interrogation room so lightly guarded."

Shvernik sagged. He'd feared this outcome when his men had reported that one of the three escaped American prisoners had eluded his net. Moments later, word had come that the interrogation room guard was dead and the enemy time beacon missing.

"Your orders, Comrade Colonel, were to . . ."

"Damn my orders! We don't have enough troops to seal off this installation . . . and we've lost heavily simply trying to recapture those escaped prisoners!"

Shvernik closed his eyes. "What are our options, Comrade Colonel?"

"Few, Major. Precious few. We will have our men fall back to the time machine. The base is lost . . . that much is obvious. With only a handful of troops here, there is little else we *can* do. The operation will have to be continued from *Moryeh Ohotnik.* . . ."

"But our base here . . ."

"Will have to be destroyed. We cannot allow it to fall into American hands."

"*Da*, Comrade Colonel." It was the price of failure. Shvernik's eyes turned to the console across the command center, where a pair of nervous-looking Soviet technicians watched them warily. The destruct sequence would be entered through the base's main computer. "I . . . will take care of it. . . ."

"*Nyet*, Comrade Major." The colonel shook his head firmly. "The responsibility is mine. I have other orders for you."

"Sir . . . ?"

"Communications with *Moryeh Ohotnik* are uncertain. They must know what happened here and . . . alter the Plan accordingly."

Shvernik nodded. It was an old problem. Without communications satellites, the far-flung elements of the Soviet master plan—of *Espahneeyah Rassvet*—had suffered from lack of coordination. Still, with the bulk of the operation's personnel across the ocean aboard the *Ohotnik*, there had been no need for continuous communications. The base, remote from the operational theater, had been a reserve installation since *Ohotnik*'s departure a week before.

"I will give you time to make good your escape. You will take *Number Four* and proceed to Point *Noyab'r*. There you will rendezvous with Krylenko aboard the *Princessa Negra*. Transfer your men and your prisoners to Krylenko's command, and proceed to Point *Ahktyab'r*. From there, you will be able to arrange your rendezvous with *Moryeh Ohotnik*."

"My . . . prisoners?"

"The man and the woman in interrogation. I've already given orders to take them aboard *Number Four*. They should be there by now."

"And the two we recaptured?"

"In the sick bay. They will die there when the base goes."

"Comrade Colonel . . . won't you come too?"

Primakov gave a shallow smile. "It is easier to stay than to explain things to our superiors. Hurry, Major! Before the Americans break through to the docks!"

"*Da, Tovarisch Polkovnik*. . . ."

"I will give you an hour. You must be well clear by then."

Shvernik knew a savage exultation as he saluted and hurried from the command center. *I will live!*

• • •

Maybe I'll live after all. . . .

Hunter had regained consciousness in what was obviously the Soviet dispensary, a starkly furnished hospital ward. Hunter and Gomez were handcuffed to two of the iron-frame beds. A nervous-looking Russian stood guard.

The sound of gunfire in the corridor outside was growing closer. When he heard the deep-throated thunder of an American M-60, Hunter allowed himself a generous smile. Roy had made it through . . . and now the Texan was back, in force!

The one potential fly in the ointment was the guard. He was painfully young, scarcely more than a teenager, and for all the military training he must have endured so far, he looked scared and uncertain. The AKM in his hands wavered between Hunter and Gomez's still-unconscious form in the next bed. If he took it into his mind not to let his charges fall into American hands . . .

He turned his smile on the boy. *"Dobroyeh ootrah, tovarisch,"* he said in what he hoped was a polite manner. "Good morning, comrade. Sounds busy out there, doesn't it?"

The AK whipped around to aim steadily at Hunter's nose. "Silence! No talking!"

"Don't be nervous," Hunter said, still speaking Russian. "I assure you I'm worth a lot more to you alive than dead. . . ."

"I said no talking!"

The uniform was that of Soviet Naval Infantry, but Hunter had no doubt at all that the guard was spetsnaz . . . and therefore well trained, unpredictable, and deadly. The *Spetsialnoye Nazhacheniye* were the Red Army's special forces and served as the military arm of the VBU. Since they generally adopted the uniform of the military arm to which they were assigned, Hunter concluded that this one was naval spetsnaz.

What were Russian elite naval forces doing on an operation in the past?

Time enough to learn that later . . . assuming he could survive the next five minutes. If he could just keep the nervous young commando talking . . .

"Say, I could help you make a deal with the Americans," Hunter said. He kept his voice smooth and unhurried.

The boy's mouth twisted in a soundless snarl, and he hefted

the AKM up to his shoulder, the muzzle still even with Hunter's face.

"I kill you now, American . . . !"

The door behind him exploded open, and Roy Anderson plunged into the room, smoke wafting from the muzzle of the M-60 slung from his neck. The Russian whirled, the AK blasting on full auto, but Anderson's machine gun was already leveled and dead on target. A twitch of the Texan's trigger finger sent a short burst of lead searing through the young trooper's abdomen, picking him up and slamming him into the blood-splattered plaster of the wall at his back.

Dark Walker was two paces behind Anderson, a Galil battle rifle in his hands. "Lieutenant Hunter! Are you hurt?"

"No problem, Sarge. You were right on time!" He rattled his handcuffs. "Now, if you could do something about these. I think our friend on the floor has the keys. . . ."

Anderson's face was white with worry. "I got back quick as I could, LT!"

"You did fine, Roy." Dark Walker unlocked the handcuffs and Hunter sat up, rubbing his wrist. "Did you get to Raye and Greg?"

Anguish twisted at Anderson's features. "No, LT. Damn it, no! That was the first place we went after we came through . . . and they were gone! Both of 'em!"

"Shit!" There was still no telling how big this base was. Rachel and King could be anywhere, and Shvernik might have a gun at their heads at this moment.

"Damn it, I'm sorry, LT!"

"Not your fault, Roy." Hunter stood, still a bit unsteady on his feet after his brush with the concussion grenade. From the next bed, Gomez groaned as Dark Walker released him. Outside, strings of armed men clattered past the dispensary at a dead run. "You did all you could . . . more than anyone could have expected. . . ."

Anderson hitched the pack off his back. "I brought you some decent clothes, LT. And your Uzi."

He still looked so upset that Hunter clapped him on the shoulder as he accepted the fatigues and the black, heavy sleekness of his Uzi submachine gun. "It's okay, Roy!"

Anderson nodded, his mouth set in a hard, grim line. "It's

just I was there in the room with them, LT. And I couldn't help. . . ."

Hunter began pulling on his uniform. "We'll find them, Roy. And if Shvernik has touched either of them . . ."

Four

The American strike force split into separate teams. They still had only a poor idea of the actual layout of the base, and there was a lot of ground to cover.

Hunter raced with Anderson and Gomez through corridors leading toward the interrogation room. Lieutenant Case split off half of the men while Dark Walker led a smaller team in an attempt to get behind the enemy.

Russian troops came boiling out of a side corridor, AKMs blazing. Hunter opened fire with his Uzi in short, precise bursts as Anderson's 60-gun hammered bloody thunder at his side. The surviving spetsnaz broke and ran for cover, pursued by a relentless, concrete-chipping hail of fire from the light machine gun.

"Strike Leader to all Strikers!" Lieutenant Case said over the communications net. "We've found their command center. We're going in!"

"Strike Leader, this is Strike Two," another voice replied. "Three bad guys down here. We're moving up!"

Battle reports continued to filter in as Hunter listened. It was strange for him to be in the middle of a firefight and not have the responsibility for leading the attack.

Anderson gave him a hasty thumbs-up and hurried forward. Their movement through the base would have been safer—and quicker—using grenades, but the strike force was hampered

31

knowing that two Americans were still being held by the Soviets, somewhere within the underground warren of rooms and corridors. They had to take each Russian stronghold the hard way. . . .

Up a short flight of concrete stairs, then, and along another. Hunter turned a corner, his Uzi already leveled in time to confront a Russian in a naval infantry uniform struggling to chamber a round on his AKM. Hunter fired first, three rounds lacing their way up the naval spetsnaz trooper's chest, pitching him against the door he'd been guarding.

Hunter and Anderson took opposite sides, out of the line of fire from the room's interior. At Hunter's nod, the Texan swung around in front of the door, raised his boot, and gave it a solid kick that splintered the thin wood and sent it crashing inward. Hunter rolled through while Anderson and Gomez covered him from behind.

Hunter had an instant's blurred impression of an office . . . of carpet, desk, chairs, and a large bookcase along one wall. A map of the Caribbean dominated one wall. In front of the desk, a Soviet colonel stood over a smouldering wastebasket, a wad of papers in his hand. . . .

The Russian reached for the Tokarev automatic holstered at his hip. *"Stoy!"* Hunter bellowed, snapping his Uzi up. "Stop!"

The officer kept reaching. A burst of fire from just behind Hunter and to his side cracked with shocking fury, hurling the Russian sideways onto his desk, papers and blood spilling in every direction.

Hunter suppressed his disappointment. It would have been a real coup if they'd been able to take a VBU colonel alive. Still, the papers he'd been burning must be important. Hunter hurried forward, upending the wastebasket to scatter its blazing contents on the rug, then stamping out the flames with his boot. Anderson joined him.

"Sorry, LT," Anderson said as the last burning document was put out. "Once he had hold of that pistol, I wasn't going to wait. . . ."

"I don't think he was going to stop, Roy," Hunter said, stooping to retrieve a half-burned sheet of paper. He squinted at Cyrillic characters, neatly arrayed in columns. "Looks like a code book. He wouldn't have surrendered with this on him.''

"Or this," Anderson said, examining a map. "Look here! Point October . . . what's that, d'you suppose?''

"I don't know," Hunter said.

"Hey, here's our stuff," Gomez said from the desk. Hunter saw his .45 and the side arms carried by the other Rangers who had been captured. Gomez picked up the items of demolitions gear he always carried: a length of detcord, a small wad of C-4, some fuse igniters.

A glint of gold on the desk caught Hunter's eye. He crossed the room and picked up a small locket suspended from a slender chain. Rachel's locket, the one with the picture of her dead mother inside.

Rachel . . .

He dropped the chain into a pocket, fighting to suppress the churning emotion in his stomach. "Right," he said. His wristwatch was also on the desk, and he picked it up. "We'd better . . ."

He got no further. Dark Walker's voice was on the tactical net, hammering at Hunter's brain. "All units, this is Walker! I've spotted King and Miss Stein!''

His hand flew to the transmitter pinned to his collar. "Hunter here! Where are you?''

Walker described where he was and how he'd gotten there. "I'm in something like an underground dock, Lieutenant! They're taking them on board a patrol boat!''

Hunter remembered the smell of salt, the sound of water as he'd come blindfolded into this base. A naval base . . . in the Caribbean?

"Let's get down there," Hunter said, gathering the others with his eyes. "Move out, on the double!''

Sergeant Dark Walker ducked low behind a double row of empty, fifty-gallon fuel drums as gunfire barked from the dockside. The concrete quays were alive with Russians, most of them readying a sleek boat for departure. Walker had seen them lead the two prisoners, King and Rachel, on board at gunpoint. Troops were crowding aboard as the craft's diesels idled. The entire dock area was underground. Sunlight streamed in through a cavernlike entrance beyond the docks, and Walker could see swampland and palm trees in the distance, with the piercing blue of the Caribbean on the horizon. The cavern's interior was festooned with lights, catwalks, and tracks for overhead cranes and loading machinery, as well as tangles of power cables and other equipment that Walker couldn't identify.

Whatever this base was, it was well equipped and large enough to accommodate a ship of considerable bulk. At the moment, there were only two boats in sight, one tied ahead of the other at the right-side concrete pier: the sleek, steel-hulled patrol boat and an aging, antique-looking craft with one sloop-rigged mast and a wooden hull. Lettering across the sloop's transom spelled the name *La Dueña*.

Other Americans emerged from the doorway at Walker's back, exchanging shots with Soviet troops as they came through. Chief Doug Morgan ran up next to the fuel drum barricade, snapped off three quick bursts from his Smith & Wesson Model 760 SMG, then dropped to cover at Walker's side. Morgan had been a member of SEAL Team 6 before the UN shut down the Navy's elite Sea, Air, and Land unit. He wore leaf-pattern camo garb and his trademark boonie hat.

"Looks like an old, stripped-down Turya," Morgan said, peering over the barricade. "They won't get far in that."

Auto-fire slammed into the steel drums, punching holes with pile-driver hammering. Walker rose to his knees, targeting a running naval spetsnaz with his Galil. He fired a three-round burst, toppling the Russian into the water. Another Soviet trooper opened fire from the deck of the wood-hulled *Dueña*. Morgan cut him down with a well-aimed triplet of shots from his SMG.

Then a heavy machine gun thundered from the patrol boat's forward deck, a twin-mount 25mm weapon designed for antiaircraft use but murderous against unprotected troops inside the cavern. A pair of Rangers climbing a ladder toward an overhead catwalk twisted and jerked, then seemed to disintegrate in bloody fragments under the hail of 25mm rounds from the vessel. Rounds struck rock and steel, shattering stone and striking orange sparks in the dim light. Walker and Morgan sprawled with their faces pressed against the concrete as the heavy fire hosed across the steel drums, knocking some over like tenpins and leaving others riddled with gaping, knife-edged holes.

The boat's engines revved louder. Walker peered over an upended fuel drum in time to see a naval spetsnaz trooper cast off the Turya's bow line and leap on board. The vessel pulled into the center of the docking basin, white foam boiling under her stern.

More Rangers entered the docking area at a dead run. A few Russians remained, scattered about the area, firing back even as they died. Walker spotted one on a catwalk high above the water, drawing a bead on the door through which the American troops were entering. The Indian's Galil spoke once; the Russian rolled off the catwalk and plunged fifty feet into the water with a loud splash.

The battle's end was marked by an almost deathly hush, broken only by the distant roar of the patrol boat as it gunned to full speed in the channel outside the cave.

Walker stood slowly. Lieutenant Hunter had just entered through the open door. The Ranger lieutenant saw Walker and lowered his Uzi. "What happened, Walker?"

"I'm sorry, Lieutenant," Walker said. *I failed.* . . . "They . . . they . . ."

"We didn't have a chance of stopping 'em, Lieutenant," Chief Morgan said. "Not when they opened up with their 25 em-em. But they won't go far."

Hunter turned his gaze on the SEAL. There was a darkness in those eyes. "Oh?"

"It was a stripped-down Turya torpedo boat."

"A torpedo boat?"

"Looked like they might be using her as an auxiliary of some kind. No aft turret . . . no torp tubes. But even with an extra load of diesel fuel, she won't have a range of much more than six . . . maybe seven hundred miles."

"An auxiliary, huh?" Hunter looked thoughtful. "Auxiliary to what?"

"I don't know, Lieutenant," Walker said. "But Miss Stein and Sergeant King are both on board. And six hundred miles covers a lot of ground."

"Or ocean," Hunter said, so softly he might have been speaking to himself. "One hell of a lot of ocean . . ."

• • •

Hunter stood once again in the office of the base commander, scowling at the map of the Caribbean on the wall. Lieutenant Case was there, along with Gomez, Anderson, Walker, and the SEAL Chief Morgan.

"We can't just let them get away!" Hunter insisted. "Give them an hour and they could be anywhere!"

"Those patrol boats can manage forty knots," Morgan said. "An hour gives us forty miles of coast to search. More, since a nautical mile is longer than a landlubber's mile."

Case shook his head. "The portal is still open, Hunter. We don't know that this base is secured yet. We should start bringing in technicians. And more troops."

Hunter frowned. "They have our people out there, somewhere," he said. "Damn it, Case, we don't even know what year it is. . . ."

"Sure we do," Case replied. "They're locked on at Time Square. We're in eastern Cuba, and this is the year 1588. Probably mid to late spring."

"*1588?*" Hunter's mind raced. He'd long held a passionate love for history, an interest that had come in useful, to say the least, during more than one excursion into the past. Though Hunter did not subscribe to the theory that the past was best understood as a series of dates and events, there were a few dates that stood out, dates immediately recognized as turning points in history: 476 and the Fall of Rome . . . 1066 and Hastings . . . 1776 and American Independence . . .

And 1588, the year of Philip of Spain's failed attempt to invade England with his Grand Armada. Hunter closed his eyes, thinking. Outside these caverns, right now, would be the Caribbean of the Spanish Main . . . of treasure fleets and galleons, of the English privateers, Hawkins, Frobisher, and, most famous of all, Drake. In England, it was the time of Queen Elizabeth, of Shakespeare and Sir Walter Raleigh.

What was the VBU planning?

"The location of this base is interesting," Morgan said, pointing at the map. "I've been here, in fact, though it'll be a few years, yet, I reckon . . ."

"Yeah?" Gomez asked. "Where's here?"

"Gitmo," the Navy man said. "Guantánamo Bay. Hell, I

was stationed here for a couple of years . . . back in '95 and '96. That was before I joined the SEALs.''

"Guantánamo . . . !'' Hunter knew of it, of course. The U.S. base there had been much in the news during American troop deployments in Central America in the mid-nineties . . . and when the Cubans moved in a few years later. It had a reputation for being one of the best deep-water harbors in the world, though it was so isolated from the rest of Cuba by the Sierra Maestra Mountains that it hadn't been used as a port until the early years of the twentieth century. In 1588, Guantánamo must be wild and deserted, frequented only by occasional pirates . . .

. . . and by the VBU.

"Did we take any prisoners?'' Hunter asked. The team had stumbled across something very large and complex, a VBU plan of startling dimensions. They needed more information.

"A few.'' Case shrugged. "Workers and rankers, mostly. They don't seem to know anything . . . not even the date.''

"Expendable,'' Anderson suggested. "The big shots boogied on that patrol boat.''

Gomez nodded toward the body of the Russian colonel. "He could've told us.''

"Maybe.'' Hunter's fists closed, a new resolve growing. "Maybe. Seems like the ones who've got the answers now are on that Turya.''

"That doesn't help us,'' Case said. "How are you going to chase them . . . fly?''

"There's another boat down there,'' Hunter replied stubbornly. *"La Dueña.''*

Case laughed. "That relic? A sailboat . . . ?''

"That relic has been outfitted with twin diesel engines and radar,'' Hunter said. He'd checked the craft over before returning to the office. It was of a type Morgan had referred to as a "coastal lugger'' and seemed to have been designed to carry supplies and cargo for the Russians.

To where? For what purpose?

"You can organize things here all you want, Case,'' Hunter continued. "But I'm taking some of my people after that patrol boat.''

"I don't like it, Lieutenant. . . .''

Hunter grinned wolfishly. While Lieutenant Case was in

command of the U.S. rescue team, he was not—technically—
Hunter's CO. "You don't have to *like* it, Case. We're not
leaving our people in Russian hands." He crossed his arms,
studying the map. "What'd you say, Morgan? The Turya has
a six- or seven-hundred-mile range?"

"Something like that. We don't know how it's been modified."

"Say six hundred miles, then." He pointed at the map.
"Look, Case. With that range, they could reach almost any
spot on the coast of Cuba . . . Colombia . . . southern Florida
. . . Hispaniola . . . even Puerto Rico. Hell, even if we can't get
our people back, don't you think the General would like to
know what the Russians are up to here?"

Case considered the map, tugging at his lower lip. Hunter
watched him, churning with a barely concealed anguish. He
didn't like thinking about the possibility that he might not be
able to get to Greg or Rachel. . . .

"You're right," Case said at last. "I don't see much hope
for your people, but they could have another base out there
somewhere."

"It might be something else," Anderson put in. "Not a
base . . ."

"Not a base? What are you talking about?"

Anderson shrugged. "Just a hunch, is all. Did you see the
electronic gear they have built into the walls of that cavern
downstairs?"

Case lifted an eyebrow. "Electronic gear? What gear?"

"Can't say for sure, but it looks like the granddaddy of all
Russkie downlinks."

Hunter nodded. He had seen the power cables and busbars
too, as though the entire mouth of the cavern housing the dock
was, in fact, a gigantic time portal. When he and the other
Rangers had been brought through from 1848 Paris, he had
heard water, felt the dampness of the concrete under his feet.
"I was wondering about that," he said. "Why would they
need such a big portal, though?"

Case turned to the desk and thumbed through the salvaged
papers, many of them partly burned: records, lists, and code
books that the Soviet colonel had been destroying when Hunter
and Anderson interrupted him.

"The answer may be here," the blond lieutenant said slowly. "Here . . . look. *'Mesto Noyab'r . . .'* Point November. A rendezvous point?"

Hunter looked over his shoulder, nodding slowly. "Eighteen twenty-eight north," he said, pointing. "Sixty-six oh-seven west. If that's latitude and longitude, we've got one of their rendezvous, anyway."

"Yeah. Where?"

"East of here. We'll have to check it on the map."

"What about this other? *'Mesto Ahktyab'r.'* "

" 'Point October,' " Hunter translated. "Five west . . . forty-eight north. Hell, five west . . . that's almost on the Greenwich Meridian! That puts it somewhere on a line with England." He was thinking of the Spanish Armada. Was that part of the VBU plan? "Forty-eight north . . . I'm not sure. Somewhere in France, maybe?"

"We'll check it," Case said with sudden decision. "This Point November could be important though, if it's not far from here. That could be where the Turya is heading."

"Yeah. Makes sense." Hunter looked up at Case. "I'm going to need some of your people. Navy people, if you can spare them."

Case glanced at Morgan before returning his gaze to Hunter. "Okay. You got 'em. But I don't want you chasing off too far, understand?"

"Well, it depends on the range we have in *La Dueña.* . . ."

"Get my people back here in . . ." He consulted his watch. "Make it six hours. I don't know how long General Thompson will want to hold the portal open, and I damn sure don't want to send more people out after you if you get lost!"

"Six hours." Hunter frowned. It would have to do. "Deal, Case. I'll round up my people now."

"I mean it, Hunter," Case added. "The General's going to want to have a long talk with you about what you saw in Paris . . . and here! Don't go getting yourself lost!"

He was about to reply, but Gomez beat him to it. "Hey, Lieutenant! No problem! I don't know how it was in Delta Force, but Rangers never get lost!"

Hunter looked again at the map of the Caribbean and hoped that was true.

• • •

Torpedo Boat Number Four's prow lifted clear of the water, her stern throwing up a crashing, foaming rooster tail as she cleaved the waves on fixed hydroplanes. To the left, the rugged, green and brown mountains of southern Cuba bulked against a cloudless sky. Ahead lay the open water of the Windward Passage.

Major Shvernik stepped off the ladder leading up to the pilot house and paced the dozen steps across the gray deck to the portside rail. The aft deck was crowded with spetsnaz troops. Some thirty men had been able to escape from the Guantánamo base in the last moments of the firefight. They would be useful later, Shvernik reflected . . . but it would make the crossing to Point November crowded.

Many of the troops were clustered around the two prisoners, their *gosti*, or guests, as the soldiers called them. Both the man and the woman were still nude, their hands and feet bound. The man was in bad shape after repeated beatings, his face swollen and puffy around the eyes and mouth.

"Enough of that!" Shvernik snapped, and a spetsnaz sergeant pulled back his hand. The woman was plainly terrified, trembling on the brink of hysteria. "Untie them," he continued. "Get them something to wear."

"Da! Neemedleena, Tovarisch Mayar!"

"We are not barbarians," he said, staring at the soldier who had been fondling the woman. He turned to her and spoke in English. "My apologies, Miss Stein," he said.

"Why should you care?" she asked coldly. "An hour ago, you were . . ."

"Our duty often demands things of us that we would wish otherwise," Shvernik said. "Your interrogation is now no longer in my hands."

"Where . . . where are you taking us?"

He permitted himself a smile. "On an ocean cruise, Miss Stein. We will meet a native craft at sea late tomorrow, transfer to her, and sink this vessel."

"You're finished, you know," she said. "The Rangers are taking your base apart right now."

"The loss of the base is inconvenient, but not serious. At worst, it will delay our evacuation of 2008."

The girl's eyes grew large. "Evacuation . . . ?"

"The Guantánamo Base was designed as a retreat, a place of safety for the VBU Supreme Command while history . . . ah . . . reorients itself. You don't think we are so suicidal as to edit *ourselves* out of existence, eh?"

"But that base . . ."

"Is no longer of importance. It has one last purpose to serve."

King scowled. "What purpose, Russkie?"

"Why, to serve as a tomb for your friends," he said. The girl started, then struggled against her bonds. "A twenty-kiloton warhead, my dear," he continued. "A small bomb, about the size of the one the Americans dropped at Hiroshima, buried beneath the base cavern. In another few minutes, there will be nothing left there but a seething, radiation-filled crater. And we will be on our way to a meeting with destiny!"

He watched dispassionately as the spetsnaz sergeant returned with two sets of fatigues and began cutting the ropes on the prisoners' ankles. As soon as the girl was freed, she turned from the offered clothing and stood with her back to him, naked and lovely, staring back toward the Cuban coast. "Travis . . . !" Her fists closed on the railing.

"It's too late, my dear. They are already dead. . . ."

Five

La Dueña wallowed in the choppy waters outside the mouth of Guantánamo Bay, her twin diesels churning the water astern in a ragged wake. Hunter looked up at the mast, with its single triangular sail furled tightly under loops of hemp, and the anachronistic spinning of the vessel's tiny radar antenna. He was happy to have those anachronistic touches on board *La Dueña*. Not even Morgan seemed to know that much about true sailing . . . using wind and canvas to travel in the desired direction.

The radar was proving just as valuable as the diesels. A screen, shielded from the light by a plastic hood, was mounted just aft of the mast on a wooden pedestal. Hunter stooped to peer at the display. Mountains showed up as a jagged mass of green light to port. Ahead was a single blip, pulsing with each rotation of the antenna.

The Russian Turya, some twenty miles ahead.

Morgan looked up from the steering tiller, set onto a post halfway between the mast and *Dueña*'s stern. A patchwork engineering job had positioned a set of throttles, a compass binnacle, and a shielded radar screen next to the pilot's station. "Twelve knots, Lieutenant," he commented. "We won't manage better than that out here."

Hunter pointed to the radar screen. "They've slowed down."

"Saving fuel," the SEAL replied. "Six hundred miles is a long trek for a Turya."

They had deciphered the longitude and latitude coordinates found in the base office. "Point November" was the port of San Juan, just within the hydrofoil's range.

The other members of Hunter's hastily organized crew were scattered about *Dueña*'s deck. Gomez, Anderson, and Walker had all come aboard, of course. Besides those three and Doug Morgan, there were five others, volunteers from Case's strike team.

Two were Navy: a tall, lean, black First Class radarman named Michael Franklin, and another former SEAL, Chief Robert Short. Corporal Gary Lynch was Army Special Forces, a Green Beret with experience handling small craft. The last two were both Marines, Gunnery Sergeant Walter Jones and Sergeant Anthony Carlucci. "Gunny" Jones, another black, claimed to have once been a lineman for the Chicago Bears . . . and looked it. He was carrying an M-60 like Anderson's, and Hunter wanted two of the light machine guns along if they managed to catch up with the Turya. Carlucci, like Lynch, knew boat handling.

Hunter had as yet no hard plan. He had requested volunteers on the basis of familiarity with boats or because of special expertise, as with Franklin and Jones. As he'd hoped and expected, the Turya was traveling slowly now after her first mad dash from Guantánamo Bay. He'd considered trying to pose as another boatload of spetsnaz refugees from Guantánamo. Maybe if they got close enough, they could board and storm— modern-day pirates in the sixteenth century.

That, Hunter knew, would almost certainly prove to be impossible. The Turya was a fast patrol hydrofoil capable of forty knots and armed with a twin-mount 25mm rapid-fire AA cannon. *La Dueña* was a wooden sailing vessel barely capable of twelve knots, with a pair of M-60s and a miscellany of assault rifles, SMGs, and side arms. A more reasonable scenario would be to confirm that the Turya was, in fact, heading for "Point November." They should be able to track the Russian boat at least across the Windward Passage. If they cut north between Cuba and the island of Haiti and headed east, it was a safe bet that their next destination was San Juan or someplace close by. *Dueña* could then return to Guantánamo. It would be a simple matter to return to Time Square and send a combat team back to 1588 Puerto Rico.

The thought gave Hunter a grim satisfaction. There was delicious irony in the thought of a heavily armed combat team, already ashore and waiting when the Turya approached San Juan.

But first, they had to be certain that Puerto Rico was the Russians' destination.

Lynch relieved Morgan at the tiller, and the SEAL walked slowly to the port rail, looking aft toward the mouth of Guantánamo Bay. Hunter joined him. "Problem?"

"No, sir, not really. I was just wondering, is all."

"Wondering what?"

"Gitmo Bay . . . it looks a lot different than it did . . . uh . . . does, up in our time."

"Sure. No towns. No Navy base. No people . . ."

"No, it's not that." He turned away from the railing. "That bay is mostly mangrove swamp and mudflat, except for a narrow channel. The Gitmo I knew was . . ."

He stopped in midsentence, staring aft. Hunter turned to see a vast, black dome heaving up against the mountains beyond the bay, climbing skyward in deathly silence.

"Everybody down!" Hunter screamed. There was a moment's stunned hesitation as *La Dueña*'s crew watched the growing horror a few miles astern. The edges of the dome turned fuzzy, mud and debris geysering out in a spreading, devastating cloud.

Long seconds passed. Carlucci hauled at the tiller, turning the lugger's stern toward the dome that was now subsiding in a boiling sea of mist. They were at least five miles from the mouth of the Bay, Hunter thought. At that distance, it would take nearly thirty seconds for the shock wave to reach them. Was five miles enough? Much depended on the size of the warhead that had just obliterated the VBU base, and on random factors such as wind speed and direction. They *might* survive. . . .

Only then did the reality of what had happened register on Hunter's numbed brain. The VBU must have left a nuclear warhead somewhere in the base, set to detonate once the Turya had escaped. The detonation of that warhead meant that Case and his people were all dead. The recall beacon linking 1588 with 2008 was gone, vaporized . . . and with it, any hope of reaching his own time.

The shock wave hit, a solid wall of wind and sea spray smashing into the *Dueña* from astern like a sudden squall, accompanied by a hurricane's roar. The lugger's nose plunged down as the wave passed under her stern. Hunter looked up into wet darkness as a sharp, rending crack sounded from overhead. Stays parted as jagged, raw, white wood showed under the varnish of the mast. Then the mast snapped clean a yard above the deck, hurtling forward into darkness, carrying rigging and fittings with it into the sea. Water crashed across *La Dueña*'s stern, drenching Hunter and the other men clinging desperately to her deck. Battered by the surge of water, the lugger wallowed, threatening to swing broadside against the waves. Hunter had little experience with boats but could feel the motion in *Dueña*'s hull; if she turned, that sea would capsize her in a moment.

Somehow, Carlucci remained standing, arms straining at the tiller as green water sluiced over him. *Dueña* balked, then shuddered, her prow plunging again. Water streamed from her sides as she rose, as sunlight reappeared overhead. . . .

The lugger's violent motions subsided, replaced by a heavy, side-to-side wallowing. Hunter released his death's grip from the portside railing and looked around. Others were slowly rising, stunned but apparently unharmed. The lugger was little more than a hulk, mastless, her rudder smashed in those final desperate seconds, but the ten men aboard were alive.

Five miles to the northwest, storm clouds bulked against the mountains of Cuba as black rain obscured the entrance to Guantánamo Bay and the ruin of the VBU base.

General Thompson looked up sharply as power died in the control room. He'd been just about to step through the blue glow of the portal and into the captured Russian base with his staff and some security people when the lights snapped off.

"What?" He looked back toward the control booth, mounted in the rear of the chamber high up on the wall. The lights flickered, then came up again. He could see Dr. David Stein in the booth, checking dials and readouts. Technicians at the array of computer terminals on the main floor of Time Square began working rapidly, as a buzz of conversation rose to fill the momentarily silenced room.

Thompson stabbed an intercom button. "Stein! What the devil happened?"

"I'm sorry, General." The voice of the Chronos facility's chief theorist sounded shaken. "We have lost our lock."

"Lost it! How?"

"Ah . . . we can't be certain yet, but it appears to have been an EMP."

The general felt a sudden chill. EMP stood for Electromagnetic Pulse and was characteristic of nuclear explosions, an irresistible surge of energy that could destroy unshielded electrical circuits, communications, computers . . .

. . . or the delicate electronics of the Chronos time machine.

"Are you saying there was a *nuclear* blast on the other side of the portal?"

"That would appear to be the only explanation," the scientist replied. Thompson heard the tremor in the voice and understood. Stein's daughter, Rachel, was still out there. *God! Hunter, Rachel . . . all of them! Gone, just like that . . .*

"A booby trap," Thompson said softly. "Or a self-destruct."

"In a way, we were lucky," Stein replied. "The EMP closed off the portal before blast or radiation effects could reach us here."

The thought of even a fraction of the force of an atomic blast channeled through the portal and into the Chronos base's underground tunnels was unnerving. Thompson stared at the now powerless and empty stage where the blue glow of the portal had been a moment before and licked his lips. "How bad is the damage, Doctor?"

"I . . . don't know yet, General. It will take time to trace circuits . . . to recover programs. Days, certainly. Weeks, possibly."

Days . . . or weeks. Thompson closed his eyes. Not that it mattered much. It was impossible that any of their people could have survived on the other side of the portal.

Damn it all to hell, he thought, suddenly possessed by a

towering, unreasoning anger. *We've underestimated the Russian bastards again!*

Hunter leaned back against what was left of *La Dueña*'s starboard railing and looked up at a murky, rain-laden sky.

There was no way to tell how much radioactivity they'd been exposed to earlier that afternoon. The wind had been blowing steadily from the northeast since before the explosion, and it was possible, even probable, that most of the fallout would be distributed harmlessly in a long oval "footprint" toward the southwest, missing the battered lugger. How much radiation they might have picked up with the blast's wave front was anyone's guess. Water, soil, and mud would have absorbed most or all of the hard stuff, just as it had absorbed the bomb's thermal effects. The base surge might have been hot, but there were so many variables Hunter couldn't begin to compute them.

In any case, learning the answer would do them little good. They would either die in a few days or weeks . . . or live, and if they lived they might suffer other effects that would make them wish they had died. Whatever the outcome, there was nothing that could be do about it. At the moment, *Dueña*'s crew was far more likely to die of thirst, starvation, or exposure than from radiation sickness.

According to Morgan, the prevailing warm water current in the Windward Passage between Cuba and Haiti should have been carrying them southwest, back toward the nuke's deadly footprint, but in this, at least, luck appeared to be with them. They seemed to be traveling east, carried slowly by a counter current just off the south Cuban coast. The coast was visible as a green blur in front of low, purple mountains to the north. No one suggested that they swim for it, though. More than once, the gray slash of shark fins had cut water nearby, and the shore was at least three miles away, far too distant for exhausted men to swim.

Eventually, perhaps, the hulk would drift ashore. What then? Hunter wondered. If they still lived, there would be food and water . . . and the Spanish who claimed these islands . . . and the Indians. The name *Carib* came to mind—bloodthirsty, cannibalistic inhabitants of the islands of the sea that bore their name.

The first thing they'd done after the explosion was check their supplies and possessions . . . which were pitifully few. Each man had his personal first-aid kit, his weapon, and some ammo. Six men had canteens with water . . . enough for the six hours they'd planned to be out, but not for much longer in the tropics. There were a collection of knives and a few hand guns, but no survival kits, no food. Shirts and scraps of canvas had been stretched out to catch rainwater, but there was no rain yet. Fishhooks had been fashioned from bent nails, but there was no bait except for blood-soaked strips of cloth torn from clothing . . . and so far, the fish weren't biting, not even the sharks. The Navy men were below decks now, checking for leaks and searching for food or water—even a rat would have been encouraging—but so far, their chances looked grim.

A shadow fell across Hunter's face and he looked up. Morgan, Franklin, and Short were all there.

Hunter stood slowly, mindful of the need to maintain appearances. "Well, gentlemen?" His throat was dry. He was desperately thirsty, and it was only evening. "What'd you find?"

"No food, sir," Morgan replied. "Or water. But we found the treasure chest."

"That's not very funny."

"Wasn't meant to be. This vessel is carrying twenty large chests filled with gold."

"Gold?" Hunter frowned. "What were the Russians doing with gold?"

"Damned if I know," Morgan replied. "Shipping it somewhere, from the look of things. Most of it's in bars, but we found this in one of the cabins."

He held out a cloth bag tied with a leather thong. Taking it, Hunter looked inside at the gold coins with Spanish words engraved on the heavy metal.

Gold . . . for Spain? "Doesn't help the food situation much," he said.

Franklin smiled. "Shorty suggested that we could all go into town and buy ourselves a fast-food joint now. We're rich enough!"

"First guy who spots a McDonald's can have my share of the treasure," Hunter said, mustering an answering grin.

"All *right*!" Franklin said, beaming. "This guy's my kind of captain!"

"How about leaks?"

"There's some water below decks," Short said. "We shipped a good bit when that wave broke over us. There's some seepage around the prop shafts. The hull seems sound, though. We're not sinking."

"The engines?"

Morgan shook his head. "I think the shafts were ruined the same time our rudder went. We can start the engine, but there's no point. The props won't turn."

Hunter smiled again. "I guess I'm not cut out to be a Navy officer."

"Oh, I don't know, Skipper," Franklin said. "Look at the bright side. With all that gold, once we make port, we're gonna have ourselves one hell of a liberty!"

They laughed, but Hunter felt a stab within. With no food, no water, no way even to make it to shore, how were they going to cash in on that liberty?

He shaded his eyes against the late afternoon glare from the water, staring across the miles that separated *La Dueña* from land.

Things did not look good at all.

On the evening of the second day, *Lohtka Nom'yehr Ch'yeteereh*—Boat Number Four as King translated the Russian name for the patrol craft—cut back her engines and idled off the green slash of a tropical coast. Rachel crossed her arms in front of her and shivered. The early evening air was chilly, despite the fact that they were in the tropics. She was grateful for the fatigues they'd given her.

In fact, they'd treated her and King quite well. The boat was crowded and there was no privacy, but Shvernik saw to it that they were well fed, and the Soviets on board had been cautioned not to mistreat the Americans.

It was a small shock to realize that gratitude—for food and clothing and an absence of harassment—was the first real feeling she'd known since . . .

She squeezed her eyes shut. *I will* not *cry. I won't. . . .*

It was still so hard to accept that Travis was dead. When

the nuke had gone off the afternoon before, the boat had been far enough away that only a low, dull *boom* had reached her ears, but Shvernik had pointed out the dark, blue-gray cloud above the coastline to the northwest and told her what it was. The cloud was not the mushroom shape she'd expected . . . probably because the bomb had been set off underground.

She'd not cried until late that night. She pictured his face, remembered his touch. . . .

Travis . . . dead?

And now she felt gratitude because Shvernik had decided not to let her be raped. A sickening blend of fear and grief and self-loathing welled up inside her.

"That is the northern coastline of Puerto Rico."

Rachel jumped. She'd not heard Shvernik come up behind her.

"I am sorry," the Russian major said. "I did not mean to startle you."

She tried to cover her fright. "We . . . don't seem to be moving."

"Correct. We have radioed ahead to another vessel of ours. He will be meeting with us here, soon. We will go aboard him and open the sea cocks on *Ch'yeteereh*."

Rachel had not yet gotten used to the Russian habit of calling ships *he*. "What's wrong with this boat?"

"Nothing . . . except that he has not the range we need. We have a long way to go."

"Where . . . where are you taking us?" The words sounded bleak to her own ears.

"To my superiors."

Rachel tried to hide her disappointment. She had no reason to think he would tell her, but she felt a hunger for information, any information, on where they were bound. Partly she was obeying the common-sense dictate of learning all she could while she had the opportunity, even though she didn't know how that information might be used later. More than that, however, was the realization that her relative comfort and freedom now was only an interlude. Once Shvernik turned her over to his superiors, she would be facing the interrogation room, or worse, all over again.

She found herself trembling.

"Are you cold?"

"A little, I guess."

"You should go inside. I . . ."

"Comrade Major!" A shout interrupted him. "We have him in sight!"

"Where?"

"South-southeast, Major! Range ten thousand!"

"Excuse me, Miss Stein. I have duties to attend to."

He left her standing by the rail. Rachel scanned the horizon toward which the Russian on the bridge had been pointing and was rewarded at last with a glimpse of something white, almost invisible between sea and the coastline.

She sensed another presence behind her and turned. Greg King looked down at her. "What was that all about?"

"What was what about, Greg?"

"With the Russkie bastard. What'd you tell him?"

"Nothing." She turned away, studying the white speck against the land. "I was trying to find out where they're taking us."

King grunted and leaned against the railing beside her. A Russian soldier with an AKS submachine gun stirred a few feet away, his eyes watching.

Rachel could barely face talking to the brawny Ranger. She knew he didn't like her, didn't trust her, and she knew that his feelings were based on her performance back in the interrogation chamber at the VBU base. *He thinks I'm weak . . . that I'd betray him.* Another shudder gripped her. *I'm not so sure he's wrong . . .*

"What . . . are we going to do, Greg?" she whispered. She didn't know if the guard spoke English.

King shrugged. "Roll with it. Take our chance when we see it." He studied the white object, now a bit larger. "Oh my God!"

"What?"

"It's a ship! A sailing ship!"

Rachel squinted, trying to make out the shape. Slowly it resolved itself, a mountain of white canvas above the plunging, gold-trimmed hull.

"What the Lieutenant wouldn't have given to see that . . ." King said softly.

His words wrenched new pain from Rachel's breast. *Travis . . . !*

Six

King watched in silence as the white spot grew, transforming itself into a three-masted ship with high, raked bow and stern. He had seen pictures of such vessels; galleons of that type had once carried the treasures of the New World back to Europe.

He still didn't know what year they were now in; that bit of intelligence was being carefully withheld by their captors. When had such ships last sailed the Caribbean? He wished Hunter were here to tell him.

Rachel was clinging to the railing, looking sick. "Get a grip on yourself," he said.

Her eyes met his, filled with anguish. He knew that she was hurting because of Hunter's death. But exactly what was going on in her head?

He turned away and watched the ship's approach. She had three masts, the two in front bearing huge, bulging, square sails, the third a slanted yard with a triangular sail. The flag whipping from the masthead was unfamiliar to King, quartered in red and white, with golden emblems in each section. As the ship turned into the wind, he heard the thunderous crack of flapping canvas, like gunfire, and the harsh shouts of her crew.

Travis Hunter had been King's closest friend, despite their differences in background. King had long made it a practice not to get close to anyone . . . but for the young lieutenant put in charge of the Ranger team before their first hazardous raid into occupied Germany a few years before, King had—at last—made an exception. It was hard to define the affection King felt for the younger man, harder still to explain it . . . except in the obvious fact that combat often turned strangers into brothers.

King had resented Rachel ever since their first mission into the past, though he could never put his feelings into words. The resentment was not jealousy—not quite—but he did worry that her relationship with Hunter would distract the Lieutenant one day when he could least afford it: He also doubted Rachel's ability to stand up under stress. He remembered her pleading with Roy, begging for death when they hadn't even touched her yet. She was afraid she might break, and King agreed. That was why he couldn't trust her. For King, Rachel had always been an outsider who had no business accompanying the Rangers on combat ops, an annoyance at best, a hazard at worst.

Now Travis Hunter was dead . . . and King was lost in time, a prisoner of the VBU, with that annoying hazard as his only resource.

He suppressed a shudder. *God, Lieutenant. We never counted on this, did we?*

The sailing ship completed her turn, and King felt the pounding throb of the patrol boat's engines as she began closing with the galleon. He was surprised to realize that the Soviet craft was at least as long as the sailing ship, though of course the sailing ship's masts towered far above the modern vessel's bridge, giving it the feel of a much larger structure. King found himself looking up the side of a wooden cliff. He could smell the warm, oily odor of tar mingled with the stronger smells of filth and unwashed bodies. Bearded faces peered back at him, mouths gaping with astonishment. Many of the ship's crew crossed themselves rapidly.

So! he thought. *Old Number Four is a surprise to them! I'll bet! A boat maneuvering without sails must look like magic. . . .*

Surprised or not, several of the galleon's sailors dropped a ladder down her side, wooden planks strung between a pair of knotted hemp lines.

Shvernik reappeared, shouting orders in Russian. Soviet

troops hurried back and forth, gathering weapons and supplies, while others made fast lines tossed down from the galleon's deck. "You two!" Shvernik said, pointing a finger at King and Rachel. "You will make no trouble, or I will have you tied again and carried across. We are going across to the *Princessa*. Now."

Princessa? The name sounded Spanish . . . *Princess*, obviously. Spetsnaz troopers crowded around the two Americans, the muzzles of their AKs leveled at them. King reached out and took hold of the rope ladder. The separate movements of the two vessels as they wallowed in the sea made the climb a queasy one. King was very glad when rough hands reached down and grabbed his arms, hauling him over a wooden gunnel and onto the galleon's deck.

Rachel was next, followed by a line of Soviets leaving the hydrofoil. King heard orders shouted in Russian to cast off, and the sharp, metallic gurgle of water already flooding *Boat Number Four*. Curious crewmen crowded around. King saw fear in many eyes, wonder in others. Most were sailors, some in baggy trousers gathered by hose that reached their knees, others barefoot and wearing little more than clouts. Soldiers were easily identified by their steel breastplates and helmets and by their weapons, which ranged from pikes to clumsy antique firearms. All wore swords and bore themselves with an aloof manner despite the hastily sketched signs of the cross several made as the strangers came on board.

Shvernik was the last man off the sinking patrol boat.

"So, Comrade Major! These are your prisoners?"

King turned at the words, spoken in Russian. The speaker wore a monk's red-brown habit, with the cowl pulled up over his head, and he carried a small gold crucifix.

"*Da*, Comrade Krylenko. Thank you for picking us up at sea."

"It wouldn't do to have the natives of San Juan alarmed by your . . . conveyance." He nodded genially at the uneasy crowd of Spanish sailors watching the Russians. "It took all my skill to keep *this* scum from panicking at the sight of you!"

"There will be no more gold coming. . . ."

"No matter. Vorosilov has enough. It may be just as well we had to meet you. We should make our rendezvous a few days earlier than expected." The hooded man turned to face King and Rachel. "Welcome aboard the *Black Princess*," he said, shifting to English. The eyes under the cowl studied King with cold appraisal, then shifted to Rachel. "You are my prisoners now. We will be getting to know one another very well indeed during our passage to Spain."

The Russian's leer was in startling contrast to his religious costume.

The night had been chilly, the day that followed hot. Daybreak had found *La Dueña*'s drifting hulk no closer to the Cuban shore than it had been the day before. By midafternoon, the men were taking turns below deck to escape from the raw burning of the tropical sun. If anything, it was hotter below and the threat of heat exhaustion was very real, but the ankle-deep water there was cool and there was no danger of sunburn.

Hunter had his crew rotate a watch on deck, however, two by two, an hour at a time. He wasn't certain what they were watching for . . . but the news that *La Dueña* was drifting toward land would help morale no end, and there was at least a chance, however small, of their being spotted by a ship.

As the sun sank toward a western horizon touched with crimson, Gomez and Anderson sighted a vessel. Their yells brought all ten Americans on deck, and moments later, *Dueña*'s entire crew was screaming and bellowing, a ragged chorus accompanied by a manic waving of shirts and arms. The ship, a low, dark hull beneath a pyramid of sails turned golden by the setting sun, was standing well out into the Windward Passage, beating her way north against a gentle breeze. Just when it seemed she would pass the castaways by, her distant hull dwindled to near-invisibility as she came about. It took long, anxious minutes before Hunter could decide whether the ship was approaching or receding. At last, though, the sails were noticeably larger, the hull clearly visible above the white mustache at her bow.

"What do you think, LT?" Anderson said, eyeing the approaching vessel uncertainly. "The more I look at her, the more I'm reminded of a pirate ship."

Hunter laughed. "You've seen too many Errol Flynn movies, Roy. This is 1588. Pirates won't be in the news for another century or so.''

"Really?''

"She might be a privateer," Hunter said thoughtfully. The ship had the raised forecastle and high-stacked stern characteristic of vessels of this period.

"So what's the difference between a privateer and a pirate?''

"Not much. Privateers were given papers that let them go pirating legally . . . under orders from the Crown. Most likely, though, she's a merchantman.''

"With all those cannon?'' The black snouts of guns protruding from a line of square-cut ports along her side were just becoming visible.

"Absolutely. Right now, the Caribbean belongs to Spain. If that ship's Spanish, she's armed against privateers. If she's not Spanish . . .''

"She doesn't belong here, so she is a privateer. Yeah. So what do we tell them?''

Hunter studied the approaching ship. He could just make out a flag flying from her main mast now . . . white with a red cross. "We tell them what they want to hear. We all look disreputable enough to pass for shipwrecked sailors, don't you think?''

"We are shipwrecked sailors," Walker said as he and Morgan joined Hunter.

"Well, some of us are sailors," Morgan added. "We could be in trouble, though. How much do you know about sailing ships?''

Hunter cocked an eyebrow. "What do you mean?''

The SEAL nodded toward the other vessel. "In the days of sail, seamen were always in short supply, Lieutenant. Always. I guarantee you the captain of that ship is going to be delighted to find ten more hands out here for the taking. I don't know what they teach you Army types, but the modern Navy doesn't go in much for swarming up the rigging or splicing the main brace!''

"I see what you mean.'' Hunter could see members of the other ship's crew now, barefoot and ragged, clinging to rigging and yards like monkeys. A line of them were extended along the lower yardarm on the foremast, their feet braced against a footrope, clinging to the yard with one hand while they fought and punched and clawed at the canvas sail with the other. As he watched, the foresail collapsed and shortened. It seemed amazing that none of the precariously balancing seamen fell.

"You're right, Doug." He considered the problem a moment more. "Okay . . . not sailors. Soldiers."

Anderson looked puzzled. "On a ship? Don't you mean marines?"

"Sixteenth century. Most ships carried a complement of soldiers. We don't look the part . . . no armor or swords. We'll just have to fake it and say we lost everything."

Gomez joined them from forward. "Our weapons are gonna look pretty strange to them," he said, slapping the M-16/M-203 combo slung from his shoulder.

"I don't think that'll be a problem, this time," Hunter replied. He was thinking of the care the Rangers usually took to conceal their weapons from the locals. "Travel's slow in this period. Anything foreign must seem pretty strange to them. We'll get by."

"I've got a question," Anderson said slowly. "Once they find our cargo, what's to stop 'em from slitting our throats and dumping us overboard?"

"Not a damn thing," Hunter said softly. "We'll have to play this one by ear." He turned to Gomez. "Eddie, get that bag of gold coins Franklin found and slip it into your pack. We might be needing it."

"Coin of the realm, huh, Chief?" Gomez grinned.

"Right. If we're going to be stuck in the sixteenth century, we'll need money. The heavy stuff in the hold won't do us much good, but the coins . . ." He trailed off, examining the ship again as Gomez hurried aft. "The rest of you get your weapons and rucksacks. Keep 'em handy. If we have to, we'll fight. But we'll try talking our way out of this first."

"If we speak their language," Walker said.

"Yeah," Morgan said. "I don't recognize that red-cross flag."

"English, Doug," Hunter replied. "Saint George's Cross. Gentlemen, I believe we're about to be rescued by an English privateer."

Her name was *Resolute*, an eighty-ton, three-masted galleon out of Plymouth. She had a crew of one hundred under the command of Captain Hugh Penvennan, a short and bristly Cornishman with a ruffled collar, baggy pantaloons, and the bluster of a small hurricane. "Haloo there!" he bellowed, as Hunter and the others were brought on board, ragged and soaking wet. "What d'we have here?"

"Travis Hunter, at your service, Captain."

"God's *teeth*, man! What do *Englishmen* here? Methought *Resolute* alone of the Queen's ships didst sail these seas!" His eyes narrowed to slits in the weathered face as his gaze swept across the rescued party, lingering on Gomez's swarthy, Hispanic features, on Walker's Amerind face, and on the two blacks, Jones and Franklin. "And who might these be . . . ?"

"*Most* of us are English," Hunter replied, thinking fast. In 1588, England's colonies of Massachusetts Bay and Jamestown were still decades in the future. Raleigh's doomed Roanoke colony was probably still in place, but in this period "American" meant "Spanish." He gestured toward his men. "Uh . . . Gomez there is Spanish, but he's on our side. This is Dark Walker, an American Indian. And these two . . ."

"I think I can tell that." He studied the blacks with a critical eye. "Not the Guinea Coast, certainly. I know *that* land well, from my trading days! Their features show white blood. Moors, perhaps . . . ?"

Franklin took a step forward, his large hands closing into fists. Hunter blocked him with his arm. "They're all my men, Captain. We're soldiers, prisoners, escaped from the Spanish. . . ."

The story that he spun for Penvennan was apparently believed, though Hunter had to feel his way carefully through the narrative, alert to changes in the man's expression that told him he'd just said something the other questioned. The task was made difficult by the fact that Americans and Englishmen had considerable difficulty understanding one another. Their accents were mutually strange, and Penvennan's speech was an odd combination of Shakespeare and a salty seafaring yarn.

"Where were you taken?" Penvennan asked. "The Netherlands?"

The name triggered memory for Hunter, scraps of information about this period of history. There was a war being fought in the Netherlands . . . the *Spanish* Netherlands, where

Protestant rebels were fighting Catholic Spain with help from Queen Elizabeth's England. He seized on that fact. A life in Holland might explain his strange—to Penvennan's ears—English accent.

"That's right. Actually, we'd lived most of our lives there. Merchant families, you know."

Penvennan nodded. "What battle were ye taken at? Old King Philip ha' been twisting our brethren and allies i' the Low Countries sore."

"I don't remember the name of the battle. . . ."

"How long ago, then? Last year?"

"That seems about right."

"Sluys?"

Hunter didn't know if the word was the name of a place, a battle, or a general. "That sounds right." He smiled. "I have trouble with these foreign words, even if I did live in the place for years. . . ."

"Hah! God's truth! So you were prisoners of the Duke of Parma! What then?"

"It's all pretty much a blur. They loaded us aboard ship and sent us to Cuba."

"Strange. Oft the Dons condemn their prisoners to life i' the rowing galleys. What wanted they with Englishmen in Cuba?" He gestured toward Franklin. "These blackamoors, yon savage, *they* weren't with you at Sluys, I'll warrant!"

"No, sir. Uh . . . neither was Gomez, in fact. They . . . ah . . . helped us escape in Cuba. We were able to capture that ship . . . *Dueña*." Hunter grinned nastily, hoping he looked the part of a convict-turned-pirate. "We held the crew at gunpoint, told them to make for England or we'd feed 'em to the sharks!"

"Ha! I like thy style, Mr. Hunter! The tale reads like an exploit of Sir Francis hi'self! What then? How cometh you to be driving i' th' windward passage?"

Hunter frowned. Driving? The word had changed meaning in four centuries. Penvennan must mean drifting. "A storm struck," he said. "Our vessel was dismasted, our crew swept overboard. We've been adrift for two days. . . ."

"And would ha' been driving for days more, I'll vow, had we not sighted you!"

Penvennan knew all about that storm. *Resolute*, it turned

out, had been in the Caribbean for the past three weeks. There were rumors, her captain said, of a Spanish treasure ship seen at various times between the Windward Passage and Puerto Rico. His search had been interrupted the day before by the appearance of a curious cloud on the Cuban coast . . . and a sudden storm swell that had damaged his mizzenmast and forced him to heave to for repairs. If it hadn't been for that storm, he insisted, he never would have seen the drifting wreck and its survivors.

"The question now is what to do with you," Penvennan said at last. "I cannot stay my quest now to ferry you to England. You will suffer yourselves to be my guests aboard *Resolute* for a few months, I trust?"

Hunter nodded, but he felt a new desperation inside. A few months? And then passage to England . . .

"What is the date, Captain?"

"The date? God's *teeth!* You lads have been hid away, in truth! The twenty-fifth of May, of course."

May 25, 1588. Another datum of historical trivia clicked into place as he thought. He could not remember the exact dates, but there was something about August . . . August and the Spanish Armada.

VBU activity in this year had to be centered on Spain's attempted invasion of England, the Grand Armada. The big question mark—and his only clue to what the VBU was up to here—was the Turya-class patrol boat. She was heading for a rendezvous; he knew that much from the papers captured at Guantánamo. The *Princessa Negra*, the ship the Turya was meeting with at "Point November" . . .

That was their only lead, that and fragments of Russian maps. If they could catch the *Princessa*, they might find what the Russians were doing in 1588.

And Rachel . . .

Seven

They cast off *La Dueña*'s hulk in the early evening, setting sail for the northeast. Penvennan and his men had been delighted to learn that the Spanish lugger carried treasure in her hold. The alien, twisting metal workings of the vessel's diesel engine were so strange that they could only assume that the Dons, as they called the Spanish, had been transporting strange Indian artifacts, relics of pagan ceremonies.

Gold, however, they understood.

There was a moment's danger for the Rangers. If Penvennan got the idea that the castaways were claiming the gold as their own, he was perfectly capable of putting them all back in the sea where he'd found them . . . and sailing off with what must have amounted to several thousand English pounds of treasure.

"We have no claim on it, Captain!" Hunter said. "It's yours! Think of it as payment for our passage to England!"

"Haw!" Penvennan slapped his thigh. "I warrant thou art a merry fellow and care for nothing!"

Hunter rubbed his chin. Two days' growth of beard scratched under his fingers. By this time, he thought, he must be looking the part of a pirate. "Perhaps we could consider it a down payment, Captain."

"Eh? What sayest thou?"

"When we took this ship, some of the crew talked." He nodded toward Gomez. "He speaks Spanish, and questioned them for us. They told us that this gold was supposed to be loaded on board another ship.''

Penvennan's face grew serious. "What ship . . . ?''

Hunter began to answer, but Penvennan raised his hand. "No! I know her name, well enough!''

"You do?''

"Her name is *Black Princess*, I warrant. . . .''

Princessa Negra! "Yes! How did you know?''

"Because that's the ship *we* seek!''

"You . . . !''

"Aye!'' Penvennan watched his men stowing the gold below decks, carefully passing each heavy box from man to man down a main deck hatchway. His eyes were hungry. "The *Princess* lay at Havana December last but did not sail with the Dons' treasure fleet. Rumor has it she's a private ship, laying up gold that was brought to her from some unknown place among the islands by coastal luggers. My guess, Mr. Hunter, is that thy escape 'twas by that self-same lugger, together with a small, small part of *Black Princess*'s cargo!''

"Then,'' Hunter said slowly, "there's plenty more where that came from. Perhaps we might work together.''

"Oh . . . aye? In what wise?''

The Russian maps, brought aboard with the rest of the Rangers' supplies and equipment when they abandoned the sinking *Dueña*, were in Hunter's pack. He pulled out the leather case that held them. "I have charts, captured when we made our escape. I'm not a seaman . . . I can't tell what they represent. But they have dates written on them, and I wonder if they might not be intended as rendezvous points.''

"Rendezvous points! For the *Princess* and her gold?''

"Possibly. It's worth a gamble, isn't it?''

"Aye! That it is. Show me these maps, and th' tenth part of the *Princess* treasure is yours! If there be one league of coastline i' all of Europe I cannot recognize, then I am no longer worthy a' th' name *seaman*!''

Penvennan led Hunter aft to a low doorway leading under the poopdeck. Another door, guarded by an English soldier in doublet and iron corselet, opened into the Captain's cabin.

Hunter stooped to cross the threshold. The cabin was cramped and low-ceilinged. A narrow bunk hung from chains along one bulkhead. Most of the room was dominated by a single table. There were a few civilized touches . . . a wooden globe on an ornate stand, an intricately carved sea chest serving as a chair. Penvennan gestured to the table, illuminated by the light from a single glassed-in candle and by shafts of late afternoon sunlight slanting through tiny round ports. Hunter found he had to brace himself with one hand against the ceiling—no, *overhead*, he reminded himself. *Resolute* was canted at a sharp angle as she clawed northeast, tacking against a heavy breeze. The hull creaked and groaned as Penvennan gestured at the map case under Hunter's arm.

"Let us have a look, sir."

"They are fragments only, Captain. The Spanish officer tried to burn them to keep them from being captured. That's why I thought they might be important."

"Indeed?" Penvennan leaned over the table, frowning. "What tongue be this?"

"Russian, Captain. I . . . ah . . . can read Russian. . . ."

"Russian, say you? What has *Muscovy* to do with Philip of Spain?"

Hunter shrugged. "Maybe their naval officers are advising him?"

"Huh! Last I heard tell, the Swedes had captured all of Muscovy's ports on the Baltic. They *have* no navy, sir, and certainly they are no power to be feared!"

That's what you think! "Then I can't explain it. But that . . ." Hunter tapped the scrawled *21–27 Yul* with his forefinger. "That's twenty-one to twenty-seven July."

Penvennan studied the map closely, then looked up, meeting Hunter's eye. "I have ne'er seen maps a' such make, sir. Came you by these in a *Spanish* ship, you say?"

Hunter could tell Penvennan did not believe him. "Perhaps the Spanish got them from some place else." *That's true enough,* he thought.

"Hmm. As you say. But these . . ." He traced lines on the map. "Such precision in lines of longitude is sheerest nonsense!"

"Why?"

"Latitude is easy to determine, sir. One shoots the sun at highest noon and reads his latitude above the equator wi' ease.

But longitude? Nay! There is no way to read i', not wi'out timepieces far more accurate than can be made! I fear these maps be rubbish!''

Oh God, no! "Well, just look at the coastline! Do you recognize any of it?"

"Oh, aye! There's no mistaking it! 'Tis the south coast of Ushant, twixt Penmarch and Quiberon. That be Belle Isle . . . and Glennan. Aye, I know the coast, though 'tis drawn wi' too much precision to be believed! This chart *supposedly* represents the Bay of Biscay!"

"And this?" He laid the map of the harbor before Penvennan.

"Plymouth!" the Cornishman said at once. "No English seaman could fail t' recognize that! See? There be the Sound . . . and Rame Head, and Torpoint." He hesitated. "Such precision! I would know this mapmaker, sir! What is this word?"

"'August.'"

"So our friends interest themselves in Plymouth between the first and seventh days of August. This bodes ill, I fear."

It does indeed! "What about this one?" He laid the final map on the table.

Penvennan stared at the labyrinth of islands and narrow inlets for a long time, his brows wrinkling. At last he sighed and leaned back. "I lose the wager, I fear. 'Tis familiar, aye, but wi'out place names . . . I'm used to rougher charts than this, I fear. It could be Norway, or on the Irish coast. 'Twould help if there were lines of latitude on't."

"It's only a fragment. They may have been on the part that was burned."

"Which helpeth us not. I cannot help wi't."

"Two out of three's not bad," Hunter said. He read the Russian words on the map to himself. *Emergency rendezvous after 7 August.* That was something, anyway, a when even if they didn't have the where.

"These dates task me, Mr. Hunter. Are they honest dates, or Popish lies?"

"What do you mean?"

"Why, perhaps you lost the knowing, while in Cuba. But it hath been full six years, now, since the Papists decreed their new calendar and stole ten honest days!"

Hunter remembered then. The Gregorian Calendar—named for the Pope who ordered its creation—had superceded the old Julian calendar in the late 1500s. He remembered neither dates nor details but knew that Protestant countries had been slow in adopting the reform. The Rangers had encountered that ten-day difference in dates before. Russia had not switched to the Gregorian Calendar until 1918.

Hunter felt cold. "So . . . this date of August seventh . . ."

"*Could* be the twenty-eighth of July as honest men tell time."

"And if these are the Gregorian dates," Hunter added, "August seventh could refer to something the Spanish are planning for the seventeenth!"

"Aye. I fear these charts may not be of much purpose."

Hunter thought for a moment. "No, Captain. They're all we have, our only lead on the *Black Princess*! Look . . . these dates on the map of Ushant."

"Aye?"

"July twenty-first through the twenty-seventh. Say we extend them as early as the eleventh and as late as the sixth of August. If we reach this area by the eleventh . . ."

"Not likely, this time a' year. *Resolute* will be hard pressed to reach Biscay before the twentieth. . . ."

"Then that might be the clue we need, Captain! If *Resolute* can't reach the rendezvous by the eleventh, than neither can *Black Princess*! The date must mean the twenty-first! The honest twenty-first!"

"Aye . . ." Penvennan brightened. "Aye! You're a bright one, Mr. Hunter, for all I wonder at the truth behind your charts! We can set course full for Ushant and seek the *Black Princess* there!"

"It'll be a slim chance." Hunter knew how big the ocean was, how small these wooden galleons. "And I'd like to know who the *Princess* is meeting."

"I think there's slight doubt o' that, Mr. Hunter. Philip's Armada."

The chill Hunter had felt returned. "I beg your pardon?"

"If these charts be no lie, I can think of no other reason. Spanish treasure galleons, Mr. Hunter, go to *Spain* . . . and seek not rendezvous with ships and times 'twixt their home and England!''

"What . . . do you know of the Armada?''

"That Philip has blustered his demands at England for months now, wi' the Armada as measure of his determination. I saw parts of it, in the raid on Cadiz with Drake, last year. Oh, aye . . . the world has ne'er seen the like o' i' before. One hundred and thirty ships and more now, some say. I feared the Dons would ne'er take heart, but leave them all to rot. This, perchance, means they plan now to venture forth!''

Hunter felt a sudden, wrenching sickness inside. If Rachel and Greg were prisoners aboard a ship mixed in with that . . .

"We'll have to find *Princess* before it reaches the Armada.''

"Aye.'' Penvennan studied Hunter closely. "There's more to this than mere gold for you, my friend.''

"What do you mean?''

"I see a fear in thee that touches deeper than a mercenary's lust for gold . . . or a captain's in the serve of his Queen. Wouldst tell me of this thing so near thine heart? Or trusteth thee not an Englishman's word?''

Hunter locked eyes with Penvennan for a long moment. The man was shrewd and a sharp judge of people and their thoughts. Behind the flowery language was a perfect understanding that Hunter was less interested in the gold aboard *Black Princess* than in something else.

"There were two people . . . people dear to me. A man and a woman. They were prisoners with us in Cuba, but they were taken away before we escaped. We'd heard they were going to be taken back to Europe on the *Black Princess*.''

Penvennan was silent for a long time. "I understand now, friend Hunter. 'Tis a long and valiant quest you've found thy-self. So far as I am able, I shall bear thee.''

"Thank you.'' They clasped hands, the interview at an end.

When he left Penvennan's cabin, Hunter felt as weak and drained as he did at the end of a firefight. Spinning tales that the keen-minded sea captain would believe was hard enough. What made it worse was his new and deeper understanding of the history the Rangers had found themselves in. Hunter had only the sketchiest knowledge of the Spanish Armada. He'd been dropped here with a handful of men and weapons but with no idea at all of where the VBU was or what they were doing.

Guilt dragged at him. *If I'd only thought about the possibility of a bomb under Guantánamo!* The VBU had installed self-destruct devices in other bases, and he should have warned Case about the possibility. He had, he realized now, been so anxious to learn where they had taken Rachel that the thought had never occurred to him. Certainly, he never would have expected anything as dramatic as a nuclear warhead!

How many Chronos Project people were dead, caught in that explosion? It was possible that the nuke had destroyed Time Square. Even if the blast had not reached through the open time portal, there was no way home for the Rangers. With their recall beacon gone in the destruction of Guantánamo, Chronos would have no way of finding them, no way of knowing they'd escaped.

So, Travis. His thoughts were edged with a bitter scorn. *Welcome to the sixteenth century! Your home for the rest of your life! Plague . . . typhoid . . . the Spanish Inquisition . . . witchcraft trials . . . oh, you've a grand future, you have!*

Roy Anderson met him as he stepped out onto the quarter-deck. The sun was setting astern and to port, lighting the sea with scarlet and gold. Cuba was now a dim, dark line of green dividing water from sky.

"How'd it go, LT?"

"He's taking us after the *Princessa*," Hunter said. He felt so tired . . .

"Well, that's something, anyway. The Russkies'll have their hands full with Rachel and Greg both. When we catch 'em, they'll be glad to get 'em off their hands!"

"That's a damned stupid thing to say!"

"Whoa, there, LT!" Anderson held his hands up. "No offense meant! I know you're worried about them. . . ."

"Sorry, Roy. But this whole mess is my fault. If we'd spotted that bomb . . . if I'd thought to look for that bomb, we might've used the time portal to head them off in Puerto Rico. Our chances of tracking them down aren't very good."

"So? You think it's your fault Gitmo blew?"

"Well . . ."

"Hey! That wasn't your job, LT! Says so in the military officer's manual."

"Huh?"

"Look it up! Quote . . . prisoners of Russian time travelers being held in secret bases in Cuba shall not be required to search for, nor be responsible for the disposal of, atomic bombs hidden in said secret base's wine cellar . . . unquote. Hell, LT . . . that was Case's job, not yours! We're just damned lucky it didn't catch us too!"

Hunter chuckled. "You got that right." He stared off across the water as the sun sank in fire. "You know we're stuck here, Roy."

"No recall beacon." The lanky Texan turned and leaned his forearms against the quarterdeck railing, his hands clasped in front of him. Somewhere forward the squeaky tootling of a hornpipe began, as a ring of sailors laughed and clapped and danced in a tight circle in front of the mainmast. "Still, I reckon our first job's gotta be stoppin' the VBU. What d'you think the bastards are up to, anyway?"

Hunter glanced at Anderson. The Texan was trying to distract him from the foul thoughts he'd been wallowing in. Usually that was King's job . . . or Raye's. . . .

"It can't be a coincidence that the VBU is here in 1588. It's got to be the Armada."

"So? I'm just a Texas country boy. By me an armada is a real *big* armadillo."

Hunter laughed. "Okay. Quick history lesson. We've got Queen Elizabeth ruling England . . . Philip II ruling Spain."

"Got it."

"They don't like each other. Elizabeth is Protestant and supporting the church her father founded . . . Henry VIII."

"With all the wives. Right."

"Philip and Spain are Catholic. *Very* Catholic. They'd like to see the heretics wiped out in England. Philip has been fighting a long and expensive war in Holland—the Spanish Netherlands—putting down a Protestant revolution. Elizabeth has been helping the Protestants, and she's also been helping herself to Philip's treasure fleets."

"Privateers."

"Right. Philip got sick of it, finally, and assembled the Grand

Armada to put the English in their place. He launched it in 1588.''

"And lost."

"And lost big. This was the first time English sea power was able to assert itself. They kept Philip's fleet from landing . . . and the Armada was finally destroyed by a storm. It was a close thing, though." He remembered the map fragment Penvennan had identified as Plymouth harbor. The situation was terrifying. Russians leading Spanish armies ashore in England would twist four centuries of history out of all recognition. "My God!" he said. "The VBU is going to help the Spanish conquer England!"

Don Alonzo de Leyva bowed low before His Most Catholic Majesty, King Philip II of Spain, his gentleman's cap nearly brushing the gleaming polished wooden floor. "Your Majesty," he said, his Spanish the cultured speech of an educated gentleman.

Philip, seated at a wooden table covered with papers and charts, motioned the young officer to rise. Spain's ruler was shockingly old, with a sparse beard and thin hands wrinkled, trembling, and blotched with age. His diseased left eye was covered by a linen bandage.

"Don Alonzo, my friend," Philip said gently. "You have news?"

"*Si, Majestad.*" De Leyva chose his words with care. "The fleet is safe once more in Coruña. The storm caused some slight damage. . . ."

"And *delay*, Don Alonzo! Again delay!" The king's weary gaze traveled the length of the room, to the wide, double windows opened above the jumbled stone cityscape beyond. It was only midmorning of an early June day, but already the sun blazed hot, reflected with tropical intensity from the tile roofs and stucco walls of Madrid. "God is impatient for the success of His enterprise!" The king's voice trembled with emotion. Philip turned suddenly on the secretary who sat at the opposite end of the table, dipping his quill in ink and scratching away at a sheet of parchment. "Leave us!"

Hurriedly, the secretary rose, bowed, and departed. In the

room beyond, white-robed priests and acolytes could be seen preparing to celebrate Mass.

"Tell me, Don Alonzo, truthfully. Was the delay Medina-Sidonia's fault?"

"Could the duke fight the winds and the sea?"

Philip nodded thoughtfully, his eyes bright and quick. "Then we must assume God has some reason for this . . . this new delay in His enterprise."

"It could be to our advantage, Majesty. *La Princessa* should reach us by the end of July with our final shipment of gold."

"As you say, Don Alonzo," Philip said. "Yours may be the most important part of God's enterprise, my son. Your personal fortune . . ."

". . . is entirely at Your Majesty's disposal." He bowed again.

Philip nodded. "All our gifts are from God. I only wish that command could devolve upon you."

"No, Your Majesty. We've discussed this at length before. His Excellency the Marquis de Santa Cruz was a brilliant admiral. When he died, it was a great tragedy for all of Spain. Think of the trouble that appointing a youngster such as myself to replace him would cause within the ranks of your noble officers! Your first choice, the Duke of Medina-Sidonia, is still the best, Majesty."

Philip made a rude noise. "Medina-Sidonia is a scion of one of the wealthiest houses in Europe, yet his debts are such that he hasn't a single *real* he can contribute to my Armada." The King of Spain swept a trembling hand across the parchment on the table before him. "I have no doubt that he is a good soldier. But all I get from the man now are complaints! He lacks provisions. He lacks ships. He complains of being seasick! Sometimes I wonder if command of a fleet is not beyond his abilities!"

De Leyva allowed himself a smile. "Is it not true, Majesty, that our abilities, too, are gifts from God? The Duke of Medina-Sidonia will be a useful tool, in His hands."

The king nodded. "Just so. Just so. And the man seeks to be friends with everyone. My officers *will* follow him." He reached out and patted de Leyva's sleeve. "And I have you, my young friend, backing him up. You will not fail me? If

Medina-Sidonia falters, you will be there to see God's enterprise through?''

The nobleman bowed. "Before God and my King, Majesty, I swear it!''

"Then I am content. You will keep me apprised of the arrival of your ship?''

"Yes, Majesty.''

The chime of a bell in another room signaled the hour for Mass. Philip rose unsteadily and made his way toward the priests waiting in the next chamber.

A useful tool, de Leyva thought. *An idiot, but a useful tool indeed!* He managed to control the laugh that rose, unbidden, behind the stony mask of his face. After so many years of preparation, everything was coming together. Medina-Sidonia might not have been able to predict the storm that had scattered the ships of the Spanish Armada after they set sail on the twenty-eighth of May . . . but de Leyva had known. The storm, and the fact that the Spanish Armada was not destined to depart Coruña for England until the twenty-first of July, were in the history books that de Leyva had studied before his arrival in Spain.

VBU Colonel Yuri Vladimirovich Vorosilov, better known in the Court of Spain as Don Alonzo de Leyva, bowed low as his king left the room.

Everything was going exactly according to the Plan.

Eight

"We have seen this point in history as the key to our success for some time now, Miss Stein. Some of our people have been here for years."

Rachel looked down at the manacles on her wrists. Her arms, the fatigues she wore, were filthy, and the cramped cubicle they'd locked her in was permeated by a cesspool stench. The chains rattled as she moved, shifting farther away from the counterfeit monk leaning over her. "Looks like some of you have done a damned good job, if you ask me." Despite the fear that overlay her every thought, the line of an old, old joke arose in her mind. "I wasn't expecting the Spanish Inquisition." She wondered if Krylenko had ever heard of Monty Python.

The Russian smiled. His English was quite good, though it carried the trace of an accent. "I suppose I should apologize for your . . . accommodations here. But there was little alternative. Women have been prohibited from Spanish ships, by order of His Majesty King Philip II himself. Only by telling the captain and crew of this vessel that you are a heretic, bound over for examination by the Most Holy Inquisition, could I bring you on board. As it was, I had to use considerable persuasion. These peasants are a superstitious lot."

She leaned back on the narrow, straw-covered wooden bench that served as her bed. The chamber had been a large stores cupboard, empty now except for her and the Russian. The creak and rumble of timbers made the ship sound alive. With her head against the damp wood of the hull, Rachel could sense the rush of water beyond.

"So why are you telling me this?" she asked.

"I think you should know the truth of what is happening, that is all. The depth of our commitment to this project."

So that I know there's no hope, he means, she thought. *And, God in Heaven . . . he's damned convincing.*

"Losing Guantánamo must have slowed you down," she replied.

"Some. But if we caught your friends in the blast, it was a small price! Bases can be rebuilt. Guantánamo was a . . . how do you say? A retreat. A refuge for our leaders, for when our operations here change history. Our failures at Munich and in your American Revolution convinced us that such a refuge was necessary." He smiled again. "Otherwise, a miscalculation could wipe out our own leadership!"

"So what does that have to do with me?" *Please, God, don't let my voice shake so much!* "Why not kill me and have done with it?"

"You are still quite valuable, Miss Stein. The VBU has had its eye on you for some time. Your insight into American time operations alone makes you worth saving! But with Guantánamo destroyed, we won't be sending you back to 2008 just yet."

Is that good? Damn it, don't show him you're afraid! "So you're going to keep me chained up in this . . . this hole instead? Straw for a mattress and a bucket for a toilet?"

He chuckled. "Perhaps when we reach the Armada, we can find more suitable quarters for you."

"The . . . Armada? The *Spanish* Armada?" Rachel did not know history as well as Travis Hunter, but she recognized the phrase.

Krylenko nodded. "The greatest fleet ever assembled, up until this time."

She furrowed her brow. "It was destroyed, wasn't it? A storm, or something . . ."

"According to the history texts, yes. But we are here to rewrite those books."

"You can't stop a storm. . . ."

"Ah! But we can see to it that the Spanish land in England! Those landings were prevented in the original history, you see, by the English fleet. It's remarkable, actually . . . a handful of ships is all that stands between the Spanish Armada and English soil. In all of England there are only a few thousand half-trained militia to stand against two Spanish armies!"

"Two armies . . . ?"

Krylenko nodded. "There are 21,000 troops aboard the Armada's transports. And in the Netherlands a superb general, the Duke of Parma, is waiting with another 30,000 veterans. Once the Armada seizes the English Channel, Parma will cross on barges. Queen Elizabeth's rabble, her so-called army, will find itself facing over 50,000 of the best-trained, the most experienced soldiers in the world!"

"But they never got that far! The Armada was beaten. . . ."

"In the original version of history, yes." Krylenko sighed. "Most historians point to the destruction of the Armada as the turning point in the power struggle between Spain and England. After 1588, Spain was never able to muster more than a shadow of the imperial power that had dominated the Old World and the New. After that date, England's power and influence grew. The Massachusetts Bay colony was founded . . . when? In 1607? That's less than twenty years from now. And Jamestown in 1620 . . . Yes, Miss Stein, the defeat of the Spanish Armada was a crucial turning point in the history of world powers!"

Rachel felt an awful chill. "You . . . you're helping the Spanish to stop England from colonizing North America!"

Krylenko nodded. "And much more. There is nothing standing in the way of the Spanish armies once they land in England! Some of our people will be there to help them, of course . . . and we have been providing the Spanish with gold."

"I always thought the Spanish had all the gold they needed from the New World."

"Believe it or not, Philip's Spain is desperately poor. He receives millions in revenues from the New World, true, but he has been paying millions for years now to fight against the Protestants in the Netherlands. He was barely able to outfit his fleet . . . and our gold is the insurance he needs to assemble his army and launch his campaign." Krylenko leaned back against the wall of the cramped compartment. "But the VBU's main task is to see to it that the Armada lands its army safely in England. There will be no Plymouth Rock, Miss Stein . . . no Jamestown. England will be a conquered nation. The Catholics will be back in power again. There will be a new round of religious wars . . . and the Inquisition will hunt down English heretics." He shook his head almost sadly. "I fear that England will be but a shadow of what she would otherwise be, two or three centuries from now!"

"You're not just changing English history," Rachel said, desperate now. "This will affect all of Europe . . . the whole world! You could wipe *yourselves* out."

"Which is why we built the Guantánamo facility, a safe base in the past, before the events that a Spanish victory in 1588 will change. However, we have other forms of insurance. The agents you have encountered before . . . protecting Lenin? With Karl Marx in 1848? They guard those times and places as much to ensure that those men follow the necessary course of history as to protect them from you Americans. Whatever happens to England, Marx will still write his Communist Manifesto. The Russian Revolution will succeed . . . and world Communism will triumph!"

The light burning in Krylenko's eyes frightened Rachel to a depth that she had not yet known or felt. The man was a fanatic, utterly dedicated to his cause.

She looked past the Russian. The door to her cramped quarters was thin, varnished wood, with ornamental bars across a narrow window looking onto a lower deck of *La Princessa Negra*. The deckhead was so low that even she would not have been able to stand up straight, and the atmosphere was close, foul, and gloomy with damp and dark. Men in ragged clothing were crowded next to one another, sleeping, talking, eating, quarreling. . . .

If they've been told I'm a heretic, they won't have anything to do with me, even if I could find one who spoke English.

He seemed to read her thoughts. "There's no help for you. They've been told you are a Jew, Miss Stein." He made the sign of the cross, lightly touching forehead and each side of his chest. "They see me here with you and assume I am trying to save your soul, poor child. Ah . . . but the Inquisition is rather harsh with Jews, I'm afraid. . . .''

She shuddered. "Where . . . where's the man who was with me?"

"Master Sergeant King is quite safe, I assure you. He has been cooperating with us completely, you see."

"You're lying!"

"Why would I lie? He is a sensible man, not given to theatrics or hopeless causes. He recognizes that you are both alone in this century, with no hope at all for finding your way back to your own time."

"You're trying to trick me! Greg would never go along with you!"

He shrugged easily. "As you will. We have spared his life . . . but that is no concern of yours. You can cooperate with us of your own accord or be turned over to the Most Holy Inquisition for . . . questioning." He rose, keeping his upper body stooped to clear the low overhead. "I will leave you to think it over, my dear. I should tell you that, if you remain stubborn, you will probably be burned alive at the stake. A grisly death. I've seen it before, in Spain. . . .''

He left her, slamming the wooden door shut with a clatter of lock and chains.

King scowled at the VBU officer. "You're lying, you son of a bitch."

"Oh, I assure you, Miss Stein is cooperating fully." Krylenko smiled. "She understands that the two of you are completely cut off from your own time and people, with no hope of ever seeing a civilized time again . . . except on our terms."

The Ranger moved his fists, short, sharp gestures that snapped to their limits the chains binding him, then let his hands fall with a clatter of iron links. He had been chained in this tiny, closed locker since he and Rachel had been brought on board . . . how long ago? The meals of dry bread or biscuit and occasional stews of questionable meat were irregular, and there was no way to tell time save by the comings and goings of the crew on the lower deck outside his door. He could not understand Spanish and had long since lost track of the number of times they'd changed the watch.

"Actually, she is quite comfortable now," Krylenko continued, his smile transforming itself into a leer. "I let her move into my cabin. . . ."

King looked up sharply. "Isn't that a bit hard to reconcile with your role as a celibate . . . father?" He spat the word.

"Oh, I've moved out, for the crew's sake. They are a superstitious lot, and it takes a great deal of control to deal with them. Appearances are important. That is scarcely your concern, however. Worry instead about your own future. As of this moment, you are utterly and completely dependent upon me. You have no one else."

King's scowl deepened. Convincing the prisoner that his comrades had already cooperated was standard KGB interrogation practice, he knew . . . but Rachel had been so damned scared back in Cuba, so convinced that she was going to break. Had she?

Not that it would make any difference one way or the other to Greg King. The Russians weren't going to get him to "cooperate" whatever they did. But if an opportunity to escape came along, it would be good to know whether he should include Rachel in his plans or not.

"You bastard, you'd say anything to twist me around," he said. "I don't believe a word of it! If Rachel's gone over to you, let me talk to her. Otherwise, I'll know it's a lie!"

Krylenko shrugged. "Frankly, I don't care whether you believe me or not. We have her . . . and the information she is providing us has already proved invaluable. If you help us, I can promise you life. Once we win, you will no longer be a danger to us and could be granted considerable freedom . . . even rewards." The voice became colder. "But I promise you, with Rachel helping us, I don't need you at all."

King shrugged and looked away. "Lucky me. Go away and quit bothering me." Through the slats in the narrow window set into the cupboard door, he could see the lower deck. It was dark there, crowded with Spanish seamen. And there were Russians with the crew as well, he reminded himself, the crew of the Soviet patrol boat. If he could get out, how would he get past them?

King knew a cold and twisting fear. He was all alone, with damned little to look for in the way of hope.

Krylenko shook his head almost sadly. "I wish I could quit bothering you," he said. "Or that I could at least grant you an easy death. There is hardly any point in torturing you for information. But, as I said, appearances are important. The crew believes you to be a heretic on his way to face the Holy Inquisition." Krylenko shrugged. "I imagine that, to keep up those appearances, you understand, I'll have to turn you over to them once we get to London."

"Idiot. There *was* no Inquisition in London."

"Ah, but there *will* be, my friend. There will be very soon now. . . ."

The locker door clattered shut on King and his darkening thoughts.

Nine

"Deck, there! Sail a' th' larboard bow!"

Hunter climbed the ladder from the gundeck, blinking into the sunlight as he stepped onto the main deck and squinted up into *Resolute*'s rigging. Dark Walker was close behind him, followed by Anderson, Morgan, and the rest of the team. Sour notes from a trumpet set *Resolute*'s crew into urgent motion. Hunter leaped aside to avoid being trampled by a rush of seamen from the lower deck.

The date, Hunter knew, was July 16 by the old calendar . . . the twenty-sixth by the new. *Resolute* had been beating her way across the Atlantic for almost two full months. The captured rendezvous log suggested that the Bay of Biscay, north of Spain and west of France, was where they might find the *Black Princess* before she could join the Spanish Armada.

Hunter made his way aft, climbing the steps to the poop. Penvennan stood against the portside railing, shielding his eyes with one hand as he searched the horizon. "A lone ship t' th' nor'east, Mr. Hunter. Leastwise, none other shows herself."

"The *Black Princess*, Captain?" Hunter frowned. They'd salvaged a pair of binoculars from *La Dueña*, but he couldn't use them. Telescopes had not been invented yet, and binoculars might seem like black magic to Penvennan's sailors.

"We'll mark her soon enough, by heaven! Helm, there! Bring her hard up!"

Resolute pressed on, heeling over under a sharp breeze gusting from the north. The other ship was running before the wind, heading south for Spain. Thirty minutes after the sighting, the Spaniard turned from her southerly course and began angling away toward the unseen French coast.

The English ship followed. A smaller, handier vessel than the Spanish galleon, her pace was faster. Hour by hour, *Resolute* drew closer, and it was clear that long before the Spanish galleon could reach land, she would have to either fight or surrender.

"We'll ha' them wi'in the hour, sir," Penvennan said, looking steadily at Hunter. "Care thee for a place i' the fight?"

"I wouldn't miss it for the world, Captain." There was no way to tell if the lone Spanish ship was *Black Princess* or not, for navies of this period had not yet begun painting names across their vessels' sterns. Still, she *could* be . . .

"Look ye to thy men, then," Penvennan said. He nodded toward the quarterdeck, where Anderson and Jones were snapping belts of ammo into their M-60s. "Yon strange weapons may yet prove their worth i' th' test!"

"That they will, Captain!" Hunter said, grinning. Penvennan was in for a shock.

Hunter had given two months' consideration to the problem. If and when they caught *Black Princess*, should Hunter and his men join the fight? There was always the danger that someone they killed might be important to history . . . and there was no way to gauge the effect such a change might have on the events of four centuries.

On the other hand, if the other ship was the *Black Princess*, Greg and Rachel would be in terrible danger as long as the battle went on. If the Rangers could shorten the fight with their modern weapons, that danger would be reduced.

Hunter joined his men on the quarterdeck. "Okay," he said, looking at each man in turn. "Remember how we planned it. Aimed fire to take out the enemy guns. Single shots or short bursts only. No rock-and-roll."

There was a chorus of "Yes, sirs" and muttered agreement.

He looked at Gomez. "Same thing, Eddie. No bangs." Gomez's 40mm grenade launcher would be a devastating weapon on board ship . . . and savagely indiscriminate.

"No bangs, Chief. You got it."

"Good. Now spread along the rail, but stay where you can hear me. Your primary targets will be the swivel gunners in the tops."

They were close enough now that the preparations for battle could be seen on the Spanish galleon's decks. Both ships were dispatching troops and sailors to platforms on the masts, where small, swivel-mounted cannons, popularly called "murderers," could be used to shotgun the enemy with small balls of iron or stone. Below decks, the big cannon protruded from the gunports. Sheets of canvas were stretched in places to hide the gunners, and nets were rigged across the gap between forecastle and quarterdeck to stop boarders.

The battle began with almost breathtaking abruptness. The Spaniard suddenly turned with the wind, presenting her starboard side to the English galleon's bow. Smoke appeared as if by magic here and there along the Spanish ship's side, followed an instant later by the sharp crack of cannons. A ragged hole appeared in the mainsail, yards above Hunter's head.

"Helm a' weather!" Penvennan bellowed from the poop, and *Resolute*'s bow slid away to the right until she was sailing side by side with the Spanish galleon, fifty yards away with the wind at her back. "Fire!" someone yelled, and English guns barked. Roiling clouds of sour smoke from the guns momentarily blotted out the target.

The smoke cleared quickly in the breeze. Hunter saw a flash of light from the Spaniard's mizzen top, on a platform shrouded by canvas well above the slanting mizzen yard. He laid his hand on Anderson's shoulder, pointing out the gun.

The Texan braced his M-60 on the quarterdeck railing, sighting carefully. The short, rattling burst from his weapon made the canvas screen shiver. A second burst tore the screen away completely, sending a trio of bodies pitching through rigging and spars twenty feet into the nets stretched across the deck.

Jones trained his 60-gun on the maintop, and in the next moment, all of the Rangers were adding their firepower to *Resolute*'s broadside.

A bugle call lilted above the crash of gunfire from the Spanish galleon's decks. Almost at once, the guns on both sides fell silent. Someone on the enemy's poopdeck was gathering in the great, billowing mass of the Spanish flag. "He's struck!" an Englishman yelled, and the words brought a resounding cheer from *Resolute*'s seamen.

Resolute drew closer as the Spaniard shortened sail. . . .

Hunter was leaning against the rail trying to catch a glimpse of Rachel or King on the other ship when the burst of full auto gunfire spat from the Spanish ship's main deck. Bullets chopped into an English sailor standing on the railing nearby, braced against the ratlines as he studied the galleon alongside. The man staggered, his face and chest shredded and bloody as he collapsed against the ratlines, rebounded, then toppled over the side into the sea. Splinters whirled from holes pocked in the deck, and a gunner holding an ornate, wooden wand with a smoking slow match attached to the end crumpled across the breech of his cannon.

"Hit the deck!" Hunter yelled. Bullets thunked into *Resolute*'s wooden hull and pared splinters from the railing above his head. That, Hunter decided, settled the question of the other ship's identity.

Hunter rolled up to peer over the railing at the other ship, searching for the source of the auto fire. Tattered streamers of smoke clotted between the two vessels, making it difficult to see.

Suddenly, Jones reared up, his eyes wide. "Oh, shit . . . !" He swung his M-60 around to point at the bow of the Spaniard in the same instant that Hunter saw the Marine's target, a man crouched over the starboard railing on *Princessa*'s main deck, the deadly and unmistakable shape of a Soviet RPG balanced on one shoulder. At his side was a shrouded figure in what looked like a monk's habit, holding an AKM. . . .

Jones squeezed his 60-gun's trigger in the same instant that the Russian fired. The rocket-propelled grenade swooped down from the Spanish galleon's side, arrowing into *Resolute*'s main deck at the tip of a trail of white smoke. It exploded close beside the mainmast, and splinters scythed through gunners crouched along *Resolute*'s port side. Fire boiled up from the gap blasted in the plank deck, and Hunter heard the panicked cries of the sailors. These old sailing vessels were tinderboxes, he knew, and fire was a sailor's greatest terror. He saw a gunner dash the flames with water from a bucket sitting near a cannon.

The fire was out, but the damage worsened. The ship's mainmast lurched to port, as a huge crack near its base appeared . . . widened . . . The English man-of-war shuddered, stricken, then swung broadside toward the Spanish galleon. Her gunners fired a last volley at point-blank range. Balls and the wicked, double-ended shot the English called langerill slashed through the enemy's rigging and boarding nets. Then the hulls touched with a slow, drawn-out crash.

The shock was enough to complete the damage the RPG had begun. *Resolute*'s mast slumped to port, tearing up lines and boarding nets and great chunks of planking as it went. A mountain of sagging canvas collapsed across Hunter's view of the Spanish ship. *Resolute*'s mainmast was suspended now, entangled in the rigging of both ships. Jones looked back at Hunter. "I don't know, Lieutenant!" he said. His eyes were wild. "I think I got the bastard. . . ."

"Serves him right," Gomez said with a manic grin. "I distinctly heard the Chief give the order: 'No grenades!' He should've known better!"

English seamen were clustered around the fallen mast now, chopping at tangled lines with axes. Auto-fire snapped again from the other ship.

"We can't see from here," Hunter said, rising. He looked up at the Spanish ship. This close, the *Princessa*'s hull seemed to tower above *Resolute*'s deck. Loose canvas cracked and banged high overhead. "We've got to get over there and stop those guns!"

"We've got a bridge now," Gary Lynch said, pointing at the mast. "Looks like the rest of the crew has the same idea!"

English soldiers and sailors were already swarming across the narrow gap between the two vessels, using the fallen mast and tangled rigging as a ladder. Hunter stood, clutching his Uzi. "Come on, men!" He could sense the fury of *Resolute*'s crew. They'd been fired on from the decks of a surrendered ship! If the Rangers did not reach *Princessa*'s deck fast, there would be a slaughter . . . and Rachel and Greg would be at the receiving end. "Boarders away!"

Hunter vaulted across *Resolute*'s railing with packs of screaming men, scrambling out into the line-infested gap between the ships on a bundle of cordage, canvas, and wood.

Each vessel had its own, independent motion, and for a dizzying moment, Hunter clung to his unsteady ladder and stared down at the seething water between them. The sides of both ships curved inboard, and footing on the Spanish galleon's water-drenched side was treacherous.

He hauled himself across the rail and onto *Princessa*'s deck. Chaos reigned there. Spanish seamen were running everywhere, but none seemed particularly anxious to fight. Hunter clutched his Uzi tightly and hurried forward, toward the spot where he'd seen the man with the RPG.

A ragged Spanish sailor lunged out of the smoke, dropping to his knees before Hunter could react. "*Cuarto!*" the man begged in naked terror. "*Por favor, Señor! Cuarto!*" A sword flashed at Hunter's side, and the seaman's face blossomed scarlet. Penvennan's crew was in no mood now to give quarter.

There . . . ! He recognized a Russian uniform, camo fatigues now liberally splashed with blood. Jones's fire had indeed found its mark. There was no sign of the man in the monk's costume . . . or the RPG.

Another VBU agent ran forward out of the smoke, marked by his camo fatigues and the AK gripped in his hands. Hunter fired a burst from his Uzi, catching the Soviet squarely in his center of mass. The man went down sprawling, tripping another running Soviet close behind him.

Before he could rise, a Spaniard clubbed him down with a billy. Hunter hurried forward and the seaman looked up from his crumpled victim. "*En el nombre de Dios!*" the man pleaded. "No kill! No kill! I help! *Mira!*"

Hunter ignored him. Beyond the terrified seaman, Hunter saw something else . . . the cowled shape of the monk, high on the galleon's forecastle, stooped beneath the unmistakable silhouette of an RPG. The Ranger snapped a burst from his Uzi. Bullets clawed splinters from the forecastle railing as the monk twisted away. *Miss . . . !*

Then Dark Walker was there, taking aim with his Galil. The Israeli battle rifle snapped once, and the monk toppled from the forecastle, landing with a thud on the deck below. The loaded RPG bounced off the railing and spun end for end into the sea.

The Spanish bugle was blaring surrender once more.

"Quarter!" Penvennan's voice rose above the sounds of screams and battle. "Give the beggars quarter, God damn you!" Slowly, the clash of steel, the crack of cannon and muskets died away. The Spanish allowed themselves to be herded forward by English soldiers and sailors wielding swords and pikes.

Hunter made his way to the base of the forecastle, where the man in monk's robes lay sprawled on his back. His chest was bloody, but his eyes fluttered open at Hunter's touch.

It was Shvernik, the VBU officer who had interrogated Hunter and Rachel at Guantánamo. A pack with a reload for the lost RPG lay at his side.

"So, Lieutenant Hunter," the Russian managed. His breathing was harsh and bubbling as his throat filled with blood from a punctured lung. "You show considerable . . . resourcefulness. . . ."

"Where are they?" Hunter demanded. He tore the robes open as he spoke, uncovering the wound. Air bubbled into the bloody hole in the man's chest.

Shvernik smiled. "Not here. You won't find them now. . . . Too late . . ."

Anderson kneeled at Hunter's side. He took a quick look at the Russian's sucking chest wound, then broke open his first aid kit. A piece of cellophane wrapping saved for the purpose plugged the wound in an attempt to stop the lung from collapsing.

"Where are they?" Hunter asked again. Shvernik's eyes were glazing. "Damn it, man! Don't die! Where are they?"

"Too late . . ."

The words turned into a rattling, choking gasp, and Shvernik died.

Ten

Both ships lay hove to, still side by side as Englishmen and Spaniards worked to repair the battle damage. *Resolute* had suffered the worst with the loss of her mainmast, but the damage to the *Black Princess* was more extensive, with large masses of her lower rigging carried away by the English ship's broadsides or entangled by *Resolute*'s falling spars. The air was alive with the shouts of seamen in English and Spanish, and with the clatter and thump of axes chopping, carpenters hammering, and masses of cordage, blocks, spars, and wreckage being lowered to the deck.

Hunter stood on the English quarterdeck, watching the activity. Most of his men were helping Penvennan's crew, at least in the heavy, unskilled jobs of chopping, hauling, and lifting, where their lack of experience with sailing ships was unlikely to get them into trouble. There was an incredible amount of work that had to be done before either ship would sail again, and time, now, was precious.

He turned to look at a clear, out-of-the-way spot on the quarterdeck, where Gomez squatted with one of the Spanish officers under the watchful eyes and 60-gun of Roy Anderson. The thought tortured him. *We almost made it in time. . . .*

"The wind's fair for England, at least," Penvennan said, coming up to Hunter's side. "I reckon a passage of three days if the weather holds."

"You think it's best to stay with *Resolute*, then?"

"Aye. It galls me leaving yonder prize, but we haven't the men to crew her aright, not with two hundred sullen Dons and damage to her stays besides." The Cornishman turned his eye on Hunter, suddenly fierce. "An' for all the gold we found i' her . . ."

Hunter spread his hands. "Captain, I'm sorry. We came so close. . . ."

"Aye, Aye. 'Twasn't your fault, lad. But it rankles, all the same. If we'd been but one day sooner i' crossing the sea . . ."

"We, too, have lost our treasure, Captain."

"Aye. Th' friend an' the damsel ye spoke of. I fear there's little hope there."

Again, desperation surged under Hunter's breast. Rachel and Greg were still alive or had been yesterday when *Princessa* had rendezvoused with the Armada a few miles to the north. Her crew claimed to have watched the two "heretics" taken, separately and blindfolded, across to one of the largest of Philip's ships. His first thoughts after the battle had focused on going after them. The captured galleon might serve as a Trojan Horse to get them into the Spanish fleet.

But any such plan was clearly impossible. Penvennan could not spare the men to man the *Princess* and *Resolute* as well, and her Spanish crew was not to be trusted with so few guards. Besides, Penvennan had his own schedule to keep. The news that the Armada was at sea had to reach England at once. They would abandon the *Princess*. The prize money for her capture was not worth the delay she would cause reaching home.

He turned from Penvennan and crossed the quarterdeck to where Gomez was questioning the Spanish officer.

"*Ay, creo que sí,*" the prisoner was saying. "*En un barque grande con el nombre de . . . de 'San Salvador.'*"

"How's it going, Eddie?"

Gomez looked up. He looked tired. "Hi, Chief. We have the name of the ship they were taken to. And I think we know where they're going."

"Oh?"

Gomez nodded. "*Princessa*'s crew wasn't in on the Armada planning, but this guy heard some gossip. Plymouth."

"Plymouth . . . !" He thought of the map Penvennan had recognized as the English port of Plymouth.

"Yeah. The idea is to have the Armada land twenty thousand soldiers at Plymouth. They'll march toward London and draw the English forces to meet them. Meanwhile, the Armada'll sail to where the Duke of Parma is waiting with another thirty thousand men in the Netherlands, and ferry them across the Channel."

Hunter closed his eyes, visualizing a map of southern England. "Putting a second army close to London and between the capital and the Queen's forces. Very neat."

"Yeah. There's more." Gomez exchanged glances with Anderson. "The gossip says 'divine angels' will prepare the way into Plymouth . . . knocking down the castle ramparts, scattering the heretics' fleet, stuff like that."

Hunter felt a cold sensation in his stomach. "Sounds pretty specific, doesn't it?"

"I was wonderin' about that, LT," Anderson put in. "Seems to me the Spanish'd be settin' themselves up for quite a disappointment, expecting walls to come tumblin' down and all . . . unless there was something pretty solid backin' up the promise!"

"Like a few RPG launchers or AK machine guns . . ."

"Or a few hundred kilos of plastique. Chief, we may have a handle on the Russian plan here."

"I think I agree." He thought of the captured map again. Plymouth was an important English seaport on the Channel coast, an excellent harbor set back from the sea by two sheltering points of land. In fact . . .

Hunter turned suddenly. "Captain Penvennan!" he called. "Where is the English fleet likely to be?"

"Why, that is a question I cannot easily give answer to. It has been four months, recall, since last I set foot in England."

"But surely you know something of the fleet's plans. Spain's been threatening to send their Armada for some time, now."

" 'Struth, but there is little enough in the telling. Two great squadrons there be, the one under Sir Francis Drake, the other under the Lord High Admiral himself, Sir Charles Howard of Effingham. Sir Charles would have the command, of course."

"And how would they know when the Armada was coming? They wouldn't stay at sea continually . . . ."

"Nay. Patrols there would be, lone ships at sea for a few weeks at a time, to fly to give the warning when the Armada was sighted."

"And where would you wait with the fleet if you were Howard?"

Penvennan chuckled. "Ah, would that I were, and not scrabbling for fortune and fame at th' toss of fate! Were I Sir Charles himself, sir, methinks I would gather the fleet, rather than remain divided, lest the Dons' vast force break mine piecemeal. From either Falmouth or Plymouth could I maintain my watch, to sally forth at need."

"Plymouth?"

"Aye. 'Tis there that I left Sir Francis, these four months past. I'll warrant he lies at anchor there now, awaiting our news. Who knows? Perhaps Sir Charles and the whole English fleet be with him there. . . . ."

Who knows indeed? Hunter thought. He didn't trust his own memory of the history of this engagement very far, but Penvennan's suppositions had triggered something, reminded him of something he'd read once. There was a story—probably apocryphal—about Sir Francis Drake waiting at Plymouth, playing a game of bowls when word of the approaching Armada arrived. Drake was supposed to have cooly suggested that there was time for one more game before sending out the fleet.

Apocryphal or not, the story tended to confirm Penvennan's supposition. Plymouth might well be a key part of the English strategy.

Now, he thought. *Put that together with a Russian map of the harbor and its approaches, and a Spanish story about angels leading the Armada into Plymouth. . . .*

Hunter was suddenly quite sure that he knew exactly how the VBU planned to change history. "Captain, we must get to Plymouth!"

"Aye. Have I not said so? Contrary winds and our missing mast permitting . . ."

"Not just to warn your fleet!" He turned, looking back to where Gomez was still questioning the Spaniard. "Captain, I can't explain it all. You'd never believe me if I did. But if you love England, you'll fly this ship to Plymouth if you have to! We've got to get there before they do!''

"They" might mean the Armada to Penvennan, but Hunter was beginning to picture a different type of invasion along the coast of southern England, one that only the Rangers could hope to stop. If *Resolute* lost her race with the Spanish, Howard, Drake, the English fleet, and England herself all might well be doomed.

King looked up as the wooden door creaked open. Two men stood there against the weak light from a lantern behind them. He recognized Krylenko, still in the dirty robes of a Spanish friar, but the other man, young, handsome, and almost flamboyantly dressed in the cape and doublet of a gentleman, was a stranger.

"I trust your new quarters are comfortable?" Krylenko smiled ironically.

The Ranger shifted his position with a rattle of chains. "They're larger."

He still did not understand why he had been taken from the *Princessa Negra*. He'd been kept blindfolded, but his ears had told him of considerable activity on the ship's deck as they'd prepared to lower him over the side into a waiting longboat. From what he'd been able to gather, he had been transferred from the *Princessa* to another ship, along with Krylenko and most of the Russian spetsnaz. Why?

Krylenko turned to the well-dressed man and began speaking rapidly in Russian. "He insists he will never help us, Comrade Colonel. I have seen no reason to persuade him otherwise. He has been docile otherwise."

"Good. We may have questions for him after the operation is complete. Watch him closely."

"Of course, Comrade Colonel."

"I must return to the *Rata* now. You will attend our council of war tomorrow, of course. You can shed those ridiculous robes and present yourself as my aide."

"That will be a relief," Krylenko said, scratching himself. "These things have been infested with vermin for months now."

"Ha! I tell you, Pavel Andreivich, if I smelled as bad as

you do now, old Philip would never let me into his presence . . . !''

The door slammed shut, and the two walked off, still engaged
in conversation. King leaned back against the side of the ship,
his eyes closed against the darkness.

What the bloody hell are they up to? King shuddered, sick
to the very core of his being. Never, in all of his life, had he
felt so completely alone or helpless.

Gregory King was a contradiction, and he was facing that
fact for the first time in his life. For as long as he could
remember, he'd presented the image of the tough, self-assured
loner, the man who could handle any situation, who preferred
going it alone.

Yet even as a teenager, back among the dirty tenements of
the Bronx where whites were in the minority, he'd gotten in
trouble more times than he could remember, running with a
gang that called itself "the British Lords." He'd managed to
make himself popular with the other gang members by actually
pretending to be British; his favorite bit of profanity—"bloody
hell"—was habit now, but back then it had been an affectation
to impress the others.

He'd quit the street gang when he'd seen the sick horror of
what drugs were doing to friends. That was when he'd enlisted
in the Army . . . and hadn't that been simply joining a larger
gang? For fifteen years, the Army had been his family, especially after he joined the Rangers and found the special camaraderie among the professional soldiers of an elite unit.
Travis Hunter had become the brother he'd never had.

Here in the stifling darkness, there were no Rangers, no
friends . . . not even the twisted brotherhood of the Lords.

Alone.

Being alone, King realized now, was the one thing that
terrified him the most.

The terror sapped his will as much as the cramped quarters
sapped his strength. He'd scarcely been able to stand when
they'd taken him out on deck for his transfer from the *Princessa,* and now his will was so battered Krylenko called him
"docile."

Slowly, his fists closed, until he could feel his nails biting
into the flesh of his palms. Sweat dripped from his forehead

in the humid darkness. He would fight them . . . he would!
Somehow he would find a way to strike back, to affirm that
he was a man, that they had not broken him!

Somehow . . .

Greg King would show the Russians a new meaning for the
word "docile." . . .

It had been a cliffhanger of a race, Hunter decided later.
Resolute was a limping cripple, coming from behind and battered by the storm that lashed her on the day after the battle
with the *Princessa*. But her opponent, a vast fleet that included
numerous galleys propelled by oars, was crawling northeast at
a rowboat's pace. *Resolute* had swung well to the west to avoid
being sighted, but made up the time with a following wind.
By Penvennan's log it was now July 19; according to the new-
fangled calendar that the Cornishman was convinced was a
Popish plot, the day was Friday, July 29.

Early in the afternoon, *Resolute*'s lookouts had sighted a sail
to the north. After a heart-stopping quarter hour of worry that
the Spanish were still between them and England, they made
out the red cross of St. George flying at the other vessel's
forepeak. Two hours later, *Resolute* rendezvoused with the
Golden Hinde, out of Plymouth under Captain Sir Thomas
Flemyng.

"I know not whether to believe this wild tale you tell, sir,"
Flemyng told Hunter warily. He was a big man, with a full,
rich beard, the points of his mustache waxed into upturned
horns. "And I am loath to abandon Captain Penvennan when
his ship doth threaten to founder i' th' waves at any
turn. . . ."

"You mayest believe, Sir Thomas," Penvennan said. "The
Don Armada cannot be more than a few hours from this spot
. . . and these men have urgent business in Plymouth. It would
be well if you could transport them thither. . . ."

"But you have not seen the Dons," Flemyng insisted. "Not
but for one stray galleon, now lost, and the word of Don
prisoners who wouldst tell thee of flights to the moon should't
please them! Thy story rests on this man's word . . . and methinks his words carry the burden of a speech as sore strange

and alien as the Spanish. How canst thou be certain the Armada is out in truth?''

''They're out,'' Hunter said. ''You can count on it.''

''Nay, sir, I cannot! You want me to return to the Lord High Admiral bearing dreams! There have been false rumors of the Spanish onslaught 'ere this. I will carry no more such ruinous fancies to shame me before my queen!''

Damn! Hunter looked around the deck of the *Golden Hinde* in mounting desperation. He had asked Penvennan to bring him along when he crossed in a longboat to speak with Flemyng, hoping to convince the man to take all of the Rangers back to Plymouth at a greater speed than *Resolute* could manage.

''Sir Thomas,'' he said, choosing his words with care. ''We have very special information . . .''

''*Yar! Deck there!*'' The shout from the maintop interrupted Hunter in mid-sentence. The lookout's cry sounded incredulous. ''*Sails o' th' larboard beam . . . thousands o' them . . . !*''

''Blast you for a fool!'' Flemyng bellowed. He turned, shaking his head. ''A pox on him! 'Thousands of sails,' the lubber says. . . .''

But disbelief changed to awe as minutes crawled by. Hunter's breath caught in his throat.

''Thousands of sails'' was, perhaps, an exaggeration . . . but it looked to Hunter in that moment as though a forest were slowly growing above the distant southern horizon. He could make out the individual masts as thickly planted as trees, each festooned with flags and banners, brightly colored and flashing in the mid-afternoon sun. Beneath the banners, white and tan sails billowed in a grand display that grew thicker and more complex as he watched. They were moving slowly, but they were moving, clawing their way across the horizon, heading toward Flemyng's *Golden Hinde* with an awesome, unstoppable momentum.

There seemed to be no way in the world of stopping or even slowing such a horde, certainly no way that ten men could turn it aside. With the Russians to help, this, truly, was the Invincible Armada.

Eleven

The *Golden Hinde* dropped anchor in Plymouth Harbor under the shadow of the frowning gray towers of the castle called the Royal Citadel. The sun had set by the time Hunter, with Anderson and Morgan, had accompanied Captain Flemyng and several of his officers in a small boat across the harbor to Phoenix Dock, climbed the dank, wet stone steps from the water to the quay, and been escorted by armored soldiers past the Citadel to the expanse of grassy field beyond known as Plymouth Hoe.

Hunter and the other Rangers slowed up as the group approached a large party of men gathered on the Hoe. The sky still carried light enough to see by. There were at least thirty men there, some in partial armor, most in colorful clothing that ran to baggy flounces around the hips, tights, capes, and long-plumed hats. Their attention was focused on the balls they were rolling across the grass.

"So it wasn't apocryphal after all," Hunter murmured.

"Beg pardon, sir?" Morgan asked.

"The famous game of bowls. Legend has it that's what Sir Francis Drake was doing when the news arrived of the Armada. He's supposed to have said there was time to play another game and still beat the Spanish after . . ."

"I'm not sure that's what's in the script," Anderson said,

nodding toward the group. "Ol' Flemyng's news seems to have them pretty shook!"

Flemyng's arrival had indeed caused a stir in the crowd. Several men were running in the direction of the castle, paced by barking dogs. Others were arguing and gesturing, waving toward the harbor. "We must move at once, sir, if we are to get out of yon narrow-mouthed sack," one man in a rich velvet cape was saying. The power behind his words reminded Hunter of Flemyng's quarterdeck bellow. "The wind i' from the southwest and pins us here like the point of a sword!"

The man he was addressing held the bowling ball, the breeze tugging at a richly ornamented cloak across his cloth-of-gold doublet. "Mayhap 'tis too late e'en as we speak, Sir Francis. With but eight ships standing to, and the rest unmanned and unready . . ."

"Then there be no time for maundering, my Lord Howard! We must move with dispatch or concede the game! We'll scour Plymouth Town for our men and warp the fleet out this night!"

The group of finely dressed men scattered in a flurry of orders, leaving the bowling balls where they were on the grass. A servant with a tray filled with wine glasses stood in blinking confusion as the party dissolved. Flemyng strode across the lawn toward Hunter. "That's done it, lad," the Englishman said. "The race is on now, 'twixt the wind and the Dons!"

Hunter looked to the east. Plymouth Harbor was in twilight now, but a full moon was rising now, casting enough light for him to make out the silent, black forms of ships, pinpointed here and there by glowing lanterns. The harbor had roughly the shape of a trident with the Royal Citadel between the middle and western prongs and the town just to the north. Some ships, including Flemyng's *Hinde*, rode at anchor in the middle prong, off the quayside below the stone castle. The eastern prong was a stubby waterway called the Catwater, and it was there that the bulk of the English fleet lay, ships arrayed close together in the midst of a horde of small coasters and provisioning craft.

"Was that Sir Francis Drake talking about the need to hurry?" Hunter asked.

"Ay, 'twas him. And he knows what he's about, that one." Flemyng pointed to the south, where the prongs of the trident joined in a short haft between two headlands, opening onto the sea. "The wind be against us, but with haste and luck, mayhap our fleet can be warped clear of the harbor by midday tomorrow. Pray God that it is so, or the Spanish will find us trapped, ripe for the plucking, able neither to sail nor fight."

Trapped . . .

"Captain," Hunter said with new urgency. "I must get my people ashore tonight."

Flemyng's gaze hardened. "Are ye so anxious to miss a fight, then?"

"It's not that, Captain," Hunter replied carefully. "I can't say much about it, but there are . . . agents. Enemy agents who want to help the Spanish win."

"Ay, the Catholics, you mean. Since Scotland's Mary was beheaded last year, they've been a devilish threat. Perchance Philip of Spain hopes the papists will rise in his cause when his army sets foot on English soil."

Hunter nodded agreement since the idea fit Flemyng's pre-conceived notions. Privately, he wondered how the Soviets would feel being lumped in with the Catholics in this war that was as much religious as it was political.

Flemyng turned and hurried back down the slope of Plymouth Hoe, followed by his officers. Hunter stood with Morgan and Anderson in the gathering darkness.

"Are you thinking what I'm thinking, Lieutenant?" the Navy SEAL asked.

"I'm thinking the Russians know the English fleet is penned up behind that narrow harbor mouth," Hunter replied. "Knowing that, we just might make a guess about what they're going to do about it."

Morgan pointed to the southeast. A land mass bulked there, almost black now against the sea in the rapidly failing light. In the trident analogy, it was the land cutting Plymouth Harbor off from the open sea, just to the east of the trident's handle and south of the Catwater's crowded anchorage. "That hill," he said. "If the Russians wanted to attack the English fleet, they could come ashore there."

Hunter nodded slowly as he strained against the darkness. "Let's see if we can round up our people and get over there."

"And do what?" Anderson replied. "With machine guns and assault rifles, we're not going to make much of an impression against the Spanish Armada when it sails into view! Or are you thinking that the noise'll scare them off?''

"I'm thinking more about the idea that 'angels' would be leading the way into Plymouth, Roy," Hunter said. "Doug's right. A Russian landing party put ashore over there could destroy the English fleet with heavy weapons. Especially if they know there's going to be a lot of confusion in the harbor tonight.''

"Maybe," Anderson said doubtfully. "But it's going to take time to get over there . . . and time to get back. If we're wrong . . .''

"At least we'll be able to see. The starlight scope, remember? If the Russians are coming from the sea, we'll be able to spot them from over there and move to a good position. What other choice do we have?''

"We'd better get our people off the *Hinde*, then," Morgan observed. "Or Jones and the other guys'll get impressed into the navy anyway. Flemyng and the other captains aren't going to be real particular about who they sweep up for duty tonight!''

Hunter nodded tiredly. "We've done the navy bit enough," he said. "I think it's time to be Rangers again.''

The three men hurried down the hill toward the quay.

Don Alonzo de Leyva, known to only a few in the Armada as Colonel Vorosilov of the VBU, leaned against the railing and stared into the darkness. He could see the pinpoint lights of the Armada's lanterns, could sense the mass of ships extending for miles all around his vessel, the *Rata Encoronada*.

There was no use in pretending secrecy now. Once the northernmost ships of the Armada had sighted land on the previous afternoon, it was certain that the English knew the fleet was here. Medina-Sidonia had celebrated the moment by breaking out an enormous banner on his flagship, the one-thousand–ton, forty-eight–gun *San Martín*. The flag—portraying Christ on the cross flanked by the Virgin Mary and Mary Magdalene—had been hoisted aloft to the resounding cheers of soldiers and sailors throughout the fleet. Priests had given blessings and benedictions, and the Invincible Armada had continued on course certain now that the final clash with the heretics of England lay just ahead.

Vorosilov stroked his yellow beard and smiled into the star-flecked darkness. The Spanish fools couldn't know how blessed they really were, with time-traveling Russian agents concealed within their midst. If not for the Russians, and the very special help they were preparing to give at this moment a few miles to the northeast, the Spanish were doomed to failure for all their giant, soldier-crowded vessels. It would be Soviet arms that would bring them victory, not prayers to their Christ.

Two Spanish ships had been infiltrated by the VBU. *San Salvador* was flagship of the stores ships and transports. His own *Rata Encoronada*, one of the most powerful vessels in the Armada, would act as flagship of the Spanish vanguard in battle.

But those two vessels were operational headquarters only, means to keep in touch with the Spanish fleet and from which Vorosilov could take command of it if necessary. The real Russian strength had been kept carefully hidden, lest the Soviets' superstitious pawns take fright and scatter. He glanced at the luminous dial of his anachronistic wristwatch, hidden under the full sleeve of his doublet.

Midnight. It would be happening now. . . .

A boat crew from the *Golden Hinde* dropped the ten Rangers on the moonlit beach south of the Catwater at a few minutes past midnight, local time. There were more than a few dark glances and mutters from the English sailors, for the longboat was crowded with the Rangers' gear, offloaded from the *Hinde* in canvas bags and stowed in the ship's cutter, making the boat heavy, crowded, and unwieldy. It took nearly fifteen minutes to unload it—weapons, extra ammo, and the starlight scope they'd taken with them from *La Dueña*. Hunter handed the coxswain a fistful of gold coins from Gomez's pack. The crew might be suspicious of the Rangers' strange clothes and weapons, but at least they were well paid.

They trudged up a path laid bare in the grass by the full moon. At their backs, across the water, Plymouth was alive with light.

In the harbor, lanterns illuminated ships and small craft everywhere, and the air was filled even at a distance by shouted orders, by men chanting in unison as they leaned into capstans, by the rattle of rigging against masts and the creak of yards being hoisted into place. By the moonlight Hunter and his men could see small boats crawling like many-legged beetles in line ahead of one of the ships in the Catwater. Rowboats were being used to literally tow the larger ships to sea, the "warping" Flemyng had mentioned earlier. The entire harbor was a hive of activity as the English ships were mustered for the coming battle, many of them packed almost hull to hull as they awaited their chance to navigate the narrow mouth of the harbor and make it to the open sea. The opening was only wide enough, Flemyng had told Hunter, for three ships to sail side by side. With some ninety English vessels inside the bay, it was going to take time to get the force under way.

The path cut back and forth, passed under some trees, then opened onto a flat-topped ridge overlooking the Channel. The wind was stronger here, still blowing steadily off the ocean, from the southwest.

The Armada would be in that direction, still unseen, but there.

"Okay, men," Hunter said softly. "Let's get set up. Don't unload everything though. We may just have to pack it again when we have to move. Where's the scope?"

"Right here." Tony Carlucci slipped the canvas bag he'd been carrying off his shoulder and opened it up. The starlight scope was cumbersome but not too heavy to be used hand-held. Hunter took it and began scanning the horizon slowly.

"You all might as well make yourselves comfortable," Hunter said as he squinted into the rubber-padded eyepiece. "It might be quite a while before . . ."

He stopped speaking in mid-sentence, the starlight scope held rock steady now, aimed at a point on the horizon.

"Whatcha got, Chief?" Gomez asked.

"Oh my God," Hunter said. He blinked several times, then adjusted the focus. He could not believe what he was seeing.

"C'mon, LT!" Anderson said. "I don't see nothin' but night! What's goin' down?"

Hunter studied the scene for several more moments. The image intensifier worked splendidly, revealing the night-darkened seascape as plainly as if it were still twilight. A patrol boat cruised slowly offshore, larger than the Turya, with wicked-looking canisters on her sides housing long-range missiles.

But it was the larger vessel that held him, stirring his guts with fear and with a new understanding of just how dedicated the Soviets were to their Spanish allies.

"I never would have believed it," Hunter said slowly. He passed the scope to Anderson, who took it eagerly and held it to his eye.

The Texan gasped. "Oh, shit!" he exclaimed. "What are they gonna do with that!"

"What the hell are you guys babbling about?" Morgan asked.

"A submarine, Doug," Hunter said. He closed his eyes, suppressing a shudder. "A very large Russian submarine. And it looks like they're offloading troops."

Twelve

Hunter studied the Russian sub through the starlight scope for a long time before shaking his head and giving his place to Morgan.

"It *looks* like an old Delta-class," the SEAL said as he squinted into the eyepiece. "That turtle back is the giveaway. But it feels too big."

The "turtle back" was a hump on the submarine's hull, joined to the conning tower and extending nearly as far back as her tail fins.

"Hey, man, lemme see," Michael Franklin said, touching Morgan's shoulder.

Morgan moved aside and let the First Class have a turn. "Uh-uh," the radarman said after a moment. "That ain't no Delta. The turtle back's been added on. I'd say she's a Typhoon . . . but with a shitload of heavy-duty mods."

"What kind of modifications?" Hunter asked. Russian submarine design was not his specialty, but he had seen photographs of both classes of vessel. They were radically different. "Are they trying to disguise a Typhoon as a Delta?"

"That's no disguise," Franklin said. "Who's gonna know the difference in 1588?"

"Tell me about Typhoons," Hunter said.

The radarman knew his facts and figures. Typhoons were the largest undersea craft ever constructed by any nation on

Earth, half again longer than the Ohio-class SSBNs that had made up the core of America's ballistic missile submarine fleet during the '90s. According to Franklin, a Typhoon was 170 meters long, 25 meters broad, and had a submerged displacement of 25,000 tons. It had an odd, stub-tailed appearance, the result of having twenty SS-N-20 ballistic missile launch tubes mounted forward of the conning tower instead of aft.

This particular vessel had been extensively modified, however. A section of the hull forward of the conning tower had been cut open to create a kind of broad hatch. It was difficult to make out the details across nearly five miles, but it looked as if the door folded out and down to form a kind of dock or platform just above the water. The turtle-backed look came from a housing attached to the submarine's after deck. This, too, was open, and Hunter could make out cranes or davits there.

"If it's not a disguise, what is it?" Hunter asked.

"See those boats, Lieutenant?" Franklin asked. "Forward, next to the big hatch."

Hunter looked. They were hard to see against the sub's hull, but now he could make out the vessels, two of them, like LCVPs with high, flat bow doors, tied alongside the submarine's rounded bow. Through the scope, he could detect what looked like masses of soldiers filing out of the sub's cargo hatch and into the two boats.

"I see them."

"T-4s," Franklin said. "Landing barges. No way those little things could cross the Atlantic. I bet they came across riding piggyback. The turtle back is a garage!"

That explained the boat davits. "What about this other boat?" Hunter asked, shifting the scope again. "It looks too big to squeeze into that . . . garage."

"That, Lieutenant, is an Osa II. Missile boat . . . maybe forty feet long. Range of, oh, seven hundred miles, max. But it could cross the Atlantic on its own if it could take on fuel from that sub."

Parts of the puzzle were becoming clearer now. He remembered the vast underground dock in Cuba, with the electronics built into the walls and ceiling that turned the entire cavern into a gigantic time portal. There had seemed to be no reason for such a design before, except for the obvious one of allowing the Turya-class hydrofoil to stay afloat as it was driven from one century to another. But that dockyard basin had been far larger than a single Turya needed. What had Dark Walker told him? Over two hundred meters long . . .

Large enough to conn a Typhoon-class through, with room to spare. That was what the underground base at Guantánamo had been for! The VBU had brought the largest submarine in the world through time, depositing it in their carefully hidden base in an uninhabited part of Cuba.

Together with a Turya, two landing barges, and an Osa. They'd left the Turya in Cuba, probably to coordinate activities with *La Dueña* and the *Princessa*. The others had come here.

Hunter felt cold. Just how many vessels did the VBU have in 1588? If there were more, where were they now?

The team continued to watch, taking turns with the night scope. The Osa was moving toward the shore now, apparently angling for the ridge-backed peninsula on which the Rangers were hiding. The landing craft were snugged up against the Typhoon's side, still taking on troops. Yellow light spilled from the submarine's interior, a beacon across the dark water.

"They don't care who sees them, do they?" Gomez asked.

"Why should they?" Hunter asked. "The Spanish aren't here yet, and if the English see them coming out of Plymouth Harbor, it'll just add to the panic."

"Yes, but what are they doing here," Dark Walker asked. "That submarine could destroy the entire English fleet simply by ramming them one at a time. Surely sixteenth-century cannonballs wouldn't have much effect on it."

"You got that right, Sergeant," Short said. "Typhoons have really massive double hulls. Four separate pressure compartments . . . and armor thick enough that anything like a cannonball'd just bounce off."

"Russian troops!" Hunter said suddenly. "Those are the angels that Spaniard told us about! They're going to take Plymouth and hold it for the Spanish!"

"With two boatloads of troops?" Lynch sounded uncertain.

"Troops armed with AKMs, grenades, RPGs," Hunter said quietly. "They're probably heading for the castle."

"What about the Osa?" Anderson asked. "Looks like she's headin' our way."

"Probably bringing in a second landing party," Hunter replied. "They could shoot straight down into the Catwater from this ridge—wipe out the whole English fleet."

"Then they turn the whole harbor over to the Spanish when they get here tomorrow," Gomez said, completing the scenario. "The militia defending the town won't stop running until they hit Scotland."

"And the Osa will run down any English ships that get clear of the harbor," Morgan said, a wondering tone in his voice. "My God, they're not fooling around, are they?"

Hunter nodded in the darkness. "This is a pretty big escalation for them." He was thinking of the VBU's intervention in the American Revolution. There, a pair of Soviet helicopters and a spetsnaz team armed with mortars had seemed like an overwhelming force, loosed on unsuspecting locals whose most impressive weapons were muzzle-loading flintlocks and smoothbore cannons. But this . . . a nuclear submarine, missile boats, and a well-armed landing party in 1588 . . . !

"That Osa's headed for a point farther up the beach," Morgan pointed out. "What are we going to do about it?"

"C'mon!" Hunter said. "We're going to follow them along this ridge! If we can be in position where they're coming ashore . . . !"

"That still leaves two landing craft full of men, plus the sub," Franklin said.

"Yeah, well . . . we'll worry about that later. For now, let's just see if we can crash their party. Maybe we can throw them off stride if they're not expecting us."

"Osas carry a regular crew of thirty," Franklin said. "They could carry more, if they need a big landing party. How we gonna face that with ten men?"

"Like I said, we worry later. Right now, move!"

The team made its way along the low, sandy ridge top, paralleling the course of the slowly cruising missile boat. A mile to the east, the coastline indented slightly around a shallow, semicircular cove. With its engines barely turning over, the Osa pulled into the bay and dropped an anchor.

From their new position, the team was able to look down

onto the waters of the cove. Through the starlight scope, the Rangers could make out a group of men on the forward deck manhandling a black life raft over the side. The Osa looked like a World War II torpedo boat, Hunter thought, except that it carried four ribbed tubes, two to a side, in place of torpedos. According to Franklin, the Styx surface-to-surface missiles in those tubes had a range of twenty-five miles, but the VBU wouldn't need to rely on shipkillers to annihilate Drake's wood-hulled fleet. He could clearly see the boat's two twin-mount 30mm machine guns in their squat turret mounts, one ahead of the bridge, one aft on the fantail. They were antiaircraft weapons, but Hunter knew that a ship like Penvennan's *Resolute* would not last long against auto fire from those guns.

The Rangers were silent now, speaking only in the slightest of whispers when they had to, cupping their hands around their mouths to prevent the least sound from carrying to the VBU team working below. As Anderson studied the raft with the scope, Hunter brought his mouth close to the Texan's ear. "How many, you think?"

Anderson handed the scope to Hunter and whispered his reply. "I see twelve in the raft, LT. Look like Soviet naval spetsnaz, to me. I see maybe another ten on the Osa, but there must be more inside."

"That's what I thought. The Osa might be traveling light, though. No need to carry extra watches when your home port is a submarine a couple of miles away."

"God, LT, how are we going to stop them?" Anderson sounded worried.

"One step at a time, Roy. That's all we can do." Hunter thought a moment, studying the Osa again. "Roy, go get our two SEALs. Tell them we're going to pull back to the other side of this hill and have a chat." An idea was forming, a nebulous plan that he was going to need to discuss with the SEALs on the team.

Thank God we have them along, he thought grimly. He'd included them aboard *La Dueña* because their boat-handling skills might be handy on the lugger. Now, though, their training would be put to even better use.

• • •

Doug Morgan made scarcely a ripple as he stroked his way across the cove with only his head above the inky water. His face was blacker than Jones's or Franklin's now, smeared with a tube of camo paint one of the Marines had found in his kit. Behind him, following at twenty-meter intervals, Short, Lynch, and Carlucci paddled silently toward their objective, which rode now on the gentle swell from the channel. The Osa was only meters ahead now. Morgan could hear the voices of some of the crew across the water, chatting amiably in Russian.

A tiny flare of light gleamed in the darkness, then dimmed, briefly illuminating a man's face. Morgan held his breath and tread water, not daring to move as the Russian on the Osa's fantail lit cigarettes for himself and a companion. The match was a pinpoint meteor arcing through the night as the Soviet flicked it over the stern.

Doug Morgan had joined the Navy at seventeen. He'd volunteered for UDT and SEAL schools out of a sense of adventure, but learned early that the Navy's elite commando arm was less adventure than it was grueling work. In the years following NATO's collapse and Europe's fall to the Russians, Morgan had swum into Germany and France on several occasions, scouting Soviet troop positions and mining ammo dumps.

But he'd never been assigned a mission quite like this.

The Russians moved away from the Osa's fantail, and Morgan forced himself to relax. Slowly, slowly, he moved forward again, careful not to let his arms break the surface with a revealing splash.

This'd be a hell of a lot easier with a wet suit and scuba, he told himself. Unfortunately, his underwater gear was over four centuries in the future, stored in a locker uptime at the Chronos base. His fatigues were waterlogged now, dragging at him with each stroke. Salt stung his eyes and blurred his vision. He was breathing hard by the time his fingers brushed against the cool, slick metal hull of the Osa.

The others joined him moments later . . . Bob Short, the other SEAL on the team; Gary Lynch, the Green Beret who claimed to have experience with small boats; and Tony Carlucci, one of the Marines. It was a mixed bag for assaulting a Soviet missile patrol boat. Bob Short he knew well from a dozen raids in Europe, but the other two were still strangers . . . unknowns.

Morgan was used to long odds, as long as surprise was on his side. He'd wanted to go in with just Bob—a two-man SEAL team, deadly and silent—but Hunter had insisted on sending the others. *I hope to God they don't screw up!*

When all of his men were assembled, he signaled silently and the team moved along the Osa's side. He had already identified the part of the boat where he wanted to go aboard, a short stretch of hull between the two port-side missile tubes. There was a narrow stretch of deck there, shielded from the view of Soviet crewmen either aft by the fantail or forward on the bridge.

Short and Carlucci moved to either side of Morgan in the water, and he placed his hands on their shoulders, steadying himself. There was nothing to stand on, nothing to hold on to, and the maneuver had to be managed with a single, precisely timed burst of strength. He lunged, boosting himself up against the other swimmers, catching the Osa's deck with both hands. The movement raised a splash, impossible to avoid. Morgan hung there from the Osa's side for a long moment, scarcely breathing, straining with all of his concentration as he listened to the night. He heard the waves against the shore, the creak of the Osa as she swung against her anchor. If her crew had heard the noise, they'd dismissed it as the jump of a fish.

He hoped.

Seconds dragged past, and no one came to investigate. Slowly, Morgan chinned himself, grasping one of the stanchions that supported the Osa's safety rail.

He could feel the slight rocking motion his climb imparted to the Osa, but he could only hope that the movement would not be noticed. The gentle swell from the Channel was heavy enough that it probably would not be felt by the Russians. Working as quietly as he could, Morgan threw one leg over the side, levered himself against the stanchion, and rolled onto the deck. He was on his feet immediately, crouched low, his Mark 3 SEAL diving knife in his hand.

The deck was clear. The three men in the water began handing the team's weapons up to him. The short immersion in sea water shouldn't have hurt them any. If it had, there would be Russian weapons around. A moment later, Short rolled onto the deck, followed by the Marine and the Green Beret.

No words were exchanged. The four men began slipping toward the stern of the Osa, moving silently with deadly purpose.

Captain Alexei Alexeivich Nagishkin was seasick. His short stay aboard the submarine had been bad enough. After climbing aboard the Osa for the slow cruise to the cove, he was definitely feeling queasy. By the time he clambered down into the large rubber raft, the combination of movement and diesel fumes had him struggling to retain his last meal.

It was ridiculous, he told himself, for an officer of Russia's naval spetsnaz to be seasick. If he became ill in front of his men, he might never live down the shame.

The raft slid over the smooth crest of another swell, and Nagishkin's stomach threatened revolution once more. He clamped his teeth down on his lower lip, swallowed hard, and took a deep breath of the clear, salt-laden air. Perhaps once he was on shore and moving . . .

Another swell rode under the raft, and Nagishkin clung to the rope strung along the edge of the rubber boat. He could hear a low, gentle surf in the darkness ahead. It was tempting to turn powerful hand torches on the shoreline, but there was always a chance that some local fisherman or smuggler was there. Better to have the landing be a complete and overwhelming surprise. There would be fewer complications that way.

The swell moved on and the bottom of the boat dropped. There was a jar and the grating scrape of sand. Instantly, the boat's ten-man crew was over the side, splashing through knee-deep water as they hauled the raft onto the beach. Nagishkin did not help, as befitted his position as an officer, but waded up onto the shore and stood with his arms crossed, gulping air and willing the sickness to pass. The night was quiet, the silence broken only by the keek and whirr of summer insects. They dragged the raft clear of the water and began unloading the bulky weapon it carried.

"Where now, Comrade Captain?"

Nagishkin turned to Korchagin, his squad sergeant. "Straight up the ridge, Comrade Sergeant," he said. He had to work to control his voice. "That hill should give us a fine view of the harbor . . . and the English fleet."

The unmistakable sound of an assault rifle bolt being drawn brought Nagishkin whirling around, his hands groping for the wZ63 machine pistol at his hip.

"*Ookroyssya!*" he screamed. "Take cover!"

Then the night erupted in flame and noise.

Thirteen

"Fire!" Hunter screamed. His Uzi bucked in his hands as he triggered a burst into the dimly seen figures moving onto the beach. Spent shell casings flashed by the strobing light of muzzle flashes, and screams rose from the foot of the low, sandy hill. The thundering yammer of Anderson's M-60 ripped through the night a few meters to his left. His machine gun's volley was matched by Jones's 60-gun opening up from the far side of the beach. The 7.62mm crossfire chopped into the soldiers clambering onto the beach, eliciting a flurry of shrieks and wildly triggered bursts of auto fire.

The other Rangers concealed in a semicircle above the beach joined in with their own weapons. The fire caught the VBU troopers clumped at the base of the hill, burning into them from three sides.

Walker fired his Israeli Galil, placing carefully aimed single shots into the enemy, while Franklin cut loose in a full-auto frenzy with his M-16. Geysers of sand spouted in the moonlight, entangling the legs of running soldiers, who twisted and went down. The machine guns continued to hammer, firing bursts now, seeking out men crawling or groping for dropped weapons.

The silence was as piercing as the gunfire had been. Hunter waited a moment, then gave a sharp whistle. Gomez and Franklin started forward, weapons at the ready, covered by the others.

The bodies of the spetsnaz troopers lay still under the moonlight.

Across the water, they could hear the alarm being given on the Osa patrol boat, and Hunter felt a stabbing pang of worry. Morgan and the three men with him were new to the Ranger team, new to the whole concept of time travel. He'd wanted to send one of his regular team members to the Osa, but he'd needed the bulk of his men on the beach to set the ambush.

He didn't know Morgan or the others the way he knew Gomez, Anderson, or the missing King. He hoped they were up to what he'd asked of them.

Morgan's hand was clamping over the mouth of the startled spetsnaz trooper at the moment gunfire erupted from the beach. The ebony blade of his Mark 3 combat knife slashed the man's jugular. Morgan lowered the corpse to the deck next to the Osa's stern twin 30mm, the sixth crewman they'd dealt with so far.

The firefight cracking away on the shore was the signal the four-man team had been waiting for. Morgan and Lynch moved up the starboard side of the craft, while Short and Carlucci went up the port. A Russian stepped out of a door a few feet in front of Morgan, and this time he squeezed the trigger of his S&W 760. The burst caught the surprised VBU trooper in the chest, spinning him into the railing and over the side with a splash. A second Russian appeared on the heels of the first. Lynch's M-16 barked once, and the man pitched backward into the dark interior of the deckhouse. Gunfire snarled from the far side of the Osa. Carlucci and Short had found targets as well.

Running now, the SEAL and the Green Beret raced forward, their bare feet slapping on the deck. In the dim light, Morgan could see a cluster of men on the Osa's flying bridge, forward of the long, narrow deckhouse and the stumpy mast with its collection of radar dishes and antennas. Morgan leaned over the after end of the starboard fore missile tube, steadying his aim, and Lynch dropped into firing position beside him. The two men opened fire together, snapping a stream of full-auto death into the backs of the officers and men crowded onto the small, open bridge.

A Russian wearing a billed naval officer's hat spun, one hand clutching a Makarov pistol. Morgan shifted his aim and loosed another burst. Bullets smashed the man's face and throat, knocking him back into the tangle of bodies.

At Morgan's side, Lynch whirled, his M-16 leveled aft. "Watch it, Navy!" Lynch yelled, and Morgan lunged to one side as the Green Beret triggered a long, ragged volley. More Russians were clambering through a hatchway onto the deck and meeting Lynch's deadly fire head-on. A lone round spanged against the missile tube a foot away from Morgan's head, and then the thunder ceased.

Lynch dropped his empty magazine and snapped in a fresh one. Morgan clapped the man's shoulder. "Thanks, Army! You hit the forward deck. I'll check the bridge!"

The soldier nodded and the two men parted. Morgan climbed a ladder to the top of the deckhouse, shot a wounded Russian he found lying just behind the mast, then made his way forward to the flying bridge. Eight men lay there, naval officers and men in the blue-and-white striped shirts and black berets of the Soviet Navy. All were dead, and the flying bridge was splashed with blood.

Movement grabbed his attention on the port side, where a VBU soldier with an AKM crouched in the shadow of the forward missile tube. Morgan shot the man. Short and Carlucci appeared moments later, changing magazines. "Port side secure!" the Marine yelled, and Morgan grinned in response.

"Keep watch aft! There're probably unfriendlies in the engine room, and they'll be coming topside to see what the ruckus is!"

"They'll wish they hadn't," Short replied.

They darted from station to station, securing the Osa. Morgan checked the enclosed control room directly beneath the flying bridge. It was deserted, the wheel unmanned.

He returned to the flying bridge as surviving members of the Osa's engine room crew spilled onto the deck. Gunfire flashed in the darkness. Bullets spanged off armor plate or punched clean through the light metal used in most of the boat's construction. Morgan crouched behind the mast, keeping up a steady fire at the almost invisible shapes ducking and weaving past the deckhouse aft.

Bob Short appeared at Morgan's side. "Runnin' low on sixteen mags, Doug," the SEAL said. His eyes and teeth were startlingly white against the black camo paint smeared over his face.

"Then grab yourself an AK, buddy! Plenty to go around!"

Short nodded and reached for an AKM lying on the flying-bridge deck. At that moment, auto fire blasted through the night, spraying the bridge from the top of the deckhouse aft. Bullets gashed the thick trunk of the mast as Morgan rolled behind it. Short staggered, clutching at his throat, which was suddenly pumping blood that looked jet black in the dim light. Morgan twisted around the side of the mast, his SMG spraying fire across the deckhouse. A half-glimpsed shape toppled over the railing.

Short was dead, his eyes staring sightlessly up at the night sky. *Damn . . . !*

He felt the slight rocking of the Osa, a gentle tug against its anchor cable. Morgan didn't look up as a fresh flurry of firing broke out astern, accompanied by repeated yells of "Yankee! Yankee!" The cry was an agreed upon signal; Hunter had not wanted the two combat teams firing at each other in the dark.

A moment later, Gomez clambered up the flying-bridge ladder, his M-203 clutched in one hand. "Yar!" the Ranger rasped in a gravel voice. "Be ye pirates?" The entire operation had taken twenty minutes from the time Morgan had boarded the Osa.

"So you finally made it," Morgan said quietly, looking up from Short's body. "Well, you're too late. Too goddamn late . . ."

"We've got a chance now," Hunter said. The eight men of his command were gathered in a semicircle about him on the Osa's forward deck. His eyes picked out the faces of the men he'd chosen because of their experience with boat handling: Doug Morgan, Tony Carlucci, Gary Lynch. Of the three, Morgan was the oldest and seemed to have had the most experience. "Doug . . . I'm putting you in charge of our little navy, here. Do you think you, Tony, and Gary can get this bucket moving?"

Morgan shrugged, listless. "I don't know, Lieutenant."

The uncaring weariness in Morgan's voice worried Hunter. The death of the other SEAL in the Osa assault appeared to have hurt the man.

Hunter hardened his own voice. "Then find out, damn it!" he snapped. "Roy, you and Jones take the raft back to the beach and gather up all that Russian gear. I know I saw a shortwave radio. Let's see what else we've got there. The rest of you start checking the Russian bodies. Look for maps . . . papers . . . anything. Jump, Rangers!"

Hunter watched as the men hustled aft. Morgan began moving toward the bridge. "Doug. Hold it a sec."

"Sir?"

Hunter walked over to the SEAL. No one else was in earshot. "What's the problem, Chief?"

"No problem, Lieutenant."

"Don't give me that. What is it? Short?"

A bitter twist pulled at Morgan's mouth. "I guess . . ."

"Friend of yours?"

Morgan shrugged. "We've been together a long time." The SEAL's fists clenched. "Damn it! He had a wife and kid, over in Moran!"

"He volunteered. . . ."

"Yeah? For this? Like we all volunteered for this? Living for week after stinking week on a damned, stinking sailboat crawling with lice . . . jammed in with stinking, superstitious primitives who don't know enough to wash their hands after using the nonexistent toilet. . . . Damn it to hell, Lieutenant! I don't know about you, but I didn't volunteer to live in the goddamned past! And I damn well didn't volunteer to die here!"

"Finished?"

"No! Where the hell were you people?" Morgan wiped his face with his hand, smearing the black paint. "We waited for you. . . ."

Hunter sagged inside, but he kept his features rigid. "And we got here as fast as we could. We knew there was a risk, sending only four men in. A calculated risk . . ."

"A calculated risk. And Bobby's dead."

"There'll be a lot more dead if we don't pull this off, Chief. We've got the whole future riding on nine Rangers now."

"I'm no Ranger." The words were stubborn, almost sullen. "Sir."

"You damn well are a Ranger now!" The whiplash fury in Hunter's voice jerked Morgan's head up like a slap. Hunter gentled his tone. "And you've got a job to do."

"Yeah. Surviving . . ."

"Forget survival! We're fighting for a future that's not going to be unless we pull together and make it happen! Fighting for Bobby's wife and kid, if you like! Fighting for a free America that the Russians are trying to smother!" He hesitated. Part of Morgan's problem was the isolation he must be feeling, with the loss of the one man on this side of the twentieth century he'd had something in common with. Once, on an earlier mission, someone had coined a name for the team: *Freedom's Rangers* . . .

"We're not 75th Ranger Battalion here, Doug. Not Marines, not Army, not SEALs. We're something new, a team for special ops like the world has never dreamed of! Freedom's Rangers . . . all of us together. And we'd damn well better pull together or there's not going to be any future. Everything we've ever known, everyone we've ever known, will be gone, wiped away because they'll never have existed." He took a deep breath, looking Morgan in the eye. "And the whole damned thing's riding on us."

Hunter wondered for a long time after that whether he'd said the right things. The words sounded hollow as he thought back on them, a cheap mix of propaganda and pep talk, a stick to goad a faltering man into motion. The truth was that even if they beat the VBU, they were stranded here in the past with no better personal future to look forward to than lice, dirt, and strangers they would never feel at home with.

But Morgan nodded and said "Yes, sir," and went to work with the team's other boat experts. Within an hour the Osa's engines were turning over gently and an electric winch was hauling the anchor line in over the missile boat's bow.

Carlucci and Lynch both knew boat engines, and Morgan posted them in the Osa's engine rooms, deciphering meters and gauges marked with Cyrillic lettering and experimenting with the valves that controlled the mixture of fuel and oil.

Gunnery Sergeant Jones knew guns. He and Roy Anderson

began assembling a weapon they'd found on the beach among the bodies of the ambushed spetsnaz troopers, a bulky, stub-snouted device that looked like a machine gun once it was mounted on its tripod on the forward deck. Then Anderson, who also knew something about engines, went aft to help Lynch and Carlucci, while Jones set to work studying the Osa's twin 30mm cannon. Michael Franklin powered up the missile boat's radar in the control room and began experimenting with the settings, while Morgan checked out the helm.

Which left Hunter to climb to the flying bridge and join Gomez and Walker as lookouts. All of the men worked in a silence that matched the dark and quiet water around them.

A team . . .

Captain Nikolai Sergeivich Tyrin had been in the Russian Navy for twenty-eight years and in submarines for twenty. He had been a squadron commander with the Far Eastern Fleet during the nuclear crisis of 2005, when the United States had backed down in the face of the Soviet missile threat.

And now he skippered one of the largest submarines the world had ever known, floating in the English Channel in an age when Moryeh Ohotnik, the *Sea Hunter*, would appear to the natives as a monstrous fabrication of sheer magic.

He'd not believed the KGB and GRU officers who had approached him first, nearly a year before at Archanglsk. The idea of sending men, of sending an entire nuclear submarine, four centuries back in time seemed utterly preposterous, the incoherent delirium of a vodka-saturated writer of science fiction.

He sighed and pressed his binoculars to his eyes, scanning the coast ten miles away. The pair of landing barges was invisible now against the shoreline. He was worried. Once he'd finally accepted that there really was such a thing as the Time Security Directorate, the VBU agents who'd approached him had insisted that, despite the somewhat exotic nature of a plan to send a 25,000-ton submarine four centuries into the past, there would be no danger.

No danger? Guantánamo was gone . . . or so the last radio report from Vorosilov had informed him. The English coast was ten miles away in the darkness, where one wrong move would leave the *Sea Hunter* stranded. It was a sobering thought: there were no other ships in this entire world that could help if his ship went aground or was damaged.

And now the first shore attack was overdue. The Osa had departed for its landing site two hours earlier, its approach timed so that the two landing craft would reach the castle in Plymouth Harbor in the midst of the utter and complete confusion of a spetsnaz attack on the anchored English fleet.

Why hadn't Nagishkin radioed that he was in position? Why hadn't he radioed that the attack had begun? Something was wrong. . . .

According to the timetable, the two landing craft should be nearing the mouth of the harbor. The glare of nearly a hundred wooden ships burning ought to be lighting up the sky, as survivors crowded one another in a frantic rush to reach the open sea.

But the shoreline was utterly, deathly silent.

Then the sky lit in a silent blaze of light, as a fireball clawed into the night. The sound reached the submarine moments later, a dull, far-off thump of exploding munitions. A party of sailors gathered on the open dock platform forward broke into another cheer and excited conversation, but Tyrin leaned against the conning tower's rim as cold fear twisted inside him.

Something was definitely wrong! That explosion had been outside the harbor!

His hand came down on the intercom switch. "Helm! Give me full maneuvering, now! Deck officer! Secure the forward dock! Ready the ship for diving.

"All hands! Battle stations!"

The giant submarine rang with the pounding feet of her crew.

Fourteen

Hunter stood on the flying bridge, watching as Gomez set happily to work.

The AGS-17, known to the Russians as *Plamya,* or Flame, was similar to the American M-174, a squat, tripod-mounted gun that fired 30mm grenades from a drum in auto-fire bursts of spectacular destruction. The Russian shore party had brought the disassembled weapon with them on the raft. Hunter had ordered it set up on the Osa's forward deck, where Gomez had taken to it like a kid with a new bike for Christmas. The grenades were not as powerful as the 40mm eggs lobbed from his M-203, but careful experiment had shown that the range was far greater . . . nearly a kilometer. Ammunition came in twenty-nine–round belts coiled inside a ten-kilogram drum and consisted of antipersonnel, HEAT, or phosphorous grenades.

Most of the loads found on the beach had been phosphorous. Hunter pictured what those incendiary rounds, dropping down from the hill south of the Catwater anchorage, would have done to Drake's wood-hulled fleet and shuddered. The bulk of Queen Elizabeth's fleet would have burned in a spectacular conflagration of seasoned wood, tar, and gunpowder that would have lighted up the coast of southern England for miles around. Any that escaped that literal rain of fire would have fled for the open sea or deliberately grounded. Plymouth would have been abandoned.

And there would have been nothing standing between England and the full might of the Spanish Armada.

The two landing craft the Rangers had spotted from shore must be a formality. Hunter decided, troops to be sent ashore to take possession of the Royal Citadel in order to formally hand it over to Medina-Sidonia's troops in another day or two. Or, he mused, the commandos who filled those barges might be expected to face the handful of survivors who might take shelter behind the castle walls.

For the Spanish, arriving to find Elizabeth's fleet in charred and smoking ruins, it would appear that angels had prepared the way!

Hunter swept his starlight scope along the coastline. *There!* The first landing craft was standing well out in the channel as it rounded the point at Rame Head outside Plymouth Harbor. Gomez fired his phosphorous rounds one at a time as Hunter marked the splashes for him through the scope. Then he switched to the deep-throated, slow-paced *thud-thud-thud* of full auto fire as the first round struck the barge squarely above the engine compartment. White phosphorus blossomed into the night, lighting sky and water in its brilliant glare. Then fuel aboard the landing craft ignited, and the fireball roiled upward against the darkness.

An ammunition supply detonated, and the concussion slapped Hunter's face and chest and left his ears ringing. Fire spread across the water . . . but of the landing barge with its cargo of spetsnaz commandos and weapons, there was no sign.

Jones called up to Hunter from the forward machine gun. "Hey, that's one, Lieutenant! Where's the other bastard?"

Hunter continued to scan the shoreline. That second barge must be along the coast somewhere . . . but where? Were both of the T-4s headed for the same landing site, or did they have different targets? One of those craft could carry thirty or forty men or more crammed into their well decks behind the squared-off bow door and ramp. If the other landing craft managed to get ashore, Hunter and his eight men would never be able to track them all down. . . .

"Radar!" Hunter yelled. "Do you have him?"

Franklin's voice came back a moment later from the weather bridge below Hunter's feet. "Nothing but clutter from the shoreline, Lieutenant! I've got a strong echo eight miles to port, though. . . ."

That would be the Russian sub. If the radar image of the second landing craft was masked by the shore clutter, it meant he must be hugging the coastline. Hunter squinted into the starlight scope, sweeping slowly . . . slowly. . . .

He caught a flash of white in the scope, the bow wake of the second barge like a mustache at its prow, reflecting the moonlight. The barge itself was almost invisible, a shadow against black water and the shore. It was hugging the land, racing to escape its companion's fate.

"There he is!" Hunter yelled. "Doug! Twenty degrees to the right!"

"Twenty degrees off the starboard bow, aye!" Morgan's voice came back from the control room below Hunter's feet. "Full speed ahead!"

The missile boat roared, the power of its twin diesels felt as a steady, throbbing vibration through the soles of Hunter's combat boots. Its own wake spread across the black water, white foam and phosphorescence gleaming under the stars.

He pointed and Gomez raised a thumb to show he understood. The roar was too loud for shouted communication now. The missile boat swept past the dwindling flame, angling toward the distant shore.

Briefly, Hunter wondered whether or not to use one of the powerful searchlights mounted on swivels at either side of the flying bridge. They had to spot the landing craft and destroy it before it had a chance of reaching shore . . . but Hunter still hoped to have a chance at that Typhoon. He wasn't sure just yet how he was going to manage that, since they had not had time yet to examine the Osa's shipkiller missiles, but if they could damage the beast badly enough that it couldn't submerge . . .

His thoughts were interrupted by a lone thud as Gomez triggered the *Plamya*. He watched the shadow of the landing barge for a long moment, then saw the white fountain of spray as the grenade struck water.

He signaled to Gomez, raising his hand in a "higher, higher" motion, then showing two fingers for two hundred meters. The AGS-17 thumped again.

Too far . . . and leading a bit.

Again . . .

Hit! The night exploded in white light once more, as white phosphorus flared into frosty brilliance. The *Plamya* thumped away in a steady stream of incendiary grenades, raining fire on the stricken barge.

Hunter saw water geysering from missed rounds, saw human torches hurl themselves into the sea. Fuel and ammo erupted in a fireworks display unheard across distance or above the roar of the *Osa's* engine. Fragments trailed streams of flame and glittering sparks as they arced through the sky, raising splashes a hundred meters from the stricken craft. There was a final flash of exploding ordnance, and the T-4 was gone, save for orange flames licking across the oily scum on the water, and a few unidentifiable scraps of floating wreckage.

Hunter turned to the open hatch and descended a ladder to the control room. Morgan stood at the helm, one hand on the wheel, the other on a pair of throttle levers set onto the console at his side. Franklin looked up from the radar scope at the left side of the room. The windows were surprisingly small, three tiny slits across the front of the bridge and two set next to each other on either side.

"Head for the sub," he told Morgan. He looked across the bridge to Franklin. "You still have him on your scope?"

"Yessir . . . but he's moving now. Coming about . . . heading south, it looks like."

"No sweat," Hunter said, grinning. "This baby'll outrun any sub. Right, Doug?"

Morgan met his eye. "Assuming we catch the bugger, what do we do with him?"

"We'll figure that out later," Hunter replied. "Hurt him, I hope. If we're lucky, those T-4s didn't know what hit them in the dark. Maybe we can pretend to be Russians coming close for a chat, then . . . wham!" He clapped his hands together. He pictured the huge, open hatch he'd seen from the shore. If Eddie pumped a stream of incendiaries through that, *something* bad would happen, no matter how big the sub was!

"Hey, Lieutenant!" Franklin called. "I'm losin' him!"

"What?"

"The radar signal's gettin' weaker! I'm losin' him, man!"

"A problem with the set?" But Hunter knew what the problem was before he'd crossed to Franklin's side and saw the blip wink out. The sub was diving, and the Osa had no sonar, no depth charges or homing torpedos.

They'd lost him.

"No, señores! No!" Colonel Yuri Vladimirovich Vorosilov pounded with the flat of his hand against the massive oak table in front of him. The richly ornamented cape he wore as part of his persona as the fiery de Leyva slipped down across his shoulder. "We must strike for Plymouth immediately!"

One of the richly dressed Spanish gentlemen turned wearily to face the Armada's commander. "Excellency, Don Alonzo speaks most eloquently, but surely His Most Catholic Majesty's express wishes in this matter are clear?"

"Well... ah... I don't know." The Duke of Medina-Sidonia was a chubby man with dark, mournful eyes. "It is true that His Majesty gave me explicit orders... and yet Don Alonzo has an excellent point. If, indeed, the devil Drake is still penned within Plymouth Sound, as he must be with this southwesterly wind, here lies our chance to deal the English fleet one single, crushing blow! We should, at least, be sure...."

Juan Martinez de Recalde, commander of the Armada's Biscay Squadron, shook his dark head. "We dare not approach Plymouth with its harbor defenses."

"Bah!" Vorosilov exclaimed. "Drake did the same thing at Cadiz last year! He didn't let a few harbor guns frighten him off! I tell you, *señores*, that this is our chance to rewrite England's destiny! Seize the port! Smash the English ships you find there! Put the soldiers ashore! And then sail to the Netherlands to escort Parma's army!"

The men seated around the table burst into a dozen conversations and protests at once. Colonel Vorosilov leaned back, his hands over his eyes.

It was morning, Saturday, July 30 by the calendar the Spanish followed. Medina-Sidonia had called a council of war aboard his flagship, the *San Martín*. All of the Armada's squadron commanders and staff officers were there, crowded into the low-ceilinged wardroom: Juan Martinez de Recalde, Diego

Flores de Valdes, Miguel de Oquendo, and all the rest. The purpose of the council was to decide just what the Armada's best course of action was now.

The hell of it was that Vorosilov himself was no longer certain, though he was continuing to urge the weak and vacillating Spanish commander to go ahead with the original plan and enter Plymouth Sound.

But only hours earlier, on board the *Rata Encoronada*, he had received a disturbing radio transmission from the *Moryeh Ohotnik*. The submarine's commander had seen the destruction of both landing barges well before they could have put their troops ashore. Vorosilov was not certain he agreed with Tyrin's reasoning. The man had submerged and left the area before the whereabouts of the *Osa* could be determined . . . or the success of the first landing party assigned to bombard the English fleet. The destruction of the barges could have been an accident—an explosion aboard one might have set off explosives aboard the other if it was close enough—but Vorosilov was not a man who assumed coincidence when deliberate malice might be at work.

The destruction of the landing craft, the possible disappearance of an *Osa* and its shore party . . . that could also be explained as the work of the never-to-be-sufficiently-damned American time commandos.

But how could it be? The American time travelers were dead, obliterated at Guantánamo. The only survivors were the two prisoners aboard *San Salvador!*

He dropped his hands and looked at the florid, angry faces around the table. *Imbeciles*, he thought savagely. *They have more to fear from their own stupidity than they do from the English!*

It was true. As Medina-Sidonia wavered, the generals and admirals under him argued, already seeking to place the blame for a disaster that had not yet happened. The Armada's commanding admiral had ordered the fleet to wait for a day, hovering a few miles off the coast west of Plymouth, to allow stragglers to catch up, watching for the English and laying their plans.

All agreed that the southwesterly wind would pin Drake and Howard inside Plymouth Sound, though Vorosilov knew from history that the English were hard at work at this moment warping their ships out against the wind. Vorosilov was not concerned about the English fleet. If they had not been destroyed, if they did make it out of harbor, he still had an ace to play against them.

It was his quarrelsome, so-called allies that were threatening to ruin everything. Vorosilov, as Don Alonzo, had only so much influence over Medina-Sidonia. He was respected by the others but was also known as a hothead, and that aspect of his character had already worked against him more than once. He had in his pocket secret orders from Philip himself, authorizing him to take command of the Armada if anything happened to Medina-Sidonia. It was so damned tempting to arrange an accident . . . but the dangers of being discovered in the act were too great aboard this crowded ship. When Medina-Sidonia brandished Philip's orders commanding the Armada to join with the Duke of Parma in the Netherlands, the others tended to lose interest in a rapid landing and a campaign on land. After all . . . Philip was God's own spokesman. To argue with Philip's orders was to argue with God, something none of these good, straight-laced Catholics dared to do. And if word were to spread that Medina-Sidonia had been murdered by one of his own lieutenants . . .

No, better to wait and watch. What was frustrating was having conflicting orders from Philip, one set giving him discretion, the other detailing minutely the plans Medina-Sidonia was to follow. Philip II, it seemed, was the world's most accomplished armchair strategist, attempting to run this campaign from his palace.

Vorosilov considered. Item: it was not yet certain that the Americans were behind the setbacks outside Plymouth. Further questioning of the prisoners might yield something, though they could know nothing about recent American operations. Item: the English fleet was no threat, not with the force Vorosilov was holding in reserve. He would contact them this afternoon and have them move up into position. Item: since his whole purpose here was to change history from Spanish disaster at sea to a land battle that could only end in a Spanish triumph, his goal was still to get the Armada's land forces ashore as quickly as possible. Whether the English fleet had been destroyed yet or not, Plymouth still offered the best and closest harbor for a landing.

He would urge that the Armada descend on Plymouth.

"Excellency!" He put a sharp edge to the word, cutting above the babble. Immediately, the wardroom fell silent. "No decision need be reached immediately, but I submit that we still are in an excellent position from which we can carry out all aspects of His Majesty's orders. There has been no sign of the English . . . and they are no threat to us in any case, I assure you! The wind is behind us, fair for Plymouth. I suggest that we close slowly on the port, allowing further stragglers to catch up with the fleet. If by this afternoon we have still seen nothing of the English, then I urge that we enter the harbor . . . and take it!" He silenced a renewal of the babble with one raised hand. "Yes! Yes! There will still be time for the Armada to meet with the Duke of Parma . . . but let us get our troops ashore first!"

"If Drake is inside the harbor, he will destroy us!" one admiral exclaimed.

"And you are allowing yourselves to be frightened by chimeras! By fantasies!"

The admiral who had spoken rose to his feet, his hand on the hilt of his sword. "Do you question my bravery, Don Alonzo? If you do . . ."

Vorosilov shook his head. "I question no one's bravery, Don Antonio! Least of all yours!" He smiled and made his words gentle. The last thing he needed now was to be killed by some damned honor-befuddled idiot in a duel! "It would be folly to squander our opportunity in argument and indecision!" He looked squarely at Medina-Sidonia. "Correct, Your Excellency?"

The Armada's supreme commander looked startled. "Eh? Yes. As you say, we needn't make an immediate decision." He held his stomach and looked uncomfortable. Vorosilov remembered how the fool had tried to turn down Philip's commission by claiming that he was always sick at sea. Perhaps the man's seasickness would steer him to the correct decision! "We will do as Don Alonzo suggests, and wait!"

The debate continued through much of the morning, but Vorosilov knew he had won at least part of the battle. All that remained now was to radio Voznesensky and set in motion the next part of the grand plan.

They would win, even if they faced an army of American time commandos. Once the English fleet met Voznesensky, there would be no power on Earth that could save them, and the Americans would be helpless.

And if the Americans met his little surprise . . . so much the better. Then, indeed, there would be nothing left to stand between the Invincible Armada and England.

It was raining.

Hunter paced the control room between one of the tiny windows and the radar scope where Franklin monitored the gathering mob of Spanish ships. The Armada was only a few miles off the English coast now, a vast, crescent shape with trailing horns, drifting in a leisurely fashion toward Plymouth. Each sweep of the radar painted them anew in green light. So far Franklin had counted over 130 ships. At their current ponderous pace, they would reach Plymouth by nightfall.

The English ships were there too, though Hunter doubted that the Spanish had seen them yet. The long, straggling line had appeared moving out of the sound early that morning. As the day progressed, some of the ships headed straight to the south, while others worked their way along the coast, angling for a position behind the Spanish Armada. The stage was being set for battle.

"There!" Franklin said suddenly. "There they are again!"

Hunter peered at the screen. Three blips glowed there, a tight cluster moving between the Armada and the coast. "Why do they keep appearing and disappearing?"

"I keep losing them behind the Spanish fleet." Franklin tapped the screen. "Those masts keep blocking our signal. But we got 'em now." He paused, his brow furrowed with concentration. "I make their speed at sixteen knots, headin' southwest."

A chill gripped Hunter. "That's too fast for one of these sailing ships."

"That ain't all. That's sixteen knots straight into the wind!"

"More patrol boats. Osas, like this one?"

"No way to tell without eyeballin' 'em, Lieutenant."

"Could they be submarines? That Typhoon and a couple of friends?"

"Can't say from this range. They act like patrol boats, cruisin' in formation."

Hunter nodded. If the Russians had shepherded one Osa across the Atlantic, why not more? "How fast do those landing barges go?"

"Ten knots," Morgan said from the helm. "Max."

"Patrol boats," Hunter said slowly. The chill grew colder, a gnawing fear. The VBU plan had evidently been calculated to destroy the English fleet in harbor and seize Plymouth for the Spanish. Four fast Osas would be ideal for running down and destroying any survivors that managed to escape the inferno in Plymouth Sound.

They also provided the Russians with one hell of a back-up. Hunter thought about what a trio of patrol boats, armed with missiles and autocannons, could do to Drake's wooden vessels. The English fleet was still in terrible danger.

"Let's go have a closer look," he said to Morgan. He kept his voice light but couldn't mask the worry there.

Hunter had read once that the British Admiral Jellicoe could have lost the First World War in an afternoon at the naval battle of Jutland. He knew now exactly how Jellicoe must have felt.

And Jellicoe had not been facing three-to-one odds. . . .

Fifteen

"Hide and seek," Gomez said. "And we're 'it.'"

The rain had given way to an unpleasant, drizzling mist that reduced visibility until the English coast was little more than a gray shadow.

"It's in our favor, Eddie," Hunter replied. "We want to get in close."

Gomez nodded and patted the automatic grenade launcher at his side. "We may be about to revolutionize naval warfare, Chief."

Hunter laughed. A jury-rigged mount for the captured AGS-17 was set onto the splinter shield on the flying bridge. The position on the bow from which Gomez had taken out the landing craft was too exposed. Worse, if a grenade accidentally struck one of the stanchions or railings along the rim of the hull, it could detonate in their faces.

A hurried discussion with Morgan, Franklin, and Jones had convinced Hunter that their one hope did lie with a close-in fight at very nearly point-blank range.

"Well, you start your revolution, Eddie. I'll be in the control room."

He climbed down the ladder. Morgan was alone at the helm. Franklin had been working most of the day on the Osa's weapons radar.

They had to assume that the VBU boats were also Osas. The

missile boats had only two weapons: the twin 30mm cannons fore and aft, and four SS-N-2b Styx missiles in their ribbed metal cannisters along each side.

The Styx was strictly a standoff weapon, with a minimum range of five nautical miles. It was basically a cruise missile with 450 kilos of high explosive packed into its warhead, an effective range of forty-three miles, and a top speed just short of Mach 1. One Styx would vaporize an Osa, but Morgan had suggested that they not count on them and Hunter agreed. Jones knew the electronics used by various missile launch systems and was working now tracing the circuits necessary to fire them, but Hunter was painfully aware that the Russians knew more about Styx missiles—and their countermeasures—than any of the Americans did. Worse still, if those three blips were Osas, then the moment Hunter launched four missiles at them they could well launch twelve in reply.

The Osa's turret guns presented them with a different problem. Designated as AK-240s, they were fully automatic and fired from the ship's fire-control center aft of the bridge. They could be used against incoming missiles—another reason not to try sinking Osas with a Styx launch—or against aircraft, but they would be deadly against small boats as well, with an effective range of over a mile. Hunter had told Franklin to leave the radar unguarded while he checked out their fire-control systems. Anderson was helping him, since Franklin could not read Russian.

Their best option, Hunter had decided, was to get as close to the enemy ships as possible. It might be that they could pretend to be Soviets suffering from a radio breakdown; they'd heard several exchanges in Russian over the Osa's radio during the past hours, but not knowing the proper codes and call signs they didn't dare respond. Unfortunately, the Russian submarine must have seen the destruction of the landing craft, and her captain would have assumed that the Osa had been lost as well. Otherwise he would not have turned and run.

If they could just get close enough to the Russian patrol boats, they could use machine guns, side arms, and Gomez's wicked little grenade launcher. If Franklin and Anderson could figure out how to work the AK-240 turrets, so much the better.

In any case, the rain was giving them their one chance to

get close. They were navigating in the dark, on the theory that if they could spot the Russian boats on radar, the Russians would pick up the signal and know they were being observed. It was a difficult choice: grope in the dark and remain invisible, or use the radar and pretend to be a Soviet Osa with a broken radio. With the rain, they were going to have to adopt a compromise plan, steering for where they thought the three targets would be, then switching on the radar for short bursts to determine their actual location. If they could get close enough before using the radar, they would cut down on the enemy's reaction time, leave him confused and uncertain while the Rangers made their final approach.

Jones walked onto the bridge, soaking wet from the drizzle outside. "Okay, Lieutenant," the black marine said. "You'll be able to launch your Styx, but I'm not promising anything. We found a manual, but it's fuzzy in spots."

The gunnery sergeant went on to explain the Styx's operation. Radar coordinates for the target were fed into the missile's guidance system from the Osa's fire-control center, and the launch was triggered from there. Once the Styx was within five miles of the programmed coordinates, its own radar switched on and it automatically homed on the largest target it could "see."

"The fuzzy part is programming ahead of time," Jones said. "There could be enabling codes or arming procedures that aren't in the manual, and we won't know until we push the button and nothing happens!"

Hunter nodded. "Right, thanks, Gunny. The way things stand now, we're not going to try to take them out with missiles anyway. Too many damn things to go wrong. For now, why don't you see if you can help with the AK-240s."

"You got it, Lieutenant."

"And send Michael up here. I want another radar sweep."

"Aye aye, sir."

"It's a damned long shot, Lieutenant," Morgan said after the marine had left. "You have any idea what those AK-240s'll do if they hit us?"

"I have a fair idea." Each explosive 30mm round weighed over a pound, and the weapons pumped them out at the rate of a thousand rounds per barrel per minute. Any one round would do as much damage as one of Gomez's 30mm HEAT grenades fired from the captured launcher . . . and these would be radar-guided and arriving in a nearly solid stream of high explosive. "But if we don't try to stop them, we'll find out what those guns would do against wooden sailing ships."

"I wasn't arguing, Lieutenant." Morgan said. "I've been thinking. You were right. About what you said this morning."

"The hell of it is, Doug, we don't have a choice. To tell you the truth, I wouldn't give you two cents for our chances . . . one undermanned boat with an untrained crew . . . against three boats and a damned big submarine. But if we do nothing . . ."

Morgan watched Franklin walk in and cross to the radar. "At least we have a chance for surprise, sir," he said. "That's the one thing going for us just now."

Right, Hunter thought. *If the VBU hasn't guessed we've got their Osa. If they don't get suspicious when we don't answer the radio. If the surprise is enough to let us take out three boats before they can nail us with those high-speed radar cannons.*

"Got 'em!" Franklin announced from the radar hood. "Range five miles, bearing one-eight-five!"

Hunter grinned at Morgan. "They won't be launching cruise missiles at us, at least. Hit the gas, Doug, and let's see what we've got."

"Aye, Lieutenant. Coming to one-eight-five. Full throttle?"

"No. Not yet." Hunter didn't want their approach to look like an attack run.

The Osa turned away from the mist-shrouded coast. The motor throbbed and the bow came up, hurling twin jets of white spray to either side.

"Should I shut down?" Franklin asked.

"Not now," Hunter replied. "Either they have their radars shut down and it doesn't matter, or they just heard us tag them. We're on their scopes by now."

The bridge radio speakers hissed and crackled. "Krasny Tree! Krasny Tree!" an urgent voice announced, the Russian sharp and urgent. "Red Three, this is Red Leader! Diamond! I say again, diamond!"

Hunter exchanged glances with Morgan.

"Too bad our radio's busted," Morgan said softly. "Otherwise, we'd have to answer that recognition signal."

"Well, we know we're on their scopes," Hunter said. "I'm going back upstairs."

Morgan grimaced with disgust. "That's *topside*, Lieutenant. If you're gonna be a sailor, you'd better clean up your language."

Hunter rejoined Gomez on the flying bridge. As the Osa thumped through the Channel swell at twenty knots, wind, rain, and spray lashed at their faces.

"Five miles," he told Gomez. "And someone over there is getting mighty nervous. Got everything you need?"

Gomez nudged a stack of drums ready by his feet. "Everything's covered, Chief."

Dark Walker appeared at their sides, holding one of the M-60 machine guns and a box of ammo. "My ancestors used to hunt plains buffalo," the Indian said with a ghost of a smile. "There was never anything in the Dakota tribe handbook about this."

Hunter grinned. "Handle the 60-gun the way you handle that Galil and we don't have a thing to worry about!"

He had agonized long and hard over how to allot his tiny crew. Morgan would be at the helm, of course, although either Carlucci or Lynch could take over from him if they had to. So far, since they'd captured the Osa ten hours earlier, Morgan had gained the most experience at the helm, so he was elected pilot. Franklin had the radar and would go to fire control if there was a problem with the radars that aimed the AK-240s or the missiles. Anderson and Jones were in fire control, hoping they could operate the Osa's high-speed guns as well as the Russians could. That left Carlucci and Lynch for the Osa's engine room, and Gomez and Walker handling an M-60 and the auto-grenade launcher from the flying bridge. Hunter himself planned to rove as needed . . . and the second M-60 was stashed in the control room if another machine gun was necessary.

The speaker on the console in front of him sputtered static. "Three miles!" Franklin said over the intercom. Hunter had to strain to hear over the engine's growl.

He reached under the console and extracted a battered white

officer's hat, its bill heavy with gold braid. They'd found the hat that morning in one of the Osa's cabins. He perched it on his head. It was too small, and he had to set it at a rakish angle to keep it from blowing off.

Gomez looked questioningly at him. "Might buy us another few moments," Hunter said. "We'll let 'em see what they expect to see."

Walker touched Hunter's arm and pointed. "There."

He peered into the mist, squinting his eyes against the stinging spray. He could see nothing but gray sea and gray sky. "I can't . . ."

No! There! The mist thinned enough to make out the ghostly shape of a large boat, just off the port bow and over a mile away. Another Osa.

"Switching to close range!" Franklin yelled over the intercom. "Range two thousand yards and closing!"

That put them within range of the other Osa's cannon. Hunter touched an intercom switch. "Roy! Do you have them?"

"If we understand this gear, we do," Anderson's voice came back. "Gunny cut the radar out of the circuit. We're using a back-up optical targeting system because we don't trust the automatics."

"Right. Wait for my order."

"We're a-waitin', LT."

Hunter brought his binoculars up to his eyes, trying to penetrate the mist. Slowly, almost magically, the Osa reappeared . . . almost dead ahead and bow-on. The Russian had turned in the mist and was closing fast. At least he hadn't opened fire yet.

"Radar! I can see the guy dead ahead. Where are the other two?"

"About two miles off the port bow, Lieutenant. Looks like they're sending this guy in to check us out."

Which meant that their surprise would be used up against one of the three. He'd hoped to open fire on several targets at once, but that was impossible now.

The question now was, would they even be able to surprise one Russian Osa? They must be damned suspicious by now. . . .

Through the binoculars, Hunter could make out a huddled

group of men on the flying bridge, every one of them training binoculars of their own right back at him.

"Wave," Hunter said. He lifted his arm. "Wave like we're glad to see them. Our radio is out and we thought we'd *never* find them. . . ."

A puff of smoke appeared by the Soviet Osa's front turret. A moment later geysers of spray walked across the water fifty yards ahead.

Gomez looked uncertain. "Are they shooting at us, Chief? Or was that the proverbial shot over the bow?"

"A warning," Hunter guessed. "If they wanted to kill us, that burst would have been right through the bridge."

You hope, he told himself. *If I guess wrong on this . . .*

He let the binoculars fall to his chest, raised his arms, and slowly waved them back and forth. He prayed the message was clear: *Don't shoot! Let us talk!* Repeatedly he pointed to his right ear. *Our radio is out! Let us get close and we'll explain. . . .*

At twelve hundred yards the other Osa turned slightly, presenting more of her side to the Rangers. Ominously, both of the Russian craft's AK-240 turrets tracked, their muzzles pointing straight at them.

Much closer and they risked having a sharp-eyed Russian officer notice details of uniform or faces through his binoculars. Hunter depressed the intercom switch. "Okay, Roy. Any time you're ready!"

Their forward AK-240 shrieked like a buzz saw, and empty brass cartridges showered off to the right. Water geysered close beside the enemy ship's hull.

Missed . . . !

"Gun it, Doug!" he screamed into the intercom. The Osa leapt forward as the Russians returned fire. Columns of white water exploded on either side.

The bow turret swiveled slightly and fired again. This time there was a flash from the VBU boat's forward deck . . . then another, and another! Smoke boiled past the Russians' bridge, but an arcing rooster tail of water exploded from the vessel's stern as the other Osa shifted to full speed.

"Closer, Doug! Get closer!"

The Osa heeled sharply as she swung to port. Something

struck the racing boat's hull with a ringing, shuddering *slam-slam-slam*. The range closed as Morgan hauled the hurtling craft's bow back to the right. The movement threw Hunter against Walker as fresh explosions churned water just astern.

"The other two are closing!" Franklin warned. "Range three thousand."

A stream of high-explosive shells crashed into the enemy Osa's side. Flame erupted from a crater yawning just behind the forward turret, as oily black smoke boiled across the surface of the sea. The Rangers' forward turret slued a bit, and Hunter saw the Russian's bridge windows explode in a cloud of tiny, whirling fragments.

From topside, Hunter heard the *thud-thud-thud* of Gomez's grenade launcher. White water spumed and geysered between the two Osas. Then a phosphorus round struck just behind the Soviet vessel's shattered bridge. Hunter felt the concussion's shiver through the deck as ammo or other explosives savaged the other missile boat and turned her streamlined sleekness into a shattered, flaming hulk.

Hunter turned and dropped through the hatch to the control room. Hurrying to Morgan's side, he pointed to the burning wreck. "Quick!" he said. "Get in close! We've got a ready-made smoke screen there!"

Morgan nodded and spun the wheel, cutting back the throttle until they were barely idling forward. Smoke billowed across the surface of the water. A single shot banged from the other craft's stern, and Hunter heard the answering hammer of Walker's M-60 from overhead, saw bits of debris fly from the Russian's fantail. The smoke thickened, cutting visibility to a few tens of yards.

"Can you still see our friends?" Hunter asked Franklin.

"Still got 'em. Bearing one-six-two, range five hundred...."

That was practically point-blank range. "Roy!" He raised his voice to be heard aft in fire control. "Stand ready!"

"You got it!"

Gently, he placed his hand on Morgan's shoulder. "When I give the word, cut across the wreck's bow and turn into them, full speed. OK?"

Morgan gave only a curt nod for answer, but there was a light of deadly determination in his eyes.

"Range three hundred! They're turning. . . ."

"Now!"

The missile boat's engines thundered to full power, and the Osa's bow rose above a foaming white knife of water. Hunter staggered and caught himself as the suddenness of the turn threw him off balance, and he heard a loud thunk from below decks somewhere, as the hurtling vessel struck a piece of floating wreckage.

Then they were in the open, slicing through the smoke cloud, autocannons flashing as they tracked across the VBU Osas. Hunter heard a bloodcurdling yell from the flying bridge as the grenade launcher thumped away in rapid-fire counterpoint to the louder clatter of Walker's machine gun. Hunter saw yellow fire flash from one of the target's deckhouses, hurling bits of deck, stanchions, and cable high into the air.

The Russians fired back. Gouts of water blasted into the sky close on either side of the Ranger craft. Something hammered into the Osa's side forward. Hunter was thrown to the deck, and he felt the missile boat lurch heavily to one side. The bridge windows exploded inward in a lethal shower of splintered glass.

Morgan stayed on his feet somehow, though blood was streaming down his face from a dozen cuts and lacerations across his cheeks and scalp. He spun the wheel sharply and the boat responded, picking up speed as smoke boiled through the shattered windows from a fire on the bow. A hot, vicious wind smelling of scorched metal whistled through the broken windows. More explosions slammed into the craft, walking aft along the deckhouse in rapid succession.

"Forward gun out!" Anderson yelled. A round had blown the AK-240 away, leaving a gaping crater in the deck. "Damn it all! Power's goin' on the aft turret too!"

Which left the Osa with nothing but machine guns and a grenade launcher.

"Oh my God . . ." Franklin was gaping at his radar screen. Blood smeared his shoulder from a bad cut, but his face, protected by the radar screen's plastic hood, had not been touched by the exploding fragments of window.

Hunter made his way to Franklin's side. Glass crunched underfoot, and he found he was having trouble standing. His forehead burned. He touched it with his fingers, and they came away sticky with blood. "Whatcha got?"

Franklin pointed at the screen. "New target, Lieutenant! A big one! It just appeared . . . !"

The submarine. "What's the range?"

Franklin did a fast mental calculation. "Eight miles . . . headin' this way . . ."

Hunter turned away and raced for fire control, conscious of new strength in his legs. The room was small and cluttered with electronic gear, dangling bundles of wiring, and control panels. A jagged hole high up on one bulkhead emitted a smoky shaft of light. Jones and Anderson looked up from an open access panel as he entered.

"Control to the aft gun is out . . ." Anderson began.

"Never mind that!" He looked at Jones. "If you think you can get one of those big missiles flying, Gunny, now's the time!"

Jones's dark face frowned. "What's the target?"

"How about a fat Typhoon-class submarine, eight miles out?"

The marine's face cleared. "We can damn well try . . . !"

Anderson looked worried. "It's going to take more than one to put a big sucker like that Typhoon out of commission."

"Yeah." Hunter remembered the Typhoon's double hull and multiple compartments. "We'll hit him with everything we've got. Get the info you need from Franklin. I'm going topside to help Eddie and Walker!"

"Better get them below," Anderson said. "If we manage to launch those things, they're gonna scorch the flying bridge but good!"

Another series of explosions lashed the Osa. Flames poured from her deckhouse as Hunter emerged into smoky light on the flying bridge. Her wake twisted behind her, marking the convolutions of her course as her dogfight with the VBU Osas continued.

Eddie gripped the AGS-17 with both hands, his face black from the smoke. Walker was next to the mast, hammering away with his 60-gun.

"Get below!" Hunter screamed into the hell of noise and smoke. "We're launching!"

The three men dropped through the hatch, back into the stifling darkness. Anderson turned from the doorway to fire-control when he saw them step onto the deck. "Punch it, Gunny!"

A hiss like a broken steam pipe sounded outside, building in seconds to a shrieking roar that engulfed the bridge, shaking it, bashing at it with raw noise. "One away!" Jones yelled. "Two . . . two won't fire! She's hung!"

Another scream made the Osa tremble. "Three away . . . four away!"

Hunter could just glimpse one of the Styx missiles through a bridge window, an intense, wavering flare of yellow light already dwindling into the distance. In that moment, he knew a heart-wrenching anguish. *Rachel . . .*

The Russian submarine had to be a special part of the VBU plans . . . perhaps a mobile HQ or operational center. Suppose Greg and Rachel had been taken there? He pushed the thought aside. It was just as possible that they were aboard one of the battered Osas and even more likely that they were already dead. He gathered Walker and Gomez with his eyes. "Let's get topside."

Gomez and Walker were already through the hatch and Hunter was halfway up the ladder when the front of the control room exploded.

·

Sixteen

The impact knocked Hunter off the ladder. He sprawled back across the chart table, rolled off, and smashed into the aft bulkhead with a head-ringing thump. He saw Morgan lurch back from the helm, saw Franklin transfixed at the radar scope, wreathed in fire. Exploding shells disintegrated the port side of the bridge, lifted Franklin clear of the deck, and ripped him open from throat to crotch.

Hunter staggered to his feet. The left side of the bridge had been torn open, and smoke was pouring in. His feet slipped and he caught himself against the chart table. Looking down, he saw blood all over the deck . . . and Franklin's severed arm. Morgan lay slumped nearby, unconscious but alive.

He made his way to the helm. A turn of the wheel brought a sluggish response. The Osa was still answering to the helm, but slowly! Slowly! Ahead he saw one of the VBU boats, ablaze, shuddering under repeated impacts from Gomez's grenades.

Hunter put the wheel over, then held his breath as the Osa changed course. The burning vessel was close. *Turn, damn you! Turn!*

There was a gentle thud as the Ranger Osa swung broadside into the ship's forward quarter. Hunter could feel the heat from burning fuel and white-hot phosphorus. If the other craft's fuel supply blew . . .

The wreckage *bump-thump-bumped* aft along the savaged port side . . . and then they were clear and picking up speed. The throttle levers were all the way forward, but the Osa did not have anywhere near the speed she'd had before the fight. Hunter wondered if they'd taken a hit in the engine room, wondered if Lynch and Carlucci were still alive.

The third Osa was a kilometer away, trailing smoke and heading toward the distant English shore. The mist had lifted during the battle, and the green hills and white beaches of the Channel coast were catching the last rays of the setting sun. The grenade launcher opened up from overhead. Hunter saw flashes along the Osa's hull where the rounds hit.

And then the VBU Osa was out of range, moving faster than the battered Ranger craft could manage toward the west, into the gathering evening twilight. It took long minutes to be certain, but the enemy was getting away.

Anderson stood next to Hunter, hands on hips. "Did we win . . . ?"

Hunter glanced at Franklin's body but stifled an acid response. *Did we?*

"I just checked aft," he continued. Exhaustion dragged at the Texan's voice. His eyes had a distant, glazed look. "Tony and Gary are okay. Cuts and bruises from an engine-room hit."

Gomez appeared from topside. "That's it for the grenades, Chief. I guess we throw rocks now." He looked down at Franklin. "Walker's running low, too."

Damn . . . !

"That submarine," Jones said, coming out of fire control. "Did we get him?"

"I don't know." With the radar out, there was no way to be sure. The sub could have had ways of jamming the missiles or shooting them down.

Hunter was impossibly weary. They'd taken three-to-one odds—four-to-one counting the sub—and they'd won. But as night fell, there was no sense of victory. Franklin's bloody death left a pall over the battered Osa. Rachel and Greg were still prisoners, or worse. The sub might have been hit, but they couldn't know, and if it hadn't been hit there was nothing they could do about it now. One VBU Osa had escaped them. They were adrift on the fringes of one of the greatest naval engagements of history, with no way of knowing whether they'd decisively beaten the enemy or not.

They'd thrown everything they had into stopping the VBU plan. And it hadn't been enough.

King had been working for days now at the eyebolts that pinned his chains to the wall behind him. The wood of the ship's hull was soft in places from age and rot, and the edge of one of the flanges of the manacle on his left wrist was sharp enough that it became a makeshift blade, digging away beneath the eyebolt and prying it loose. After two days of steady work, the bolt wiggled loose and pulled free. The bolt's sharp point became the tool with which he attacked the pin on his other side.

Docile . . . that's the key, he thought as he dug away at the wood with quick, scraping movements. *I've been docile for so long they won't be expecting me to resist.*

It was the unexpected that he was counting on. For hour upon hour, sitting in the darkness, he'd been maintaining muscle tone with rigorous isometrics, stretching out with hands and feet pressed against opposite bulkheads and pushing. By this time, his captors probably expected him to fall over the first time he tried to stand up.

The door to the cramped cupboard that served as his cell did not look sturdy enough to hold him. Even chained shut, a few hard kicks would probably bash it open. But if he waited until someone opened the door, he might have a better chance. Twice each day, a sailor came to bring him food and empty the waste bucket, backed up by a mean-eyed Russian with an AKM. If he could take them by surprise, he would have a weapon, and that was worth both the extra wait and the extra risk.

It was the middle of the night when he finally pried the second bolt free from the hull. Working carefully so the noise would not be heard by the soldier standing guard outside, he wrapped the chains around his forearms to keep the loose ends from getting in his way. Then he sat back on his bench and waited.

Docile . . .

The watch was called, and he heard the noises of hundreds of men waking and going about their morning chores. The faint light of dawn, gleaming through open gunports, illuminated the wooden grate in his door. He smelled breakfast fires, heard men chattering in Spanish as the day grew older.

He waited, but the sailor and the guard did not appear with breakfast. Instead, he heard a yell, and moments later drum rolls and trumpet blasts sounded an alarm. He couldn't understand the urgent, shouted Spanish exchanges, but one phrase caught his attention: *"La flota Inglesa!"*

The English fleet.

His captors had other things to think about.

They heard the opening rounds of the battle from the cove south of Plymouth where they'd grounded the captured Osa in the middle of the night. It was Sunday morning, the twenty-first of July by the English calendar, the thirty-first by the Spanish. The opening rounds of cannon fire were isolated thuds, muted by distance. To the south a forest of masts rose from the horizon, hazy and indistinct.

The English had worked their ships clear of Plymouth Harbor. While the Rangers dueled with the three Osas on the previous afternoon, they'd placed their fleet behind and upwind of the Spanish, winning a vital tactical advantage.

"So what do you guys know about radar?" Hunter asked. He was standing on the Osa's forward deck, near the gaping, knife-edged hole where the forward 30mm turret had been. Gunny Jones exchanged glances with Lynch and Carlucci.

"I've worked with AN-PPS-15 tactical radars in the field, Lieutenant," the marine said. "That's not the same as this Russkie junk, of course, but . . ."

"Leave it to the Marines," Carlucci said, grinning. "I've had to tear down the GE Vulcan jobs, and I've gone troubleshooting in small-boat radars lots of times."

"Yeah," Jones said. "If the parts are there, we should be able to get it working."

"Then do it," Hunter said. The blast that had killed Franklin had knocked out the Osa's radar, but the damage did not appear bad. "We're going to need that radar if we're going to have a chance in hell of finding that missing Osa . . . or the sub."

"Aye aye, Lieutenant," Jones said, snapping a salute.

"You'll have it if we have to build printed circuits from beach sand!"

Hunter's gaze wandered across the water to the gathering storm of battle in the southwest. Cannon fire sounded like distant thunder. Repairing high-tech gear was one of the nightmares of time travel. There were no tools, no parts, and no trained personnel when you needed them. It was lucky that the marines were experienced with electronics. Otherwise, there'd be no hope at all of finding the enemy again.

He carefully did not think about what they would do if they actually found the surviving Russians. Assault rifles would not be much use against that Typhoon.

"Right," he said at last. "Doug, I want you to stay here. Keep a lookout for stray Russians. I don't want them finding the Osa."

"We'll keep an OP on that ridge, Lieutenant," Morgan said.

"You two," Hunter told Jones and Carlucci, "get me a working radar." He turned to Lynch and Anderson. "Gary, Roy . . . it looks like it's up to the Army to get us a working boat engine. Can you two handle it?"

"No sweat, LT," Anderson said. "We have some holes to patch on the engine deck."

"Fuel okay?"

"About three-quarters."

Hunter nodded. "Walker, Gomez, and I are going out again."

Morgan looked surprised. "In what, Lieutenant?"

"The *Golden Hinde*." He pointed to the ridge in the distance. As soon as the Osa had reached the cove, Hunter had sent Anderson and Gomez to the ridge top to have a look at Plymouth Harbor. "She's still in port but getting ready to leave."

Carlucci looked worried. "So what do you expect to prove out there? You still thinking about your friends?"

Hunter shook his head. "I'm thinking about a Spanish ship with VBU agents on board." The *San Salvador* had been preying on his thoughts since he'd heard of her. Greg and Rachel might be aboard, but . . . He shoved the thought aside. "With the shortwave we captured, we might get a lead on the submarine. Maybe we can get a chance at the VBU people with the Armada."

Morgan smiled grimly. "Once we get 'em, what'll we do with 'em?"

"We kill them."

But he still didn't know how.

Krylenko clutched *San Salvador*'s poop-deck railing until the rough wood gouged the palm of his hand. Damn the English bastards! And damn the American time commandos! It was clear now that there were other U.S. Rangers here. The confused radio messages from the trio of Osa missile boats suggested that the fourth boat, lost during the spetsnaz landing at Plymouth was being used by someone to upset the VBU plan. That someone could only be the Americans.

And so the English fleet under Drake and Howard had escaped the trap set for them at Plymouth, escaped the bottleneck of the narrow harbor, escaped the Osas waiting to annihilate any ships that beat their way into the open sea. The English ships were here, just as they were supposed to be according to a history that was looking more and more gloomy to the Russian officer. If things continued to run this close to the unaltered version of events, the VBU mission here would fail.

His hand clenched, and he slammed the fist into the railing. *No!*

"Birasten!"

"*Da*, Comrade Major!"

"Go below. Raise *Moryeh Ohotnik*!"

"They will not yet have completed repairs, Comrade Major."

"I know. The plan has gone too far wrong now for us to risk staying here. We will abandon the *San Salvador* and return to the submarine."

"*Da*, Comrade Major!"

Krylenko pulled the cowl of his priest's robes up over his head and watched the unfolding spectacle of the battle. The English fleet was gathering behind the vast, sprawling crescent of the Armada. In the middle of the morning, Howard, aboard the giant, four-masted *Ark Royal*, had passed the southern horn of the crescent, exchanging volley for thundering volley with de Leyva's squadron. Little damage had been sustained by either side, but it was clear now that the battle was joined in earnest.

He turned and looked north, toward the low green smudge of the English coast. Plymouth was there; he could see the gap in the hills that marked the Sound. Vorosilov had said that further attempts to convince Medina-Sidonia to land there would be useless. Now that the English were out, what was the use? Better to run before them and hope that a prolonged engagement would draw them out and finish them.

That hadn't worked historically, and there was nothing the Russians could do from the Spanish decks now that would change that.

But if they could reach the submarine . . .

Moryeh Ohotnik had been damaged in the unexpected engagement the previous afternoon, but the damage was relatively slight and easily repaired, given time. The Russian back-up plan allowed for such minor setbacks. Yes, they could still pluck victory from the deteriorating situation.

And they would crush the American time commandos at the same time.

Although he had no way of telling time, King estimated that at least six hours had passed since the battle began that morning. During the early afternoon, the fighting had dwindled away, a lull that dragged on into the afternoon as if the two huge fleets were wrestlers cautiously circling one another, unwilling to come to grips.

He heard the rattle of keys, the clatter of the chain at his door. He tensed himself, gathering strength and courage. The doors were flung open. . . .

He'd expected the Spanish sailor and one guard, but there were two Russians facing him as he lunged forward. The one standing in the door held a Skorpion machine pistol, while the other carried an AKM. King shifted as his shoulder collided with the first VBU trooper's gut and stepped aside as the Skorpion twisted toward his face. He swung his arm, heavy in its tightly wound coils of chain, and felt a satisfying crunch as the iron links swept the pistol aside and cracked the side of the man's skull.

The second spetsnaz fumbled with his rifle, caught off-guard by the attack. King's momentum carried him to the floor. He rolled once, rose, and hurled himself forward, hitting the VBU soldier before he could bring the AKM into position. King struck with a chain-wrapped forearm once more and felt the thin bone at the man's temple shatter. The Soviet trooper went down in a heap and King grabbed his weapon.

He was standing on the lower gun deck of the *San Salvador*. The ceiling with its heavy, white-painted wooden beams was so low he had to crouch, and the floor was a tangled maze of coiled lines, gratings, cannons, and bearded, ragged-looking men. Many of those men were gaping at him now, surprised by his sudden appearance.

There was nothing behind him but a wooden wall, with a doorway opening onto mounds of wet cable. His only way out was through the room crowded with sailors. Wondering how long he could hold the advantage of surprise, he hurried forward.

"*Alto!*" someone yelled.

Not long enough, he thought, turning to meet the attacker. A man with a trim mustache and a steel helmet advanced, swinging his sword for a cross cut at King's face. The Ranger threw up one armored forearm, and steel struck steel with a spray of sparks and a shock that jolted King up to his shoulder. The Spaniard staggered, thrown off balance. King lashed out with his foot. His opponent was armored, but there were other parts of the man's anatomy that were not so well protected.

The Spaniard gasped and turned white, dropping the sword, crumpling to the deck. King turned away, just in time to see a soldier lunge at him with a pike.

He blocked the thrust with one arm and swung the AKM with the other. The barrel cracked hard across the man's face, dislodging a spray of blood and teeth. King sensed other Spaniards closing in from behind. He didn't want to open up with the assault rifle on unarmed men who could not possibly know what the weapon was or what it could do, and yet . . .

King dodged around a massive, white cylinder rising from deck to overhead that he knew must be one of *San Salvador*'s masts. He loosed a burst of auto fire into the deck, sending a shower of splinters into a nearby group of gunners. The thunder of full auto fire in the enclosed space stung his ears and left them ringing. Someone screamed, and King broke through the crowd, pounding aft in a head-down crouch.

"Stop, American!" The order, bellowed in English, brought him to a halt. Krylenko stood at the aft end of the gun deck, a Russian soldier on either side of him. He held Rachel with one hand around her upper arm, a Makarov pistol at her head.

"Drop the weapon!" Krylenko snapped. "Or I splatter her brains on the deck!"

The Spanish gun crews stood frozen in place around the squat, metal monsters they tended. Though they couldn't understand the language, the strange yet obvious weapons, the crackling tension in the air held them transfixed, waiting.

The details of the instant were burned into King's mind, made crisp by the adrenaline pounding through his bloodstream. The cannons ranked on either side of the deck were a surprise—two-wheeled field guns instead of the blocky naval carriages with four small wheels he expected from the pirate movies he'd seen. Light from the gun ports highlighted dust motes in the air, the beads of sweat on faces and naked backs. The gunner nearest the Russians tried to back unobtrusively away, a smouldering wooden tube carved in the shape of a crocodile held in front of his face like a talisman.

"Go to hell, Krylenko!" King growled, raising the AKM. "We're dead anyway...."

"No! We're taking you aboard a pinnace. We'll go to our submarine. Our time machine is there! Think about it, man! That's your only way out of this time!"

A time portal...aboard a submarine? The surprise nearly made him lower the weapon. But then, why not? The VBU had hidden the things before, in the turret of a castle, even aboard a railway boxcar....

Rachel acted.

Until that moment, King had not been absolutely certain that she was, indeed, still on his side. The pistol at her head suggested she hadn't broken as Krylenko had claimed...but that could have been a bluff.

The black-haired girl twisted free of Krylenko's grip, reaching out as the Russian lunged to grab her again. She plucked the carved staff from the gunner's unresisting fingers, spun, and drove the shaft with all her strength into Krylenko's eyes.

The staff was a linstock holding the slow-burning fuse that fired the cannons. Krylenko screamed and clawed at his face, the Makarov clattering to the deck. Rachel ran past King as the Russian guards dove for cover behind cannons on either side of the deck, their weapons raised.

"Dive out a gun port!" King yelled.

"You come, too!"

"Get out of here!" he roared. He cut loose with a ragged burst from the AK, driving the VBU troopers' heads down. It would be a long swim to England, but she might make it . . . or she might be picked up by a ship that had no Russians aboard.

King had already made a lightning assessment of facts. The VBU troops were under cover, and more were rushing forward from the door at the far end of the gun deck. Krylenko, screaming orders, had his pistol again. The Spaniards wavered on the verge of panic. He would never win a firefight here, not with only half a magazine left. And he had to make sure the Russians were killed!

He swung his arm, aiming at a stack of wooden kegs along the far bulkhead, squeezing off the last of the rounds remaining in his AKM. Bullets burned down the length of the deck, smashing through the kegs' sides, scattering black powder. . . .

King didn't hear the blast, but suddenly the dark gun deck turned white.

Then blackness drowned the light in spinning, burning pain.

Seventeen

The *Golden Hinde* was standing out into the Channel, her sails close-hauled on a starboard tack. The fifty-ton barque, handier in tight waters than the larger ships of the English fleet, was not as hampered within the narrow boundaries of the harbor and had required only a few hours to get clear of Rame Head and raise full sail.

Hunter, Gomez, and Walker had heard the distant cannons fall silent at one o'clock in the afternoon and wondered what it meant. The Rangers were still concerned at the escape of one Osa and the Russian submarine; either by itself would be enough to disrupt the English fleet, though Hunter thought the Russians would probably exercise caution in any direct attack on it. The appearance of magical craft could panic the Spanish as well as the English, which explained why the Osas had been standing well clear of both fleets on the previous afternoon.

Hunter glanced up at Flemyng pacing the *Golden Hinde*'s narrow quarterdeck. The Englishman had accepted Hunter's explanation that their mysterious, middle-of-the-night mission had succeeded and that Plymouth was now safe.

"Safe," Flemyng had said with a scowl. "Safe unless the Dons decide to enter, English ships or no! They lie between us and Lord Howard now, I fear!"

He was steering the *Hinde* past the Armada now to join Howard and Drake. The English strategy assumed that the

Spanish would not enter Plymouth with an enemy fleet behind them. Hunter hoped the assumption was right. It appeared sound; he'd heard tales about Drake's raid on Cadiz in the previous year, how Spanish ships had been trapped inside the harbor and burned like kindling.

Hunter glanced at his watch, set now to local time. It was four o'clock in the afternoon, and the battle had still not resumed. It would take hours yet to reach the English fleet, and sunset was due at 7:44. He paced across the deck to where Gomez and Walker crouched in the shade of the starboard side bulwark. "Anything?"

Gomez had a headset over his ears, the captured shortwave radio still in its pack lying on the deck between his knees. He looked up and shook his head.

"Our Russian friends are not being talkative," Walker said quietly. The Indian glanced around, but none of the English sailors or soldiers were paying them any attention. The Rangers had been careful to keep the radio hidden. This was not a good period of history in which to be suspected of witchcraft.

"Keep on it," Hunter said. "If the VBU is going to make a move, it's . . ."

The concussion hit the *Golden Hinde* as a dull, booming thud. Hunter could feel the blast as a palpable blow against his body, strong enough to rattle the windows of the houses in Plymouth. The ship's masts shivered with the impact, and the English sailors began rushing to the port side of the ship, looking and pointing to the south.

Hunter turned, craning his neck to see past the crowd. He could see the Spanish Armada, a blur of masts and sails sprawled across the horizon. Rising from the center of that mass like the discharge from a volcano was a black cloud of smoke, slowly unfolding into the sky as he watched.

"What is it?" Gomez asked. Tied to the radio, he couldn't see past the crowd of jabbering, excited sailors. He pulled the headset off. "What do you see?"

"An explosion," Hunter said. He turned and looked at the others. "I think one of the Spanish ships has just blown up."

Rachel felt the sharp, rasping pain of a burn on her left arm, knew without looking at it that the skin was blistered. She didn't want to look, dreading what she might see. The girl drew a breath and choked. The air was thick with smoke and foul with the sour stench of sulfur. Her eyes burned.

I've got to get out! The smoke would overcome her in minutes, she knew. She forced herself to take shallow breaths.

It took her a moment to collect herself. She was not badly injured, though her arm hurt like hell. Several minutes passed before Rachel realized that the ship was unnaturally silent. The ringing in her ears focused her attention on them. It wasn't that the ship was silent; the blast had deafened her, though she was becoming aware of sounds through the roaring in her ears. The deafness seemed to be temporary.

Her thoughts were jumbled and confused, muddled by the sheer, violent shock of the explosion. She remembered falling behind the wheel and massive carriage of a Spanish cannon just as Greg raised his rifle. That had been what saved her, she decided, the bulk of the gun that deflected the blast. Greg must have fired into a store of gunpowder . . . and the explosion had detonated a larger quantity of powder stored nearby and scoured the gun deck with flame. Through boiling smoke, she saw dim light aft. It looked as though the stern of the *San Salvador* had been blown away, the gap imperfectly plugged by fallen, smouldering wreckage.

Greg! As memory returned, Rachel groped for a handhold on the cannon and tried to stand. The metal was hot and she jerked away, then got to her knees.

Only scraps of her fatigue shirt were left hanging from her shoulders, but she didn't bother trying to cover herself as she sat up. The men nearby did not even see her. Those not wounded were in a brain-numbed daze, stumbling through the smoke to reach the ladders leading to the upper deck. Many were naked, their clothes torn away by the blast. Some were hideously burned, stumbling aimlessly or helped by less badly injured comrades. Rachel had trouble taking in some of what she saw, the charred and blackened masses of flesh too graphic to be easily seen and understood.

Yes, her hearing was definitely returning. She could hear a keening, insistent noise, but far away, as though her ringing ears were stuffed with cotton. What were those sounds, anyway? She concentrated, frowning, before she recognized them.

The screams of horribly burned and wounded men.

She found King lying on the deck and for one, wrenching instant she feared he was dead. Rachel touched his throat and felt a pulse. The Ranger was burned, but not as badly as some of the Spaniards. His face was blackened, but it looked more like soot or grime than burned flesh. She remembered he'd been standing behind the massive cylinder of the ship's mast when he raised his gun to fire. Perhaps the mast had sheltered him in the same way that the cannon had protected her. Perhaps . . .

She felt giddy with relief when King stirred. "Greg! Greg! Are you okay?"

His eyes opened and he said something she couldn't hear.

"I can't hear you!" she shouted. She bent closer, trying to hear what he was saying. It was difficult to make out his words over the screams.

"I . . . told you to go . . ." Her ear was nearly touching his blackened lips. "Go . . ."

"No, Greg! I'm not leaving you!"

"Have to. Leave me . . . here."

"What's the matter?" She looked at his body anxiously. Could he have injuries she couldn't see? If his back was broken . . . "Can you move? Can you feel your legs?"

"You'll have to make it on your own," he said. His voice was stronger now. He turned his head, and as she looked into his eyes she realized what was wrong.

"Greg!"

"It's no good, Rachel. I'm blind."

Captain Nikolai Sergeivich Tyrin stared at the Cornish coast, passing slowly ten miles to starboard of the *Moryeh Ohotnik*. The land there was rocky: the long, slender neck of cliff and beach stretched west to the point sailors knew as The Lizard.

His exec climbed through the lookout station hatch and saluted. "Damage report, Comrade Captain."

"*Da*, Vladimir Vladimirovich," Tyrin replied. "How is he?" Like all Russians, he thought of his ship as masculine, rather than as the western "she."

"We are on reduced power, Captain. The reactor chief informs me that we should remain at forty percent output for at least another three days. He wishes to inspect the cooling systems on both reactors for leaks or cracks. The patching to the hull is nearly complete, but the damage control officer suggests that we not dive to any great depth until more substantial repairs can be made.''

Tyrin considered this. "There should be no problem, then. There is no sign of pursuit. We should need neither to dive nor to run at flank speed." He closed his eyes, remembering the attack. They had surfaced only moments before radar reported the trio of fast-moving objects skimming across the waves, locked on the sub. Tyrin had sounded battle stations, had ordered chaff fired to distract the oncoming missiles.

One missile had been diverted by the chaff, but two more had slammed into the submarine's hull. The first had smashed the Typhoon's "hangar," as the men referred to the tacked-on shelter for the two lost landing barges. The second had hit just aft of the conning tower, severing power leads, damaging the reserve batteries, and very nearly destroying both of the ship's nuclear reactors. Only the fact that Typhoons were so heavily armored, with massive double hulls, had saved them.

"What is your intent, Comrade Captain?"

"To reach the rendezvous point in one piece. After that . . ." He shrugged. "Perhaps Uralskiy will have further word for us. What of the time-gate equipment?"

"The technicians say there was some damage, but nothing major. The power grid is off but can be restored. In any case, with the reactors cut back, there is insufficient power to open a gate while the submarine is in operation . . . but the attempt would be useless while we are under way in any case. They need a stable, unmoving platform in order to cross from one time to another."

"That much I know, Vladimir Vladimirovich. Tell me something I do not . . . such as how soon we will be able to reestablish communication with our own time."

"The technicians say five days, Comrade Captain. A week at the most."

"Very well." He sighed. "Order radar to maintain a close watch. I want no . . ."

He was interrupted by the buzz of the ship's intercom. "Captain."

"Communications, Comrade Captain," a voice said. "Transmission from the *Rata Encoronada*."

Tyrin frowned. The *Encoronada*? "Patch it through."

A moment later, the voice of Vorosilov crackled through the speaker, static-torn and faint. "This is Vorosilov! Do you read me?"

"*Ohotnik* here. Go ahead."

"*Ohotnik!* There has been . . . an explosion. The *San Salvador* is a wreck. I fear . . . I fear Krylenko is dead."

"What! What happened?"

"We don't know yet. The ship is a burning hulk, adrift and out of control. Other vessels are having difficulty approaching him."

"Is it the Americans?"

"Impossible yet to determine. It may have been another missile. You said only three hit you yesterday, which leaves one unaccounted for. But how did they know *San Salvador* was one of ours?"

Tyrin's frown deepened, and his eyes strayed to the patched-over scars aft of the conning tower. The VBU had consistently underestimated the Americans here in 1588.

"Perhaps you should rejoin me here, Comrade Colonel." He went on to explain what he'd just been told about the ship's condition. Tyrin could not give orders to Vorosilov. The Colonel was in operational command of the VBU forces in 1588. The fact that the time machine would be functioning within another week, however, would shape Vorosilov's thinking.

"*Nyet*, Comrade Captain," was the reply after a moment. "At least, not yet. The Spanish are shaken, and I believe we've lost our chance to force Plymouth Harbor, but we may yet be able to link up with Parma. We will know within the week."

"And your orders for me?"

"Continue to the rendezvous. As soon as the time-gate equipment is operational, open a link with Uralskiy, and have them prepare to set the reserve plan in motion."

"It is to be the reserve plan, then?"

"Of course. Perhaps we can still arrange to ferry Parma's army across the Channel, once the English get word that an unexpected army is on the march in Scotland!" There was a pause, as static hissed from the receiver. "If it proves impossible to move Parma, I will join you at the rendezvous.''

"We will be there, Comrade Colonel,'' Tyrin said. "And the army will be waiting.''

"Excellent. We are counting on you, Nikolai Sergeivich. The success of *Espahneeyah Rassvet* depends on you!''

Tyrin ignored the pep talk. "Understood. *Ohotnik*, out.''

He looked at his exec, who had stood by in silence during the conversation. "Well, Vladimir Vladimirovich. It looks like there will be a Russian invasion of England, after all, and not the Spanish invasion the planners first envisioned.''

"*Da*, Comrade Captain. Swords and primitive muskets against assault rifles and grenades! It should be an impressive exercise.''

Tyrin looked away, unwilling to risk an answer. Bringing modern troops and weapons through the submarine's time gate to attack the English army would be neither an exercise nor war.

It would be a bloody slaughter that the tough old submarine skipper did not even want to think about.

Eighteen

The worst part of that night was the sounds, Rachel thought. The moans of wounded men transformed the battered hulk of the *San Salvador* into a Dantean hell. The wind picked up at sunset, and throughout the hours of darkness the *San Salvador* wallowed in heavy seas, threatening with each rolling swell to capsize. A smaller Spanish vessel, with a high, ornate stern and banks of oars that gave it the curious look of a seaborne centipede, managed to get a line to the *Salvador*'s prow and keep her moving, but all attempts to save her appeared doomed.

Rachel stayed at King's side. Immediately after the explosion she had guided him onto the upper deck and found a shelter for them out of the wind. Once she left him and went back below decks, returning with a bucket of water. Shock had made him thirsty. She used a rag to clean his face and burned eyes, bandaging them with a strip torn from a Spanish flag. She couldn't tell how bad his injuries were. Burning powder had imbedded itself in his face. His eyes were filled with blood, but she didn't know if the blindness was temporary or permanent.

Grimly, she corrected the thought. The blindness was permanent . . . unless they could somehow return to 2008 and decent medical care. They might both die when their burns became infected. In 1588 antibiotics were three centuries in the future, and people still believed sickness was caused by an imbalance of bodily humors.

Rachel left again as the evening air grew cool and King began trembling with the chill born of his shock. She found a wool blanket for him and a linen shirt for herself in a canvas bag that had once held an officer's possessions. Remembering her first aid training, she elevated King's feet and kept him warm. He slept, but Rachel did not. She found a dagger, razor-edged and vicious, lying on the deck and kept it as a last resort weapon, sitting with her back against the bulwark, watching *Salvador*'s crewmen working to save their ship and each other.

Her hand strayed to her throat, fumbling for her mother's locket, before she remembered it was gone. The Russians had taken it, of course. As they'd taken everything else . . . as they'd taken Travis.

Rachel thrust the thought from her mind. She was still afraid, but the sense of helpless terror was under control, chained at the back of her mind with a cool and calculating sense of purpose. Greg needed her. She was there. It was as simple as that. Later, perhaps, there would be time for the luxury of falling to pieces . . . but not now.

Rachel had no idea at all of what later would bring. The ship's survivors ignored both of them; there were scores of wounded, and men scattered here and there across the deck caring for them. No one noticed the two Americans. For now, at least, Rachel was content to leave it that way.

When King awoke again, it was daylight; he could feel the sun's warmth on his face. He had vague memories of a lurching, wallowing sensation as the hulk was towed through rough seas during the night, but now the wind had died away to a gentle, almost nonexistent breeze. He was still blind but told himself that it could be just that the bandages on his eyes kept him from seeing. He didn't believe it—he had felt the burning powder searing into his eyes—but the thought brought reassurance enough that he could speak without having his voice shake.

"Who's there?" The words were more croak than speech.

"It's me, Greg. Rachel." He felt something cold and wet

against his lips . . . a wet rag. He sucked at the moisture greed-
ily.

"And what the bloody hell are you doing here?" he said.
"Told you to go over the side. Can't you swim?"

"I can swim." There was calm assurance in the words.

"Then why are you staying?"

"I like the company."

"Yeah, but . . ."

He was interrupted by a man's voice close by, an unleashed
torrent of Spanish.

"*Nein!*" Rachel said, whip-crack authority in her voice.
"*Gehen Sie weg!*"

King wondered for a moment about Rachel replying in German to a statement made in Spanish . . . but he could hear
someone mutter, then turn and walk away.

"Since when do they speak German on a Spanish ship?" he
asked.

"I've been listening to them all night," she said. "There
are lots of Germans on board . . . Dutch too, I think. I figured
this guy would understand 'go away' at least." He heard the
grin in her voice. "Maybe the dagger I showed him helped the
translation."

"What did he want?"

"Beats me. I don't know Spanish. He pointed at you. I think
maybe he wanted your blanket."

"He can have it, for all I care."

"Uh-uh. You just stay put. I'll keep an eye on our friends."
He heard her hesitate. "Sorry. I didn't mean . . ."

"Never mind," he said. It didn't bother him to be reminded
about his eyes. He just wished he dared rub them, to rid himself
of their itching, gummy feeling. "Looks like you're going to
be my eyes for a while." He groped toward her voice with
one hand, felt her hand close over his fingers. "I'm glad you're
here."

King faded in and out of consciousness for the next several
hours. Rachel kept him informed of what was going on when
he was lucid. By midday, it was obvious that the Spanish had
given up trying to save the *San Salvador*. Rachel described the
scene as Spanish soldiers came aboard and carried heavy crates
on deck, lowering them onto smaller, single-masted ships

alongside. From her description, King thought the crates must
hold gold . . . the VBU's gold from the *Princessa,* perhaps. The
boarders also tried to lower the wounded to safety, but the
renewed screams of the burned men were so terrible that the
rescuers abandoned the attempt. Rachel asked if he wanted to
go, but King refused. He was feeling weak and sick. The idea
of being lowered blind into a pitching, yawing boat alongside
the *San Salvador* was more than he could think about. He urged
Rachel to go. They'd decided that the man they'd spoken to
earlier must have thought she was a teenaged boy. It was
possible that she would be able to blend in with the sailors and
escape.

"And do what?" Rachel had countered. "If the Armada is
destroyed the way history says it's supposed to be . . . well,
let's just say I'd rather take my chances here?"

He agreed.

In the early afternoon, the galley cast off the towline, and
the *Salvador* was left to drift alone as the breeze carried the
Armada ponderously toward the east.

But King felt less lonely now than he had during his captivity.
Rachel held his hand as they listened to the shriek of seabirds
keening overhead.

"Yon lies *San Salvador,*" Flemyng said. "God's teeth, look
at that!"

Hunter felt his pulse quickening as he leaned over the rail.
They'd joined the English fleet early that morning and spent
the rest of the day pursuing the Armada up the Channel. There
were no radio calls to monitor. If there had been Russians
aboard the *Salvador,* Hunter could understand why. The vessel
was a drifting wreck.

There had been little fighting that day. Sometimes opposing
ships would close the range and loose volleys, but there was
none of the large-scale chaos that Hunter associated with what
he knew about the Spanish Armada.

He was surprised, too, by the relative sizes of the Spanish
and English ships. Always in the past when he'd read about
the engagement, the writers would speak of the disparity between the two sides . . . the huge and clumsy Spanish ships
towering above the smaller, more nimble vessels of Drake and

Howard as they skipped in to deliver a broadside, then danced away before the Spanish could reply.

The reality of the battle was nothing like that, another instance, Hunter decided, where history had been distorted by both victor and vanquished for reasons of propaganda and politics. There were more Spanish ships, it was true, but a large number were towed hulks or oared galleasses, armed with cannons but so clumsy they were next to useless in a fight. Most of the Spanish ships were taller than their opponents, with forecastles and sterncastles stacked to dizzying heights that must have made them next to impossible to control, but ton for ton the Spanish were out-weighed and out-gunned. Hunter was beginning to understand just how important the VBU operation to destroy the fleet at Plymouth had been to their plans. The English fleet might be all that stood between the Spanish and England . . . but it was a quite substantial all, one that the Spanish did not dare challenge head-on.

There was a difference, too, in the cannons carried by the two fleets. Hunter could see that the Spanish were not reloading after they fired. From what he could make out, their guns were two-wheeled field pieces, while the English had naval cannons with blocky carriages and four wheels, guns easily hauled inboard for loading after each shot. Hunter suspected that the Spanish guns were simply too large and clumsy to be reloaded during battle; they were fired once and serviced later, when the sailors were able to clamber onto the muzzles outside the hulls.

Still, the Spanish fleet looked impressive and deadly. The English captains kept their distance except for brief forays, snapping at the Armada's heels.

The *San Salvador* was far larger than the little *Golden Hinde*, but she looked anything but warlike as the English barque closed the gap between them late in the afternoon. The gilded, carved gingerbread of her high-stacked sterncastle had been splintered as though by the blow from a monstrous sledge hammer, and the wreckage had collapsed upon itself in a jumbled tangle of wood and tattered rigging. Her masts were gone except for stumps. There was evidence that a great deal of rigging had been cut away to free sails and wreckage dragging in the water.

Hunter's experienced eye confirmed what he'd expected. The *Salvador* had been mangled by an internal explosion. It couldn't have been her magazine or there would have been nothing left. Someone might have dropped a match in an open powder cask.

But he found himself wondering if Greg or Rachel might have had something to do with it. Their Spanish prisoner had specified this ship as the one where Rachel and Greg had been taken after their removal from the *Black Princess*.

Evidently, the *Salvador* had been abandoned by the Spanish and allowed to fall behind the Armada. Two other English ships, *Victory* and *Golden Lion*, had already pulled close alongside and put troops aboard her. Hunter hurried to Flemyng's side. "Can you put a boat across, Captain?" he asked. "I'd like to get aboard her. That is the ship where my friends were held prisoner."

" 'Twas my intent, aye," Flemyng said. "Besides, I would see this Spanish monster which has fallen into our hand."

It took nearly an hour to clear away a longboat—little more than a rowboat with a single collapsible mast and one sail—and lower it beside the *Hinde*. Even with her stern blown away and her upper decks collapsed, the *Salvador* was too large for the *Golden Hinde* to board directly. Flemyng went across, together with several of his officers and men, Hunter, Gomez, and Walker.

It was a long climb up a rope ladder to the *Salvador*'s deck. The stench from the shattered vessel was awful, a mingling of burnt hemp and wood, hot tar, charred flesh and death. Besides the English boarders already there, perhaps fifty Spanish survivors remained, a pitiable huddle of burned and exhausted men.

And Rachel . . . alive!

Rachel had seen Hunter from the deck of the *San Salvador*, recognized him while he was making the crossing in the tiny sailboat to the Spanish ship's side. For one dizzying moment, she thought she was seeing things, that the strain and exhaustion had pushed her over sanity's ill-defined edge. Travis was dead . . . vaporized in the nuclear blast on the Cuban coast! He couldn't be . . .

. . . here!

She was in his arms the moment he set foot on the deck. The armored men who had come across with him in the small boat looked at them curiously, then moved off to where the captains of the other English ships were examining *San Salvador*'s damage.

Her lips found his as his arms encircled her. "Travis! How . . . ?"

"Never mind," he said. "It's . . . good to have you back." He pulled back, fumbling in his pocket. Gold flashed in the sunlight. "I thought you'd want this. . . ."

Her locket. She took it, blinking back tears. "Thank you." She snuggled close. "But you're what I needed. Oh!" How could she tell him? "Travis! It's Greg . . . !"

Moments later, the Rangers knelt by King's still form. "Howdy, Lieutenant," the wounded man said. "We were wondering when you'd show up. "

"Expecting me, huh?"

"Hell, Lieutenant. I figured it'd take more'n an A-bomb to stop you. How'd you manage it, anyway?"

"It's a long story."

"You can tell me after we get back home."

"Greg . . ." Rachel saw the anguish in Hunter's face. He looked up, meeting her eyes. "I'm sorry. We're stranded here. We didn't have a beacon when the VBU base blew."

Rachel felt as though the deck of the ship had dropped from beneath her. Mingled with her first delirious joy at seeing Hunter impossibly alive had been the realization that they would be able to get home.

"There's another way," she said slowly.

Hunter looked at her sharply. "Huh? What way? What do you mean?"

"Did . . . did you know the VBU have a submarine here? A big one?"

Hunter nodded. "Typhoon class. We took a shot at her the other day, but we don't know if we hit her or not."

Rachel closed her eyes. "Oh, God! If you destroyed it . . . !"

"Why? What are you talking about?"

"The VBU officer, Krylenko," she explained. "He said they have a submarine with a time portal aboard!"

"A VBU downlink . . . on the sub?" A dark, wild emotion

swept Hunter's eyes. He reached out and grabbed her arm, and she gasped as he touched the burn under her borrowed shirt. "Sorry . . ." He released his grip. "Is that possible . . . ?"

She dragged her fingers through her hair. It was matted and dirty and she gave up the attempt. "They had one inside a boxcar. I imagine if they had something to pull out, they could replace it with the portal electronics and gear easily enough. They'd have to be stationary to use it, of course . . . so their space coordinates wouldn't change."

"Nuclear sub, Chief," Gomez added. "Plenty of power from the reactors."

"That would explain a lot," Hunter said, nodding.

"Like how they got all those soldiers out of a submarine . . . enough for two landing craft and a small shore party," Walker said. His dark eyes were bright with sudden understanding. "I was wondering at the time. I've never been on a submarine, but I gather they can be . . . cramped."

"Space is at a premium, even on the big nuclear jobs," Hunter agreed. "But they were feeding troops straight from 2008 onto the landing craft! No crowding at all!"

"And they have a working time machine!" Rachel reminded them. "At least, they did until you guys started shooting at it!"

"If you're suggesting we try capturing it, Raye, I don't know." Hunter looked uncertain. "We don't know how many people they have on board . . . and it sounds like they can just bring as many reinforcements through as they want, any *time* they want."

"We've got to find it, Chief," Gomez said. "We might've stopped 'em here, but . . ."

"Yeah," Hunter said. " 'But . . .' "

Rachel finished the thought. "The mission's not done until we find that sub. Otherwise, the VBU will just keep pumping more men and weapons back here until something gives. Until history gives."

Hunter nodded. His eyes held Rachel's. "Right. Listen people. If we can find a way to . . . ah . . . borrow the VBU time machine, that's great. But if we can't . . ."

Rachel laid her hand on Hunter's arm. "The VBU time

machine must be destroyed,'' she finished for him. ''It *must* be.''

Hunter smiled, and she knew he understood. They would be together, no matter what the year was. Her eyes strayed to King, wrapped in the blanket and lying on the deck. If only there was something they could do for him.

Nineteen

Hunter used the last of the Russian gold in Gomez's pack to hire passage on a two-masted fishing smack heading back to Plymouth. Flemyng's orders from Lord Howard were for the *Golden Hinde* to take *San Salvador* in tow and head for Weymouth. Hunter considered staying aboard, but Weymouth was a good eighty miles by land from Plymouth, and time now was vital.

Vital, too, was the need to rejoin the Osa as quickly as possible. The captured missile boat was their only hope of tracking down the Russian sub; Hunter didn't want to squander more of her limited fuel supply by sending her farther east when the sub's last course had her going west. Besides, it was entirely possible that the Russians would hear Hunter's short-wave transmissions and guess that the Rangers were coming.

The fishing smack *Mary Beth* brought the five of them into Plymouth well after dark. The captain, a villainous-looking rascal with one eye and the air of a pirate, was surprised when Hunter asked that they be put ashore in the small cove south of Plymouth, but agreeable. Hunter's gold guaranteed the profits of a month of smuggling, and he'd already been paid by the citizens of Plymouth to carry news of the Armada fight back to the city. He was willing to cater to the strangers' whims . . . and if he was curious about the strange, mastless craft anchored in the cove as his men rowed the four men and the person he took to be a ship's boy ashore, he gave no sign.

The Osa set out that night, moving slowly to save fuel. Hunter didn't know how far the submarine might have gone, but he was gambling that there was a rendezvous point someplace . . . and that it would be close enough for the surviving Russian Osa to reach. Again and again he fingered the anonymous fragment of map identified as an emergency rendezvous. Somewhere among those unnamed islands the Typhoon was waiting . . . but where were they?

He was not even certain that the sub had gone west. Their last brief radar sighting of the vessel was all they had to go on. Daylight of August 2 found them off the point of land known as the Lizard. Dark Walker was sharing the watch with Gomez on the flying bridge, and his call brought Hunter up from the control room.

"There," Walker said, pointing to the shore. He handed Hunter the binoculars.

Hunter stared for a long moment before he realized just what he was seeing. In the water, heavy on the rise and fall of the Channel swell, was a thick, silver sheen.

It was a common enough sight along the coastlines of Hunter's time, but 1588 had neither industrial pollution nor leaking oil tankers. "We hit him," Hunter said as the significance of what he was seeing struck home. "My God, we hit him!" Then he frowned, puzzled. "But I thought Typhoons were nuclear powered."

Walker shrugged. "They still use lubricants. The most likely explanation is that we holed a tank carrying fuel for the Osas."

"Right!" Hunter remembered the sub's high, added-on turtle back. "They could have been carrying thousands of gallons aboard her!"

"Or they had equipment to pump it back through time. But there would be a storage tank of some kind, certainly."

Gomez looked at Hunter. "Nothing more dangerous than a wounded submarine." The words were joking, but worry lay behind them.

"That Styx missile that hung in the launch tube, Eddie . . ."

"It's safe."

"Right . . . but could you make it *unsafe*?"

"Easy enough, I guess. Disconnect the arming mechanism and jigger something mechanical. Why?"

"Because we need something to fight that monster when we catch it, and the explosives in that warhead are all we've got. See what you can come up with, Eddie."

"Sure, Chief. Just keep us out of storms, okay? There won't be much left of this tub if that warhead blows while I'm working on it!"

"I'll keep that in mind."

"We still have that RPG round, don't we?" Gomez asked.

Hunter nodded. The rocket grenade they'd captured on the *Princessa* was aboard, stowed in Lynch's rucksack aft. "Sure do. Why?"

"Oh, you never know when you might need something that makes a nice bang." Gomez grinned wolfishly. Hunter left him to his work.

It was not a sharp or clearly defined trail they followed, but it was a trail of sorts, leading them around the Lizard and Land's End north through St. George's Channel and into the Irish Sea. After two days of sighting nothing, they saw the sheen of oil once more along the beaches of Caernarvon Bay. On the afternoon of August 5 they sighted oil again off the Isle of Man, but by the following day, Hunter realized that the Rangers stood a good chance of losing their quarry entirely in the tangle of islands off the west coast of Scotland.

That evening, he called the others together on the weather bridge and spread out the map fragment they'd not been able to identify.

"Mull," he said quietly, and the others bent forward to see. "There was no way to tell before, but now that we know where to look, the shape of the land is right. Look." He traced the outline of the largest island on the map fragment, comparing it with the contours of a navigational chart found on the *Osa's* bridge. It was a close match.

"The Isle of Mull," Anderson repeated. "No⸱ much there."

"A few villages. A deep, sheltered sound between the island and the mainland." Hunter straightened.

"So what's the plan?" Morgan asked. "Cruise in pretending we're lost and looking for mama?"

"I doubt that they'll believe us, especially if that other *Osa's* already at the rendezvous.'' Hunter smiled. ''No, tonight we're going to go on a little hike.''

''Suits me,'' Gomez said, grinning. ''I'm tired of playing sailor.''

''We're hunters now, Eddie.'' He tapped the sound northeast of Mull. ''And unless I miss my guess, our prey is waiting for us right there.''

It was the eighth of August, 1588, and the cannons of the massed fleets boomed and thundered across the shallow stretch of water north of Flanders known as the Gravelines. Colonel Vorosilov leaned against the poop-deck railing of the *Rata Encoronada* and clenched his fists in wordless, angry frustration.

Since they'd turned away from Plymouth a week before, nothing had gone right. A running fight had developed, with the English snapping at the Armada's heels all the way from Plymouth to Calais. At midnight the night before, Sir Francis Drake had launched a fire-ship attack. None of the Spanish ships anchored off Calais was damaged, but the Armada's discipline had finally broken under the assault, as captains cut their anchor cables and fled before the wind. With the Armada in disarray, the English had seen their chance, and attacked.

In other words, Vorosilov mused, so far all of the VBU efforts in this year had come to nothing. He, himself, had spent years studying the role of Don Alonzo de Leyva, nobleman, hero, and favorite of the Spanish court. The real Don Alonzo had died to a VBU agent's dagger thrust in a Lisbon alley the previous December. Vorosilov, his face altered by surgery, had replaced him. So much had gone into the effort to penetrate Philip's court, with the sole purpose of placing Vorosilov here. . . .

The VBU colonel watched the smoke billowing above the clashing fleets and wondered again what history said about de Leyva's end. His briefing had not extended beyond the historical events of August, a purposeful bit of security designed to allow him the greatest freedom of decision.

Well . . . what more was there to decide now? He could still replace Medina-Sidonia, but to what purpose? Now that the

Armada was scattering into the North Sea, the chance to ferry Parma into England was lost.

His last radio communication with Tyrin had brought good news on that front, at least. The sub was at the rendezvous point, its battle damage repaired, its downlink operational. Perhaps Parma's army would not be necessary after all. Once Russian troops started coming through into Scotland, much of *Espahneeyah Rassvet* could still be carried out. It wouldn't be quite as elegant, but it would serve its purpose.

Vorosilov's own destiny might still be in question, but that didn't matter as much as the success of the VBU plan. He hoped he could still be in on the final triumph.

Simple enough. All he had to do was live long enough to reach the submarine.

Hunter lay on the damp ground, peering into the eyepiece of the night scope. They'd left the Osa hidden in a narrow channel on the east coast of Mull that opened into the Firth of Lorn. Their midnight hike had carried them across the lower flanks of a thousand-meter hill called Ben More to a position where they could look down into Mull Sound from less than two miles away.

Any locals in the area would be fleeing with tales of witchcraft and black magic, Hunter reflected. Jules Verne could not have written a stranger scene, with the black form of an injured sea monster lying close to the rocks of the shore, the coast and the water bathed in a harsh and eerie radiance unknown in an age of candles and oil lamps. Men worked on the submarine's steel decks, adding to the strange light with the sputtering glare of welding torches. The forward hatch the Rangers had seen before was open, serving as a temporary wharf. Hunter could see the surviving Osa tied up aft of the improvised dock, partly blocked from view by the Typhoon's conning tower. Russian seamen appeared to be transferring cargo from the missile boat to the sub.

Anderson touched Hunter's arm and pointed. The Ranger lieutenant shifted the night scope, and a VBU sentry came into focus. He could see several of them standing guard along the shore, carrying flashlights and AKMs. Other sentries maintained a watch over the waters of the sound from the sub's deck and conning tower.

"Well, there she is," Morgan said. "Now what?"

"I've seen enough," Hunter said. "Let's get back."

Two hours later the Rangers gathered in a circle around the Osa's chart table. "That's the plan," Hunter said. The words were blunt, without emotion. He had worked things out in his head during the hike back but still didn't like what he'd come up with.

"It's gonna be a bitch," Anderson said quietly.

"Why go in with a combat swimmer team?" Jones asked. "It'd be simpler if we didn't have to board the damned sub."

"Simpler, yeah," Hunter agreed. "But this'll be our only chance to get out of here." He looked up, searching faces. "Unless you guys want to take up fencing and try living as sixteenth-century gentlemen."

"If it doesn't work, that's what we'll have to do," Gomez observed.

Hunter steadied himself by leaning forward, his hands braced on top of the table. "I have to stress one point. We have a chance, a very small chance, of getting home. It all depends on Rachel . . . and on what she finds when we get her aboard. But . . ." He paused, letting that one word hang in the air for a moment. When he continued, he paced each word, hammering them home. "It is absolutely vital that we blow the VBU time gate. Nothing else matters, even if it means spending the rest of our lives sounding like Shakespeare: If we don't shut that gate down permanently, the Russians'll use it again."

"Maybe it'd be better to just blow the damn thing and run," Lynch said.

"*If* we can blow it," Gomez added. "We have one warhead . . . one chance. And it's going to have to be planted inside that open hatch for it to do any good."

"That's why we're sending swimmers in," Hunter said. "If we have the chance for some of us to get back to 2008, great."

Rachel's brow furrowed. "There's so much we don't know," she said. "Is the equipment damaged? Is it powered up? Can I set the coordinates from memory?"

"You can do it, Raye," Hunter said softly. "We'll buy you the time, and you do what you have to."

"You realize, of course, that I'm drawing hazardous duty pay after this," she said.

They laughed, the tension broken, but Hunter continued to wrestle a gnawing doubt.

There were only ten of them . . . too few for an all-out frontal assault on the Typhoon. Hunter was forced to dispassionately consider each one in the group as a military asset, a *thing* to be used to accomplish the mission.

But people were not impersonal things, and they never acted like it in battle. Hunter was faced with a command problem for which there was no easy answer. Small, elite military units such as a Ranger Team—or Morgan's SEALs, or one of Jones's Marine Recon units—worked only because each person in them knew his own job and knew that each of his teammates knew his. Such squads relied on trust, on mutual, long-term respect. It was dangerous, Hunter knew, throwing so many individuals together this way and expecting them to work smoothly as a unit.

Unfortunately, there was no other choice. He'd been worried about Morgan, but the ex-SEAL seemed to be meshing smoothly with the rest of the team. When Hunter had told him his part in the plan, he'd accepted it without question, even though it might have been more logical to include him with the swimmers.

Rachel was the unknown who troubled him most. She seemed okay now, despite her weeks of imprisonment. But so much was riding on her, on her being able to carry out her task, to make the right decisions at the right time.

Hunter had fretted about that one for hours, turning at last to Greg King. "Can I trust her?" Hunter had asked when they were alone.

King had laughed. "Trust her? God damn it, Lieutenant! That girl went through hell, and she's still up and swinging!" He'd sobered. "Yeah. She's solid, Lieutenant. We can depend on her, no matter what."

That had decided the matter, but Hunter was still troubled. *If Greg is wrong . . .*

Twenty

Two hours after the last preparations aboard the Osa, Rachel waded into the ink-dark waters of Mull Sound, her face and hands blackened with grease paint, an AKM slung across her back. Despite the fact that it was August, the water was frigid. Her clothing clung to her body unpleasantly as she leaned forward and began a gentle sidestroke that carried her along the curve of the shore.

There was a tiny splash to her right, farther from the shore. She knew it was Tony Carlucci, though she couldn't see him in the darkness.

The seven people assigned as combat swimmers were organized into two groups. Hunter, Anderson, Gomez, Jones, and Lynch were in Team One, several hundred yards ahead by now. Rachel, with Carlucci as escort, was Team Two. Somewhere on the night-shrouded hill to her left, Dark Walker was doing what he did best, laying in ambush with his Galil rifle and the Rangers' night scope. Morgan was aboard the Osa behind the point of land that formed the northeast corner of Mull, while the blinded King waited on the crest of a ridge with a radio.

Rachel didn't like having so much of the plan depend on her. She still felt shaky after her weeks as a prisoner. It was as though she were somehow incomplete. Would she be able to do what Travis was asking of her?

Surprisingly, the knowledge that she would be facing the Russians in a few moments steadied her. It was strange, she thought, that only now she was realizing that the battle she'd been fighting for years was not with the Russians, but with herself. Russians she could handle. Her own fears and self-doubt were something else . . . but now that she knew them to be her real enemy, she thought she could face them.

Her heart pounded with anticipation. She *would* face them . . . now. . . .

Hunter moved through the water with a steady breaststroke. He could see the Typhoon now, looming monstrous against the glare of the work lights. Team One was approaching the sub's bow. From his fish's vantage point, the Soviet vessel looked like a black steel cliff rising from the water, vast and threatening. He could hear the muffled thump of cargo being unloaded, the low voices of sentries walking the forward deck. Somewhere overhead, someone laughed.

He touched the cold steel of the submarine's hull, slick with a scum of marine growth. Treading water, he waited as the other Rangers caught up with him. he found himself holding his breath. There was enough light scattering from the work area here that an accidental scrape of gun butt on metal would raise an immediate alarm, and black faces and silent swimming would not help them then.

The men around him were sensed more than seen, shadows against darkness. Hunter began swimming again, moving toward the dock.

Up close, Hunter could see how the Soviets had actually cut away a portion of the sub's hull, hinging the section at the bottom to allow it to drop down and lock horizontally just above the water's surface. He could see into the sub's interior now, could see the double-hull structure that made the Typhoon-class submarines so difficult to kill. By cutting through both hulls, the designers had sacrificed some protection. Though the panel would be closed when the vessel was under way, the design certainly must restrict the depth to which the Typhoon could submerge. That wouldn't be a problem, Hunter reflected. With no sonar to worry about, deep dives simply weren't necessary in 1588. Nuclear-powered, large, well-armored, it was the perfect mobile base for VBU operations in this century.

He touched the black hull again. He could clearly see the men on the dock section now, less than twenty yards ahead, their boots less than two feet above the water. The light spilling from the open hatch was dazzling, and Hunter felt nakedly exposed. If one of the Russians even glanced in his direction . . .

But we're committed now. Grimly, he continued stroking. The range narrowed to ten yards . . . to five. He could hear one of the Russian sentries standing above him now, telling an elaborate and obviously dirty story to his companion. Beyond them, Hunter could see four more men unloading crates from the damaged Osa, which was moored against the sub's hull aft of the dock. Another guard stood inside the open hatch, silhouetted against the light. More sentries paced restlessly on the open deck above.

In a move carefully rehearsed with the others earlier, Hunter stopped and let himself submerge. Underwater, he slipped the AKM from his shoulder, then allowed himself to surface slowly. A hand touched his arm . . . then another. One by one, the four other men in Team One slipped past, each touching him in turn. He could see four heads now, silhouetted against the light reflected from the water as they approached the dock.

For at least the hundredth time, Hunter wondered if he'd made the right decision about Morgan. This was the sort of op the SEAL was trained for. But Doug Morgan knew the captured Osa better than any of them, and Hunter wanted a sure hand at the missile boat's helm when the time came.

The four heads were gathered now immediately below the dock. Hunter raised the assault rifle from the water, careful not to splash. All of them carried AKMs picked up in the battle at the cove near Plymouth, a precaution made necessary by the salt water swim. While short immersions didn't usually affect American firearms, this was one time when they couldn't afford a fouled weapon. Soviet AKs were virtually indestructible. You could drop the things in the mud, thumb the receiver clear of gunk, and open fire with almost no chance of a jam.

He saw an arm snake up out of the water, the hand closing on a sentry's ankle. There was a shout as the guard's arms pinwheeled against the light.

Hunter squeezed the trigger. Despite the weapon's legend of invulnerability, he felt relief when the rifle blazed, sending a burst over the heads of the swimmers and into the Russians on the dock. Recoil drove him down, and he spat cold salt water.

A splash from just ahead marked a VBU sentry's plummet off the dock. *"Amerikahnets!"* someone yelled. *"Strelyat! Strelyat!"*

Gunfire burst wildly from the upper deck of the submarine, and geysers tracked across the surface of the water in jittering, choppy bursts. Lynch was half onto the dock now, his AK spraying VBU soldiers only a few feet away.

Hunter held his rifle high and kicked out, managing a clumsy, one-handed stroke toward the dock. Another Russian fell with a splash, as Jones hoisted himself from the water, his AKM snapping at the enemy.

Now, Hunter thought. *Now, Walker . . . !*

•

Five hundred yards away, Dark Walker rolled away from the night scope and took up his Galil. There had been some discussion as to whether the starlight scope could be mounted to his rifle, but in the end he'd vetoed the idea. There hadn't been enough time to sight in a new scope mount, and he was familiar with the sights he already had. He raised the rifle to his cheek, drawing down on a sentry standing on the submarine's forward deck. Five hundred yards should be just about right. . . .

He squeezed the trigger. An instant later, the target staggered, then pitched forward, his assault rifle spinning into the water. *Got him!*

Walker tracked left. He could make out the flash of auto fire on the conning tower bridge, a VBU trooper spraying the dock. He fired, paused to check through the night scope, then fired again. He couldn't be certain he'd hit the target, but the flashes of AK fire from the bridge had stopped.

Squinting through the night scope again, Walker thumbed the button on his radio. The device was small and short-ranged, part of the equipment he'd worn through the portal back at Guantánamo. "Action begun," he said.

"Copy," King's voice replied in his ear.

King would relay the message to Morgan aboard the Osa on the far side of the ridge. He saw another flurry of movement near the base of the submarine's conning tower, VBU troopers racing onto the deck with assault rifles at the ready. He shouldered the Galil again and began squeezing off single shots.

The Dakota warrior guessed that he had at least another minute before his targets figured out where the deadly sniper fire was coming from.

Meanwhile, he would kill Russians.

On board the Osa, Morgan heard King's voice over the radio. *"It's started, Doug."*

He'd already heard the distant crackle of auto fire, but the radio message was a necessary backup. It was impossible to know in advance how well sound would carry. He checked his watch. "Copy," he said. "The clock is running."

Ten minutes, he thought. *Ten minutes to doomsday.*

Hunter scrabbled for a handhold on the edge of the dock, then dragged himself clear of the water. Anderson extended a hand and helped him up. There were bodies on the metal platform, sprawled in pooling blood. The other Rangers scattered across the dock area. There was a cry from the upper deck, and an AKM clattered down the sloping curve of the submarine's hull and splashed in the water nearby, followed a moment later by a dead VBU trooper.

Thanks, Walker. He hadn't heard the shot. The Indian was giving Team One the time it needed to get on board the submarine.

Hurriedly, he checked his watch. They should have ten minutes now.

Gunfire spat from astern. He spun, crouching, his AKM cracking off a rapid-fire burst. Gunmen aboard the damaged Osa cut loose with a long, chattering volley. Splashes chopped at the water, and ricochets sang from the metal platform. Hunter fired again, aiming for the flashes. He caught a glimpse of Lynch, briefly illuminated by the light from inside the sub, racing forward, cocking his arm, letting fly. . . .

"*Grenade!*" the Green Beret yelled. A pair of seconds later, an orange flash lit the superstructure of the Osa, and a savage boom made the surface of the water shiver. Hunter ducked as fragments rained from the sky around him, then dashed for the cover of the submarine's hull.

"Nice toss!" he snapped as he passed Lynch

"Struck 'em out," the soldier replied. Hunter saw the man's easy grin as he pulled another grenade from his combat harness. "Now the fun begins."

Before he could reply, Hunter felt a shudder of sound and movement through his boots, heard the grating creak of machinery. He staggered a little as the dock platform began lifting from the water, grinding up toward the Typhoon's hull.

The open hatch was closing, with the Rangers still on it!

"Do it!"

Just inside the open hatchway, a massive drum mounted on brackets against the inner hull ground slowly around, hauling at a length of steel cable. That cable fed through gasket-sealed eyes and attached to the corners of the platform like the chains on a drawbridge. As the winch turned, the hatch closed.

Gary Lynch was already nestling the grenade between the cable and the winch. As the motor continued to grind, the cable closed over the grenade, effectively securing it tight against the drum under a steel coil.

"Ready!" Lynch yelled.

"Ready!" Anderson answered from the other side of the hatch, where he had just finished the same process with another grenade on the second moving cable. Gunfire barked from inside the sub where the other Rangers were rushing the VBU defenders.

"Now!" Hunter yelled. "Yank 'em and run!"

Lynch pulled the pin on the grenade as the rotating drum brought it up and around. "Fire in the hole!"

Anderson, Lynch, and Hunter raced back into the night air. Hunter took three long steps and launched himself headfirst into the water, counting to himself as he plunged into cold blackness. *Three . . . two . . . one . . .*

The explosions boomed out an instant later, two dull, heavy pulses of sound hammering at his ears through the water. Hunter broke the surface and began paddling back toward the sub. The lights were out now. Somewhere inside, gunfire mingled with the eerie whoop of an alarm.

He clambered back onto the dock platform. As planned, the grenades had jammed it open, one cable split, the other frozen in place by a fouled winch. He helped Anderson out of the water, then stood a moment, both arms extending above his head.

On the hillside, Dark Walker saw Hunter's signal through the night scope. The platform was locked open, leaving the submarine helpless.

He keyed his transmitter. "They've done it," he said. "The door is open!"

"Copy," King said. *"I'll pass it on."*

Movement caught his eye, dragged his gaze away from the sub and to the left, where low, scraggly bushes clung to the slope. *Here we go,* he thought.

"They're on to me, Greg," he said. "I'm going to be busy. Walker out."

He raised his rifle, holding the sights on the shadows where he'd seen motion. *No more targets on the sub anyway,* he thought. *Now it's up to them. . . .*

Soviet troopers rushed from the darkness and Dark Walker opened fire.

The alarm sirens blasted their raucous keening through the submarine's gray passageways. Gomez leaned back against the bulkhead as he snapped a fresh magazine into his AKM and exchanged nods with Jones. The big marine flashed Gomez a grin, then rolled around the corner of the passageway, his assault rifle hammering out three single shots. The noise was deafening within the enclosed, steel-walled corridor. Gomez followed Jones. A pair of bodies in naval uniforms lay sprawled beside a watertight door, testimony to the accuracy of Jones's fire.

"That's it, Gunny," Gomez said. He could hear excited voices beyond the door, muffled shouts of "They come!" in Russian.

Jones put one hand on the heavy wheel set into the center of the door and tried turning it. "Damn!" he said. "They've dogged it!"

There were a dozen points in the op where the unforeseen

or the unfortunate could foul up the whole mission, and this was one of the big ones. The Rangers had not known what kind of doors the time-portal room would have but had to assume that the Russians used the sub's original construction where possible.

Gomez ran his hand over the steel surface. This had probably been the original watertight door leading into the sub's missile-tube room, though he could see signs of hasty or sloppy re-welding. The launch tubes had been pulled, but the bulkheads and fittings were the same, rugged and solidly built. The three-quarter-inch steel was designed to be sealed shut in case of flooding, and it was more than strong enough to stand up to grenades or ordinary munitions. The Rangers had hoped they could reach the door before some bright young Russian thought to close and latch it.

That much of the plan had failed.

"I don't see a doorbell," Jones said, scowling at the barrier. "Looks like you get your bang, Eddie."

Gomez gave his best imitation of a maniac's grin. The Hispanic Ranger's penchant for demolitions work—his love of what he called "nice bangs"—was a running joke with the Ranger team.

"Here's just what the doctor ordered," Gomez said, setting a canvas satchel on the deck and removing the RPG warhead they'd taken from the *Princessa*. He'd completed work on it the day before, separating the grenade from the motor-fuse assembly and priming it with the wad of plastique and length of detcord he carried in his pocket. Now he attached a fuse igniter. It would have taken several kilos of high explosive to breach this door, but the shaped-charge warhead would penetrate easily.

Working carefully, he wedged the rocket head into the locking wheel in the center of door, securing it in place with a length of electrical tape. The entire process took only seconds, with Jones scanning the passageway for signs of movement. So far, the assault seemed to have left the sub's crew stunned. That wouldn't last long.

"Ready!" Gomez said. "Hit the dirt, if you can find any."

"I'm way ahead of you, man!" Jones slipped back around the corner. Gomez waited until the marine was clear, then yanked the fuse igniter's pin. A telltale wisp of smoke curled from the fuse, and Gomez sprinted for the end of the passageway.

"How long do we have, Eddie?" Jones's voice was tense, a harsh whisper.

"I cut the fuse for ten seconds, but it won't be exact. I had to guestimate the . . ."

The explosion was deafening in the metal-walled, enclosed space and set the submarine's hull ringing. Gomez and Jones made their way back to the door, probing the thick and acrid smoke with their AKMs.

The grenade's shaped charge had blown the locking wheel out of the door, leaving a ragged, gaping hole in the center. The dogging latches had been unseated and the hinges sprung; Jones slammed a foot against the door and it sagged inward.

Gunfire spat from the smoke-filled interior of the room, and something yowled off the steel door in a searing ricochet. Jones ducked, bringing his AKM up. The marine fired once . . . twice . . . then pushed ahead, stepping over the foot-high sill of the open door and dropping into a shoulder roll to the left across the shiny deck, just in case the enemy was waiting with an automatic weapon trained on the opening. Gomez followed, cutting to the right.

The blast must have stunned the defenders, for the two attackers were not met by machine gun fire as they rose, weapons tracking. The room was huge, far larger than anything Gomez had expected to find aboard a submarine . . . even a sub as big as the Typhoon. Curving steel walls appeared to dwindle into the distance. The room had once housed twenty missile tubes arrayed two-by-two. Now it was filled with computer consoles and the wire guts of complex electronic systems. The ceiling was low, slabs of white insulation paneling hung with fluorescent light tubes.

And there were men. . . .

Gomez had a blurred impression of a spetsnaz trooper raising a wZ63, a wicked little Polish machine pistol with a snap-down front handgrip and a pistol-butt magazine feed like an Uzi's. He swung his AKM up and triggered a burst. The Polish chattergun ripped off a high-speed burst of flame and metal that chewed into the insulation panels in the ceiling, as the soldier tumbled backward over a chair.

Jones's captured assault rifle spoke again, still in precise, single shots. Another spetsnaz trooper clawed at his face as it turned bloody, dropping the familiar VBU Skorpion machine pistol with its heavy, silenced barrel. A third Soviet bolted and ran for the far end of the room and began frantically turning a locking wheel on another watertight door. Jones's deadly fire tracked him, slamming him into cold steel.

That one wore a white coat . . . a technician, Gomez decided. Another cowered behind a bank of instruments across the room, only the top of his face showing.

"Watch it," Gomez warned as Jones raised his rifle. "Don't ding the equipment!"

"Hey, you!" Jones bellowed. "*Zdavahetees'*! Surrender!"

In answer, the technician jumped suddenly, both hands folded around the grip of a 9mm Makarov. Gomez and Jones fired together, the rounds smashing the Russian back into a steel bulkhead.

The room was suddenly very quiet except for the ominous, low-throated hum of electrical equipment. There was a sharp tingle in the air, a metallic taste like ozone, and Gomez felt the hair at the base of his neck standing on end. With time now to look, he saw more computer consoles and monitor displays, wiring like clumps of braided spaghetti snaking across the deck, massive busbars and power conduits that gave the steel-walled room the atmosphere of Dr. Frankenstein's laboratory.

At the far end of the room, near the second door, a stage nearly ten feet long had been set up, the focus of the power buses and conduits. A blue haze of light shifted and crackled between upright strips of silver metal, an auroral glow that told Gomez the Russian time portal was operational.

"Oh, shit!" he said. "They've got the damn thing up and running!"

Twenty-one

Hunter crouched beside Anderson and Lynch, trying to watch all directions at once. The broad gap in the Typhoon's hull opened onto a passageway, with the inside bulkhead walling off what had once been the sub's missile room. Entrance was gained by following the passageway around the room to either end. Several Russian sailors and naval spetsnaz had been killed in those approaches; how many more were lurking in unchecked rooms or blind corners was unknown.

At least the submarine's upper deck was clear now. What would their next move be, and how long did the Rangers have? Not long, Hunter guessed. The Soviets would be mustering some sort of countermove at that moment.

Running footsteps sounded on the metal deck, and Hunter swung, still crouched, his AKM seeking a target.

"Yankee!" Jones's rasped exclamation was the unit's password. "Don't shoot! I'm coming in!"

"Come on!" Hunter replied, but he kept his weapon ready. The marine appeared around the far corner above Hunter's gun sights, and he looked worried.

"The portal chamber's secure," he said breathlessly. "But power's on and it's up and running! Gomez is watching it, but . . ."

"But we could be neck-deep in time-traveling Russians any time," Hunter said. They'd faced this situation before. There was no way to know how long the temporal lock had been established, no way to know how long it would be before VBU reinforcements started coming through from the future. When they did, Hunter's tiny force of Rangers would quickly be overwhelmed. "Right," he said. "Get back and keep watch with Gomez. I'll bring in Team Two."

The faster we get this over with . . .

He sprinted to the end of the submarine's dock, faced toward the bow, and extended his arms to either side. Somewhere in the darkness, he heard a splash.

C'mon, Raye, he thought. He was sweating now, though the evening was cool and he was still wet from his swim. They were rapidly running out of time. *We need you at those controls, fast!*

Kapitan-leytenant Voznesensky—his rank corresponded to that of a U.S. Navy lieutenant commander—saluted the KGB major. His left shoulder was heavily bandaged and the arm in a sling, making the movement stiff and painful. He gave his report in crisp, concise statements, neither elaborating upon nor hiding the events of the past few downtime days.

Major Andryanov's eyes widened as he heard that the *Moryeh Ohotnik* himself was under attack. "The Americans!" Andryanov said, his voice a harsh whisper. "They are aboard the submarine . . . now?"

"Now," of course, was a relative term. Voznesensky accepted it as he knew it was meant. "*Da*, Comrade Major. When I left, a small team had seized the fold-out dock."

"How many spetsnaz troops are left aboard *Ohotnik*?"

"Not many. Five . . . perhaps ten. Only two were in the time-gate chamber as I left . . . Lieutenant Simonov and one trooper. Simonov feared an attack on the control center at any moment."

"Well he should," Andryanov said. "If what I fear is true, we have faced *these* time commandos before!"

Voznesensky swallowed hard. He was—had been—boat captain of *Krasnoyarsk Komsomolets*, squadron leader of the four Osa IIs transported back in time as part of Operation *Espahneeyah Rassvet*. He'd been wounded in the sharp, brutal firefight with one of his own boats, Morzov's *Sverdlovsk Komsomolets*. Obviously that vessel had been captured by the American time commandos. The battered *Krasnoyarsk* had only barely made it to the primary rendezvous with the Typhoon.

And now they were being attacked again by these same commandos.

The Soviet naval officer looked around the room. Uralskiy Station was a massive base, buried far beneath the sandstone slopes of a mountain on the rugged frontier between Siberia and Europe. The facilities here were similar to those aboard the *Moryeh Ohotnik*, but vaster by far, with a monstrous transport stage that could transport platoons of soldiers at a time. The blue light wavered and swam like rippling sheets of glass between the power-charged uprights . . . a few steps and 420 years from a submarine resting in the waters of a Scottish sound.

"What shall we do then, Comrade Major?" Voznesensky was thinking of his men, the ones who were left, the handful of sailors who had helped him manhandle the limping *Krasnoyarsk Komsomolets* through the Irish Sea.

"We attack, of course." Andryanov paused, thoughtfully tugging at his lower lip. "The Americans must have more people trained for time operations than we believed possible. Perhaps they deduced our plan after losing their assault force in Cuba."

"They could have an army in 1588, Comrade Major, waiting for us!"

"I doubt that, Comrade. I know these Americans. They do not wish the shape of history twisted. Perhaps the force attacking *Ohotnik* is not so large after all . . . a few men . . ." Andryanov appeared to reach a decision. "Captain!" he yelled.

An officer with KGB collar tabs dropped the clipboard he was holding and hurried over. "*Da*, Comrade Major!"

"Grab as many armed men as you can . . . now! The sentries in this room, those outside, anyone with a weapon! Muster them and take them through . . . there!" He pointed toward the blue light.

The captain followed his gesture, a worried look on his face. "But Comrade Major . . . the KGB guards here have had no experience with . . . with *special* operations!"

"They won't need it. You will enter a command center similar to this but smaller. Secure it. Kill any American raiders you find. Try not to damage the equipment." He gave a wry smile. "We will need it to get you back."

The captain looked pale. "*Da*, Comrade Major."

"Don't worry, Captain. While you hold our base in the past, I will be marshaling an army to come to your aid."

"An army, Comrade Major?" Voznesensky asked. "What army?"

"Our reserve. Actually, it is only one Guards regiment, but it should be sufficient. We were holding them in case direct military intervention in Scotland was called for in this operation. Apparently, it has come to that." He shrugged, staring at the light. "But first, we must kill these interfering Americans and save our downtime base! *Now . . . !*"

The first VBU trooper stepped through the blue glow and into the submarine's time gate chamber holding his AKM at high port. Gomez was waiting, his rifle trained on the wavering sheets of light, his finger already closing on the trigger as the indistinct shape became solid. The second Russian soldier tripped over the body of the first. Jones fired as the man fell, killing him before he hit the deck.

Then it stopped being easy. The portal stage was wide enough for many soldiers to walk through at once, and Gomez could make out the shimmering forms of a dozen men or more materializing. "Watch it, Gunny!" he yelled. "They're mad now!"

He flicked his selector switch to full auto. The roar hammered in his ears as hot brass bounced across consoles and keyboards. Gunfire stabbed from the portal gate in response, gray-uniformed men yelling as they ran . . . and dying.

Gomez jerked back behind a console, fumbling for his last thirty-round magazine.

He rose again, aiming the assault rifle across the top of the sheltering console. The attackers were returning fire, but hesitantly, in single shots, evidently afraid of damaging the submarine's electronics. They continued to die and fall in the Americans' twin streams of lead, but there were so many of them. The unequal fight would not last for more than another few seconds.

His last magazine went dry. Desperately, Gomez looked

around the chamber. The nearest Soviet AKM lay ten feet away
and out in the open. It would be suicide to try for it, and the
Russians were spilling off the stage now. With a shock, Gomez
realized that Jones's weapon was silent now, presumably for
the same reason. He reached for the Sykes-Fairbairn sheathed
to his leg. . . .

A new volley of auto fire burst from behind him, snapping
into the advancing Russians and cutting them down. Gomez
dropped and rolled. Hunter, Anderson, and Lynch were plunging through the blown door, weapons blazing. ''Hey Gunny!''
he yelled. ''Here comes the cavalry!''

Jones didn't answer. He was slumped against an instrument
console, clutching at the red stain spreading across his shoulder
and chest.

Shit, Gomez thought. *Maybe for once the cavalry didn't
come in time. . . .*

Morgan opened the throttles and guided the Osa into deeper
water, giving the rocky headland to port a wide berth. Water,
overcast sky, and rocks mingled in impenetrable blackness.
Morgan didn't cut in the missile boat's spotlights. There was
no way of telling how many eyes might be watching, and even
a few extra seconds of surprise could help. He held his breath
as he rounded the point off to his left, a black mass against
blackness. All he needed now was to throw a prop on a submerged rock or run aground on an uncharted sandbar.

Then he caught a glimmer of light against the sky and beyond
the land. *There . . .* His hands turned the Osa's wheel. *That's
from the sub. I should be into the main part of the sound by
now.*

He centered the wheel and secured it, snagging its spokes
in loops of line attached to either side to keep the vessel moving
in a straight line. Certain that the Osa would maintain its present
course, he left the bridge, walking through an open hatchway
and hurrying aft toward one of the missile cannisters.

He could make out the missile's shape by the faint sheen of
light reflected from sky and water, but he used a small flashlight
from the Osa's tool locker to inspect the warhead. Gomez's
handiwork was easy to see. The demolitions expert had opened
an access port to the Styx's fuse assembly, and a tangle of

wires led now to a precarious-looking wooden framework tucked into the cannister next to the warhead. Morgan reached into the contraption and extracted a block of wood. The missile was now armed; a hard enough shock—a collision, say—would drive a set of battery contacts into an electrical trigger, unimpeded by the wooden plug.

Doug Morgan knew that the force of the resultant explosion would be enough to blow the Osa into fragments. The question was whether it would destroy the Typhoon. At least two of the Styx missiles they'd fired at the sub earlier had hit, and they hadn't been enough. It was Morgan's job to make sure the warhead was placed in the best possible spot to make certain of the job this time.

Again, he contemplated death.

According to the plan, he was to line up the Osa with the Typhoon's open cargo hatch, lash down the wheel, and dive overboard, letting the untended missile boat rocket into the opening in the sub's massive double hull. The message relayed by King told him the assault team had been successful in blocking the hatch open.

But Morgan knew how chancy the approach would be. A wave could bump the Osa off course, and anything less than a direct hit on the cargo hatch would be useless.

Worse was the thought of the people, his comrades, still on board.

Would they be able to capture the time machine and escape? There'd been no message from Walker or King on that point. That meant the battle was still going on, that they'd not been able to take over the VBU equipment or set their own coordinates . . . or Walker and King had been killed themselves. Maybe they were all dead.

He checked his watch. Only seven minutes remained.

Once before, the ex-SEAL had felt this kind of loneliness, back at Plymouth when Bob Short had bought it. He'd found a new camaraderie among these time Rangers, and he was about to guarantee the deaths of all of them. He didn't care to be the last Ranger survivor in this alien past.

Perhaps it would be better if he steered the speeding Osa directly into the submarine . . . a clean death for them all.

Grimly, he returned to the bridge, slipped off the lashings, and took the helm once more.

Rachel stepped into the submarine's time-gate chamber, instinctively ducking her head as stray rounds thunked into the insulation of the ceiling yards away. Smoke hung in the air like fog. Ahead, Hunter, Anderson, and Lynch were gunning down the last of a tangled huddle of Russian soldiers in front of the portal stage.

Carlucci was right at her heels.

"Here goes, Tony," she told the marine. "Curtain going up."

"You'll do fine, Miss Rachel," Carlucci grinned. "We're all behind you!"

Just what I need, she thought. *A cheering section instead of about three days to check out this junk!* Hunter waved to her from the far side of the chamber, and she managed a weak smile in response. *Oh Travis! I don't want to let you down!*

"Roy! See to Gunny!" Hunter stood in the middle of the aisle between the consoles, shouting orders. "Eddie! Tony! You two watch the platform and sing if they start coming through again! Gary! Watch the busted door!"

Rachel found the primary programming console and slipped into the seat. She ignored the bloody Russian body lying on the deck at her feet and concentrated on the Cyrillic letters glowing on the display monitor in front of her. Tentatively, she tapped at the keyboard, watching new words appear.

"Well, Raye?" Hunter asked at her side. "What do you think?"

"I . . . don't know." She felt a surging tide of inner panic. *I can't do it!*

Besides being an expert temporal programmer, Rachel was the team's expert on Russian time-gate technology. She'd led the technicians who had studied a captured VBU downlink in 1918 Siberia on an earlier mission.

But she didn't have a technical team here. There was only herself, and scant minutes to work in. Her Russian was less than fluent, limited to recognizing certain key words on the VBU computer display. She'd worked out the programming sequence for linking Russian portal gear to Time Square before, but . . .

She felt gentle pressure on her shoulder, knew that Hunter's hand was there. "You can do it, Raye."

The touch steadied her. She began pecking in the numbers for a coordinate change, desperately hoping she understood the sequence. Fortunately, she was being asked to change the spatial coordinates only. The Russian gate must already be linked to 2008. All she wanted to do was shift the downlink's lock from the Ural Mountains to a particular spot in Wyoming.

The numbers glared back at her from the screen. "I *think* that's it." She reached toward a key. "This should initiate the new programming. . . ."

"Incoming!" Gomez yelled. Auto fire thundered.

Hunter whirled away from Rachel's side, his AKM stuttering white flame. On the stage, more VBU troops were materializing.

Rachel's finger came down on the key. There was a ripple in the curtain of blue light as the gate's focus shifted, and a piercing, ear-grating shriek of agony. She looked up, her eyes wide with a new horror. A Russian soldier collapsed onto the platform, falling out of the light . . . or, rather, half of him did. Crimson blood geysered from arteries severed by the shift of the temporal field's interface.

Lynch put a mercy round into the screaming, writhing upper half of a man, and Rachel looked back to her console, shuddering.

New readings appeared there. She stared at them as she struggled to swallow the sour lump rising in her throat. The blue glow on the platform should now open into the Chronos Complex above Jackson Hole, Wyoming.

She hoped.

"We need full power!" Captain Nikolai Sergeivich Tyrin grimaced as he touched his shattered arm in its sling. The bleeding had stopped, but pain and loss of blood left him fuzzy-headed. That sniper in the darkness had come within a hand's breadth of ending Tyrin's career right there on the bridge. "We must get this vessel under way!"

"Reactor output has been diverted to the missile room, Captain," his engineering officer reminded him over the bridge intercom. "Missile room," of course, was the ship's euphemism for the time travel equipment located forward. "We cannot move until reactor output is available for engineering!"

"Stand by!" Tyrin turned to face a spetsnaz lieutenant. "You say you've lost all contact with your people forward?"

"*Da*, Captain! The Americans may have already occupied the gate chamber!"

"Then we needn't worry about pulling the plug!" He keyed the intercom again. "Very well, Pyotr! Switch full power back to engineering. Our passengers are finished with their toys forward!"

"Aye, Captain! Switching now . . ."

Rachel saw the shift in numbers on her display and realized that power to the VBU gate was dropping. There was a momentary dimming of the overhead lights.

She was technician enough to realize that someone was switching off the power supply from the submarine's two reactors to her console. They might lose all power in seconds, at the flick of a switch on the sub's engineering deck.

They hadn't counted on that.

There was no time to shout a warning, no time to do anything except act. Rachel was up and racing across the deck almost before the lights stabilized after the first flicker. She crashed into Hunter, knocking him aside, then bounded up two metal steps and onto the platform. Gray-clad bodies sprawled everywhere. Her foot came down in a puddle of gore surrounding what was left of that last Russian attacker, slipped, pitching her forward. She recovered and plunged toward the glow.

"Raye . . . !"

Hunter's voice came from very far away. Time itself had taken on a curious, dreamlike quality. She was aware of Hunter, rising, shouting . . . could hear the dwindling hum of the chamber's power coil, feel an odd, twisting sensation as the field interface began its collapse. All the things that could have gone wrong flashed through her mind . . . if the coordinates were off . . . if the field collapsed before her headlong plunge could carry her through . . .

If . . . !

Twenty-two

The blue glow snapped off as though it had never been. The room lights dimmed, then came back up to normal, but every one of the consoles and display panels was dead. Hunter realized he was shaking as he stepped up onto the platform, studying the mangled bodies lying there. Had Raye . . . ?

After the horrible death of that last VBU trooper, he more than half expected to see her legs, left behind when the time field snicked off. It had been that close. . . .

But there was nothing. *No!* He stooped and picked up a fragment of leather. It might be a piece of the sole of a combat boot. Rachel's? Or did it belong to the shredded corpse at his feet? There was no way to know. Perhaps she'd made it after all.

Or had she panicked? He remembered the wild look in her eyes as she'd shoved him aside. His thoughts returned to the doubts he'd had about her, his talk with King.

No! That wasn't panic! Only now was the enormity of what Rachel had done sinking in. She must have guessed that the Russians were cutting power, guessed that in another second the time gate would be closed. With no time to argue, no time even to give warning, she had dived through headfirst, knowing that she might well suffer the fate of that last VBU trooper.

Or worse. She couldn't know the new coordinates were accurate, either. Hunter closed his eyes. She might have mater-

ialized out in the Wyoming wilderness, or half a mile above
the ground, or far out at sea. . . .

No time to think about it now. "C'mon, men! Time to pull
out!" He glanced at his watch. Morgan would be making his
approach by now. "Blow what you can and move!"

Their first responsibility was still the destruction of the VBU
downlink. If Morgan's attack with the Osa failed, they could
at least make certain that the Russian equipment was smashed.
Grenades sailed through the chamber, clattering across consoles
and power leads. Explosions filled the chamber with shrill
thunder as they ducked through the door into the passageway.

"Hurry!" Anderson yelled from outside. "The Osa's coming! For God's sake, hurry!"

Tyrin squeezed through the hatch onto the conning-tower
bridge. The lookout extended one arm, pointing, and the submarine captain saw the luminous bow wake of the approaching
boat. He felt the shudder of *Ohotnik*'s props as they began to
churn the water astern. Slowly, majestically, the great submarine began to move.

"Get someone on board the *Krasnoyarsk Komsomolets*!" he
snapped to his deck officer. "Manual control! Blast the Osa!"

Morgan gripped the spokes of the Osa's wheel tighter as he
peered forward into the night. Spray off the missile boat's bow
splattered across what was left of the windshield, cutting visibility even further. Wind shrilled through missing windows.
He could make out the light spilling from the Typhoon's open
cargo hatch and moved the helm over just enough to bring the
opening directly ahead.

Water geysered with a thunderous roar alongside the racing
Osa. He became aware of a tiny, rapidly strobing flash of light
to the right of his target and realized that the Soviet Osa moored
there was firing at him. So much for surprise, he thought. The
speeding vessel shuddered, lurching hard to port. He brought
the bow back in line . . . then another blast savaged the captured
missile boat. A wall of foam and water broke across the mangled bow, drenching the SEAL as he clung to the wheel.

God! His thoughts flashed to the armed Styx in its portside
cannister. A hit from that 30mm cannon ahead could detonate

it, ending the attack right there. Explosions bracketed the Osa close alongside, threatening to shred the hurtling missile boat with concussion alone.

Had the Rangers gotten off the target? His eyes flicked to the silent radio, then back to the target. There was no helping it now. He was committed.

All he could do was ensure that his comrades had not died in vain.

"Out! Out! Out!" Hunter yelled, waving his men past him. Anderson staggered past with the unconscious Jones slung across his back in a fireman's carry. Rapid-fire flashes stabbed against the night from the Osa's bow gun, tracking the dimly seen mustache of a bow wake far out in Mull Sound. He could feel the pulsing vibrations of the submarine's engines as it got under way.

Carlucci! Hunter looked around the cargo platform, urgency hammering in his chest. He hadn't seen the other marine go past. Where . . . ?

There! A spotlight snapped on from the bridge of the submarine, silhouetting Tony Carlucci's form as he vaulted onto the deck of the Soviet Osa. Hunter saw him pulling the pin from a grenade.

Machine gun fire spat from the submarine's conning tower, lashing past the searchlight and lancing through the marine's body. Hunter twisted, bringing his AKM up, triggering a long burst from the weapon that shattered the light and chopped into the dark shadows behind it. There was a scream, and the sound of something metallic clattering down the side of the sub.

Carlucci swayed on the Osa's deck, the grenade still clutched in his hand. The sub began grinding forward, and the missile boat, still moored to its side, lurched, nearly throwing the marine to the deck. Somehow he recovered. By the light from the cargo hatch, Hunter saw the man stagger through a door in the Osa's deckhouse.

Seconds later there was a flash, and a savage detonation that blew out the missile boat's ports and lit the interior with fire. The autocannon fell silent, the barrels snapping up, uselessly trained on the sky. Flame licked from behind the bridge, casting a dazzling glare across the waves. Carlucci's grenade must have ignited combustibles on board, a paint locker, possibly, or a store of ammo. Hunter didn't stay to watch but took five running steps and dived into the water.

Walker's battle was over, the last of the Russian perimeter guards gunned down in a series of sharp, savage firefights in the darkness of the hillside above Mull Sound. From his vantage point, he watched a pillar of flame light the sub and the waters of the sound for a hundred yards around. The Typhoon was moving now. He could make out the wake churned up by its propellers. The burning Osa suddenly broke free of its huge guardian, though he couldn't tell whether that was because of the fire or someone cutting its lines. The cargo hatch was still open, dragging at the waves.

Morgan's missile boat hurtled forward into the circle of illumination from the fire, water spraying past its bow. Walker saw it shift slightly to anticipate the submarine's forward motion.

Jump, Walker thought. *Jump . . . !*

The speeding vessel struck the Typhoon squarely on the platform, skipped into the air, and plunged like an arrow into the nuclear submarine's open hull. The explosion was shattering, a blaze of light spearing across the Sound followed seconds later by the rumbling boom of the detonation. The first blast was followed moments later by another . . . and another, as fuel tanks or stored ammo contributed their pent-up thunder to the rolling fireball scouring the night sky.

Incredibly, the Typhoon continued moving, turning a slow, almost leisurely circle now into the middle of the Sound. Walker suspected that the ship's captain must have been killed. Perhaps the rudders had been jammed in a port turn . . . or perhaps the helm was simply waiting for an order that never came.

An oil slick was spreading from behind the conning tower as fuel reserves for the Osas poured through ruptured seams. As the sub turned, Walker could see that it was listing heavily to port, the open cargo hatch dragging beneath the water. Inner bulkheads must have given way, and watertight doors must have sprung.

Another explosion lit the night from the burning Osa. The

oil slick took flame from the blast, and in a moment the water was covered by leaping, searing flames. The Typhoon wallowed, slowing now, its conning tower leaning at a forty-five–degree angle as the bow began the long plunge into the cold, deep blackness of Mull Sound.

Silently, Walker stood, staring at the spectacle of the dying ship. Distantly, he heard screams floating above the roar of the flames. Some of the submarine's crew, at least, had abandoned ship . . . and were burning now in that inferno.

He wondered if any of the Rangers could possibly have lived. Grimly, he slung his Galil and started hiking up the slope. He would find King, then go down to the beach and look for survivors.

I wonder how many got away. Hunter staggered onto the rocky beach and collapsed, utterly spent. His desperate swim against the undertow from the submarine's propellers as the night around him dissolved in flame had left him exhausted.

But alive. How many others had made it?

He heard the click of pebbles scuffed by boots and opened his eyes. Anderson grinned down at him with a nightmarish face streaked with oil and camo paint. "Glad you're still with us, LT."

Hunter struggled to sit up. "Roy! Did the others . . . ?" He saw Gary Lynch and Gomez crouched behind the Texan, bandaging Jones's shoulder.

"No sign of Doug," Anderson said softly. "The rest of us made it, but . . ."

"Maybe he didn't want to make it." Hunter remembered Bob Short and the bleak look in Morgan's eyes when his friend died. "I wonder if he ever really thought of himself as part of the team," he said. Then he thought of Rachel's dive through the closing portal. Was Morgan's suicidal attack any less of a sacrifice . . . *for the team*? "On the other hand, maybe he did. Maybe that's what he died for."

Slowly, with Anderson's help, he got to his feet. In the waters of the sound, the fire slowly died. Of the submarine, of either Osa, there was no sign.

"Looks like we're really shipwrecked this time, Roy," he said. They were as badly off now as they had been after the destruction of Guantánamo. Their weapons, ammo, and some supplies were cached on the other side of the headland, but they were stranded on a sparsely populated island now with no way of getting off.

"Rachel'll come through for us, LT."

Hunter closed his eyes. "Yeah. Right." If she had made it back to Time Square. He didn't want to think about her chances.

"You don't sound convinced." Hunter whirled at King's voice. The master sergeant stood a few yards behind him, his eyes still bandaged. "I told you, she's solid. She'll be back and with the whole damn army."

"Greg! How'd you get here?" The rocky, brush-strewn hillside would have been impossible for a blind man to navigate.

"Walker brought me down. He heard something and went to investigate."

"Where . . ." Hunter paused as Dark Walker materialized out of the night. He was supporting another man, dripping wet and oil-covered.

Another Ranger. "Doug!"

Morgan grinned weakly as Walker let him slip to the ground. "You guys weren't planning on running off without me, were you?"

Hunter questioned Morgan about his escape from the fiery crash, but the SEAL would say very little. From what he was able to gather, Hunter decided that Morgan had jumped at the last possible instant . . . and only when he'd glimpsed the Rangers on the submarine leaping into the water. It suggested that the Navy man had been unwilling to live after causing the deaths of the other Rangers.

Perhaps Morgan had found a home with Freedom's Rangers after all.

Hours passed, until the east lit with the first pale smudge of dawn against a leaden, overcast sky. The fire in the sound died away completely. Some bodies on the shore burned beyond recognition and a few scraps of unidentifiable debris adrift on the water were all that remained of the VBU vessels.

"Do you think Rachel got through?" Jones asked. He was lying on the beach, his feet propped up on a rock. "Is anyone gonna find us?"

"She made it," Hunter replied. "Remember, it'll take time

to figure out the coordinates for this island. Hell, I don't know how accurately they can open up a portal to 1588 based just on what she was able to carry in her head. It may take a while, but she'll come through.''

Jones chuckled softly. ''Seems strange for time travelers to be worrying about running out of time. . . .''

Hunter grinned, masking the worry he felt. The marine had lost a lot of blood and was desperately weak. They needed to evac him to a better hospital than sixteenth-century Scotland could provide. King's eyes needed treatment. And the rest of them . . . How long could they sit here, waiting? Suppose Rachel's best guess opened the portal from Time Square, say, sometime in the middle of next week? Suppose . . .

No. If anyone can do it, Rachel can! She's part of this team too!

''Lieutenant!''

He looked up at Anderson's shout. There, on the hillside above them, a blue haze was shimmering against the gray dawn. Shadows materialized within the light. . . .

Then Rachel was there as Hunter stumbled forward. He scarcely noticed General Thompson or the squad of troops from Time Square deploying across the slope. He took Rachel in his arms, pressing her close, his lips searching for hers.

''I knew you'd make it,'' he said.

Epilogue

Hunter stood on the northern coast of Ireland, looking out to sea. Rain lashed him, wind-driven by the gale thundering down across the waters of the North Channel. It was October of 1588, nearly three months after the battle on Mull. He was standing on the headland near the rocky beach known as the Giant's Causeway, not far from the brooding, cliff-top towers of Dunluce Castle.

He was here to keep a date with history.

He felt a touch at his side. Rachel was there, hair plastered across her face, water streaming down her cheeks. Hunter jerked his head toward the patch of blue radiance above the rocks a few yards away. "You should get inside," he said. "Out of the rain."

"And miss this?" Her tone was bantering, but there was a sadness in her eyes.

"I'd miss it," Hunter said softly. "If I had the choice."

"We have our part to play in the history books, Travis," she said. "We're part of the past, too, like it or not."

"I just wish there were another way."

The relationship between history as they remembered it and their own actions was still not well understood, but they were learning. After their rescue from Mull, they'd returned to Time Square and learned what history had to say about Philip of Spain and his Grand Armada.

Drake and Howard had played their parts harrying the Spanish up the Channel, of course, but the Armada's real enemy proved to be the weather. After the Battle of the Gravelines on August 8, the fleet had turned north, driven by winds that now prevented them from approaching England. The winds grew worse. Storms broke the Invincible Armada into smaller flotillas scattered across the North Sea . . . then into individual squadrons and isolated ships. All thought of an English landing was abandoned. Now they beat north along the Scottish coast, seeking to reach not England but home.

Of 134 ships, as many as thirty were sunk or driven to pieces on the coasts of Scotland or Ireland. Thousands of Spanish soldiers drowned. Thousands more clambered ashore, only to be hung by English troops or murdered and stripped by half-savage tribes lurking in the hills above the wind-torn bays and rocks. It was a disaster of unparalleled magnitude. Protestantism was safe, the independence of the Netherlands assured, England triumphant, and Spanish dreams shattered.

In the Chronos Facility's historical library, Hunter had learned something more about the end of the Spanish Armada. The Duke of Medina-Sidonia, aboard his battered *San Martín*, had made it safely back to Spain, where he would eventually die in disgrace. But his most illustrious lieutenant had been lost in the storms off the Irish coast . . . the young and dashing Don Alonzo de Leyva.

The story of de Leyva's trials after the Armada's defeat read like fiction, too fantastic for reality. Sheltering from the storm in Blacksod Bay off Ballycroy in western Ireland, de Leyva's *Rata Encoronada* had been driven ashore, but the Russian and most of his men had managed to reach another ship, the *Santa Ana*, that was anchored in a cove nearby.

De Leyva had then made a remarkable decision, to turn north again in a desperate attempt to reach Scotland. The history books suggested he hoped to reach a neutral kingdom from which he could eventually reach the continent, but Hunter had read those words with the chill certainty that the VBU agent's actual destination had been the Isle of Mull, and a rendezvous with a submarine now lost in the soft ooze at the bottom of the sound.

The *Santa Ana* had battled north along the Irish coast. She made it as far as Loughros More Bay before being driven onto the rocks. Again de Leyva escaped, though the Russian was injured and some of his men were drowned.

For over a week they encamped on the hostile shore. The histories remarked that de Leyva's discipline and guidance alone had kept the company of nearly seven hundred men together. How many of those men, Hunter wondered, had been VBU? How many more had been Spanish soldiers and seamen, following the one man who appeared to offer them hope in a hopeless situation?

Hearing a tale from the local Irish of other Spanish ships nearby, de Leyva led his men in a march across the Malin Mor Peninsula to the south. His injury prevented him from walking, so he had his men carry him over the rugged hills in a chair. Reaching Donegal Bay they found the *Gerona*, a Spanish galleass.

On October 14, de Leyva put to sea one more time. They made slow progress, but now de Leyva's ship was propelled by oars as well as sails. They crawled along the Irish coast, at last reaching North Channel with Mull less than a hundred miles to the north.

Hunter wiped the rain from his eyes, peering into the night. According to the histories, *Gerona* had foundered here, within sight of Dunluce Castle. And the Rangers were here to make certain that this was so.

He hated the idea. De Leyva—Colonel Vorosilov as Rachel had identified him—had performed an almost superhuman feat to get this far, and it seemed tragic that his attempt had to end on these rocks. There was no submarine waiting for him, though he couldn't know that if his radios were lost or dead. But with an unknown number of Russians with him, with hundreds of troops at his command, Vorosilov could still play havoc with the histories of England and Scotland.

The Chronos Project could not permit that.

"There!" Anderson said behind them, peering through binoculars. "About a mile off the coast."

Hunter looked in the indicated direction, raising his own field glasses to his eyes. He could see her now, wallowing heavily, her canvas tattered by the wind, but still making headway with her oars.

"She doesn't look too bad off," Gomez said. He was standing beside the heavy-barreled TOW missile launcher, mounted on its tripod on the rocks.

King squinted through the launcher's sight. "They're in range, Lieutenant." A week in the Chronos Facility infirmary had restored his vision, though he would need glasses for close work from now on. "I make it two thousand yards."

"Take 'em, Greg," Jones said.

"Easy there, Gunny," Morgan said. "Lieutenant's call . . . right, sir?"

Hunter nodded and walked back to the TOW launcher. "I'll take it, Greg." It was his responsibility.

King moved aside and Hunter took his tube-place leaning forward, pressing his eye against the optical sight, taking the weight of the launcher on his shoulder. *Gerona* appeared blurry, a shadow behind the curtains of rain.

"What are you waiting for, Travis?" Rachel asked.

"I'm still hoping we don't have to do this." His finger caressed the launcher's trigger. "Maybe they sank without our being here, without our interference. . . ."

"They're moving off, LT," Anderson said. "I think they're going to make it."

"Right." He'd already arrived at the same conclusion. "Stand clear!"

He squeezed the trigger and the launcher roared. The missile leaped beyond the headland. Hunter held the cross hairs steady on target. His movements were interpreted by the launcher's computer and communicated to the missile through the wire unreeling behind it. For a horrible moment, he thought he'd waited too long. Despite his commands, the missile was drifting off course. It was going to pass astern of *Gerona*, to miss completely. . . .

No. A last course correction swung the TOW missile back in line and it struck. There was a flash and a geyser of water at the galleass's stern, an explosion that splintered her rudder and sent her lunging before the wind, hopelessly out of control.

Within minutes it was clear that she would never clear the rocks of the Giant's Causeway. Already she was breaking up. Treasure hunters would pick her bones four centuries hence, Hunter knew. He wondered what they would make of the corroded remains of an AKM . . . or would those clues to *Gerona*'s commander and passengers remain forever lost?

Hunter stood up, watching the ship die. Nine Spanish soldiers would survive, he knew, out of a crew of hundreds. Philip of Spain would later say that the loss of Alonzo de Leyva meant more to him than the loss of the entire Armada.

"It had to be done, Chief," Gomez said. "*Had* to be."

"Let's get back, Rangers," Hunter said. The blue glow was waiting . . . a hot shower, dry clothes . . .

And Rachel. She took his arm and together they walked into the light.

243a